AUTHOR'S BIBLIOGRAPHY

1970 - **Un Garbanzo (negro)**. Relato autobiográfico.
1970 - **Del Amazonas al Perú**. Relato de viajes,.
1971 - **A través de La Argentina**. Un viaje a la Patagonia.
1972 - **El Séptimo Rollo**. Críticas de cine.
1976 - **Florilegio de Santa Política**. Sátira política.
1977 - **Los Cuentos de Juan Terbury**. Romances de ciego.
1978 - **Los caballos de la Noche**. Colección de cuentos.
1979 - Al **filo de la edad madura**. Nos han robado la vida.
1984 - **Liturgias y Vejámenes**. La Danza de la Muerte hoy.
1985 - **Confidencias,** historias de la gente. La gente común.
1990 - **Dios y yo**, la Verdadera Historia del Verdadero Dios.
1992 - **Desde mi ventana**. Comentarios de la actualidad.
1994 - **Las mujeres mandan, los hombres obedecen**.
1997 - **El tercer milenio.**   (Los Carientismos de   Ulrico 2)
1998 - **En aquel tiempo…** (Los Carientismos de Ulrico 3)
1999 - **Crónicas del final de un siglo.** (Los Carientismos 4)
2000 - **Carne de jarrete**. Un niño gallego del franquismo.
2001 - **Con ojos de niño**. (Los Carientismos de Ulrico 5).
2001 - **Un foro macabeo**. Colaboraciones en un foro.
2006 - **La papisa Juana**. Una mujer del siglo IX que fue Papa.
2006 – **Pope Joan**. An English translation of La Papisa Juana.
2007 – **La Papesse Jeanne**. Une traduction française.
2007 – **Giovanna**. Una traduzione italiana.
2007 – **A Papisa Xoana**. Unha tradución ao galego
2008 - **El Hijo de Dios**. Autobiografía de Jesús de Nazaret.
2008 – **The Son of God**. An autobiography of Jesus of Nazareth
2009 - **El famoso Millennium**. El foro de Bubok.
2012 – **Hock meat**. An English translation of Carne de jarrete
2013 – **Girls rule, as it should be**. An English translation
2013 – **Los hijos no cuentan**.
2013 – **Amor de padre y madre**
2013 – **El oficio de escribir**
2013 – **The horses of the Night**
2013 – **A life only dreamed**
2013 - **De Ribadeo a Santiago por el Camino del Norte**.
2013 - **The Northern Way to Saint James**.
2013 - **Después de Franco, los demócratas**
2013 - **Memorias de un gallego en Sudamérica**

2013 – De Santiago a Finisterre por la costa de la muerte
2014 - **Cartas desde El Camino de Santiago**
2014 - **Letters from the Way to Saint James**
2014 - **Galicia a pie.**
2014 – **Han asesinado a un travestido**
2014 – **They have slain a travestite**

Publicados como eBook por Kindle Amazon y en papel por Create Space Amazon

POPE JOAN

Pope Joan

a woman Pope

The true story of a IXth century woman who disguised herself as a man and was elected Pope.

An autobiography

translated by

Cerinto

from his Spanish original

La papisa Juana, una mujer que fue Papa

Copyright © 2006 Cerinto
First Printing: may 2010

All rights reserved

(Registry number: 10/102338)
Nº VG–44/2010 intellectual ownership registry

I.S.B.N. -13: 978-1463718909

Printed in USA

"... Women keep silence in churches, because they are not permitted to speak, rather showing restraint. That if they want to learn something, let them ask their husbands at home ..." -

Saint Paul (1 co. 14, 34-36)

"men are over women because God has distinguished."

A commentator on the Qur'an.

CONTENTS

CHAPTER 1. The birth and baptism, her early years.

The childbirth — 21

Gunilda the midwife — 26

Some shepherds worship her. — 28

The prophetess sorceress — 29

Two saints announce to Gudrun the birth of Joan — 32

My father suspects — 35

My father's character — 36

Joan's father meets her mother for the first time — 39

Some heavenly signs announce the birth of Joan — 40

Joan was baptised — 43

Three wise women worship her — 44

A queen favours her — 48

Presentation in the Temple. Mass at birth. Purification — 55

Some strange signs frighten everybody — 58

Louis orders the death of newly born children — 61

My parents offer me to the Holy Virgin Mary — 63

CHAPTER 2. The first childhood of Joan

Joan's father had been an oblate in England _____ 65

My parents' characters _____ 67

My fate written in the stars _____ 70

My early education _____ 73

My mother chastens me _____ 77

An episode among many _____ 80

Corporal punishment is effective _____ 86

Some other ways of educating children _____ 88

I grew up in virtue and grace in the eyes of God _____ 90

My early rebellion _____ 92

My first devotions _____ 96

CHAPTER 3. From childhood to adolescence

They educate me in suffering _____ 101

My father tells me about martyrs _____ 106

The idealism of puberty _____ 110

Lost and found in the temple _____ 112

My school years _____ 113

The then prevailing ideas about education _____ 118

A devout portrays me _____ 124

CHAPTER 4. Joan knows love

The exemplary lives of saints moved me _____128

I decide to go and convert Muslims _____130

My pious attempt fails and I return home _____135

The first love of Joan _____136

CHAPTER 5. The second departure and life in wilderness

The pros and cons of blessed matrimony _____149

Rather dead than married _____152

I decide to consecrate myself to God _____156

I run away from home disguised as a man _____161

Community life does not satisfy me _____164

Hermit life _____168

I felt called to an even more secluded life _____173

I live as an anchorite _____177

The devil tempts me _____187

The temptation of vanity _____190

The temptation of gluttony _____194

The temptation of political power _____196

The temptation of lust _____199

CHAPTER 6. My fame spreads, people come, acclaim me and confer on me the holy orders

The temptation of heresy — 202

I see the devil, he appears to me — 202

I perform some miracles — 207

My exemplary life attracts imitators — 209

St. Romuald did not wash his frock — 215

My devotees want my relics — 218

I talked to animals — 218

They set me a trap — 220

CHAPTER 7. Joan is Pope, loves God, becomes pregnant and gives birth to a child

They urge me out of retirement to be bishop and Pope — 223

The scene of my coronation — 227

I am Pope, become pregnant, they find out and intern me — 229

My mystical loves. Ecstasies, swoon, rapture, levitation — 231

Others had preceded me in loving the divine beings — 242

I conceive by virtue of the north wind — 245

The streets are my Golgotha and my Way of the Cross. — 248

They shut me in a convent — 257

About the author — 259

FOREWORD

Brief historical notice of Pope Joan

In the mid-thirteenth century, Martin Polonus, then chaplain of the Pope in charge and his confessor, wrote about John VIII, a ninth century Pope, the following:

Johannes Anglicus, of English descent, was born in Mentz and it is said he came to the papacy by diabolical arts, as being a woman disguised as a man went to Athens with her partner –an educated person- where under the doctors who taught there she progressed in wisdom so much that on arriving later to Rome found few that could match her and even less who exceeded her even in the knowledge of the Holy Scriptures. By her knowledge, her reading and her success in intellectual disputes, she was respected to such an extent that at the death of the Pope Leo and with everybody's consent she was elected to take his place. Going to the Lateran church, between the Colosseum and St. Clement, she was in labour, and according to some she was killed right on the spot and was buried without ceremony. others say she survived the birth of her son but lived the remnant of her life imprisoned in a monastery. Her pontificate had lasted two years, four months and ten days.

The legend spread quickly. One of the best known versions had it that in Ireland or England a young monk reached to seduce the daughter of a local notable and made her pregnant, so to hide her fault and avoid the wrath of the father both had fled to Europe, where after having brought to the world a girl, whom they named Joan, he had preached the gospel to the heathen Saxons.

It did not take long for him to die, followed soon by his partner, so that their 15 year-old daughter, Joan, suddenly found herself alone and homeless in a land that, despite being her birth place, she did not know.

Forced to earn a living and having noticed that in places and villages preachers were welcomed, it came to her mind to copy her parents and be also a preacher, something for which she felt herself well prepared and besides provided her a substantial income.

But being a woman was a nuisance because she was constantly badgered and wooed and arrived the night, in inns and farmhouses, she had to fight and defend herself from those who leaving aside good manners sought to obtain by force what they were not given willingly.

Also male evangelists obtained more out of their job than their female colleagues. so she decided to dress as a man and to go head and shoulders into the pitfalls of the world.

John English, as she was called since then, cultured and refined, preached with such grace, eloquence and knowledge, linked to a youthful and seductive face that he started to become famous and attract people desirous of hearing him.

Thus she met a young monk of the monastery of Fulda, who carried by the passion that had inflamed him, discovered the true sex of the girl and possessed her without any delay.

They spent thus many years, preaching when they were not fucking, copulating when they were not preaching, until little by little they came to Greece first and then to Athens, where, disguised as a boy, Joan met the students of the philosophical schools of the time, studied and argued with them and took profit of lessons in such a way that soon surpassed them in knowledge and tricks to emerge triumphant in dialectical disputes.

Such living began gradually to bore her, and because she felt already prepared for higher flights, helping her that the monk who had hitherto accompanied her fell ill and was of no avail all the knowledge of Hippocrates and Aesculapius together, died and left her alone, she left Athens and went away to Rome.

There again she won over everyone's friendship, nobles as well as commoners. Nobody had ever met someone who by his learning and eloquence could match her. First literate people, later the bishops and cardinals of the papal curia, all sought her company and conversation.

Finally the Pope appointed her his secretary. Again at this new position she showed herself more than enough, so when Leo IV fell ill and perhaps poisoned died, the Romans and the diocesan curia, who at the moment hesitated between two candidates for the papal see very close in intent to vote and faced in politics and alliances with the worldly powers of the time, decided to settle the matter quickly and decisively and temporarily be in agreement upon electing Johannes Anglicus Papa. So John the English, actually Joan, was appointed Pope.

Her reign lasted just two years, four months and a few days. She ruled with wisdom and won only praise. But life in the papal palace was monotonous, and the hours were long, especially at night; the honours and power grew boring to her and besides she was surrounded by distinguished cardinals and clerics in the prime of life. Thus being in her thirties and still young and fertile, she fell pregnant of one of them.

Things followed their natural course, and at the feast of Corpus Christi, year 857, when she rode in procession through the streets of Rome, she felt labour pains, and inevitably, there, in the presence of everybody she gave birth to a baby.

According to some, the Romans, amazed, confused and fearful in the face of such unheard-of and never seen event, furiously pounced on her and her son and without anyone could prevent it, killed them and made them disappear as soon as possible.

According to others, the members of the curia trying immediately to avoid scandal, picked up in a hurry both the woman and the fruit of her womb and took them to a remote monastery where they remained until the final hour arrived to them both.

There is no reliable proof that such thing had ever happened. There are many arguments for and against.

Was ever a woman Pope? Nobody will ever know, probably.

Introduction

JOAN - They have locked me in this monastery. I'll spend here the rest of my life. I have committed a crime and deserve a punishment. Because I have dressed as a man I have sinned before God. They appointed me to be the Pope of Rome. I gave birth in public, when in a procession. As a penance I have been ordered to write these memoirs. I must obey.

CHAPTER 1. The birth and baptism, her early years.

The childbirth

JOAN - On November 1st, Anno Domini 822, after midnight, they were awaiting my arrival in the hut. Everywhere was quiet. In a corner a mule and a cow were asleep. There were two women in the room and both were keeping silent. You could hear only the crackling of the fire and the whistling of the wind on the roof. In the lareira or fireplace, a log of wood opened up, and out of a thin crack came a bluish flame engulfing the iron casserole in which the water that would later be needed was heating. Outside, the soft wind dragged itself, blowing bits of clouds that from time to time unloaded some showers. It had rained again during the day and the sky was already clearing. In the hut a birth was about to happen. In order to make the opening of her vagina easier, my mother had been forced to sit on two chairs, one buttock and thigh on one of them, one buttock and thigh on the other, and, in this position, she waited patiently. The midwife was around for what might be necessary; she was a "practice", as they used to be called those who -in the midst of general ignorance- were supposedly more skilful than others. Such people still exist, but those just mentioned did not know anything, not even how to wash themselves.

To pick up what was about to come out, an apron had been spread over the ground. In the semi-darkness of the kitchen, the largest available space, with only the light of the fire and one dirty oil lamp, beside the hearthstone, which occupied half the surface of the floor, smelling the smoke, that dry and sweet smell so characteristic of such places, a cobweb in a corner, in a room without a ceiling, with blackened walls, they were patiently awaiting my arrival.

Suddenly my mother had exclaimed, here he comes! And the other woman had stretched out her hand to pick up what was about to fall. 'Oh my God, how little it weighs!' she exclaimed, disoriented, while at the same time pulling the apron nearer in order to get a closer look at what was there. And at that precise moment I came out. Instead of falling onto the prepared cloth, I fell straight on the floor and thus I began the journey of my life amidst suffering; I started being treated rudely in the hands of women who believed themselves knowledgeable when truly they knew nothing. They washed me and thus started everything – the whole story of my life in this world.

THE AUTHOR - Thus Joan recounted her birth. It happened at Ingelheim, a small German town on the left bank of the Rhine. Into the world had come a girl who would give luster and fame to the female gender. She was born at the stroke of one o'clock in the morning on that rainy night in the incipient winter, and in childbirth a healer called Gunilda had attended her mother - the sole physician at the place.

Gudrun, the mother, was Basque. Recently baptized and converted to Christianity by love, she had not entirely abandoned the traditional practices of her people and origin. She had placed under the bed, at whose side she rested expecting the birth, a rusty iron bar. According to ancient customs it facilitated the matter and ensured the successful arrival of the nascituro, i.e., the one about to be born.

There was no iron bar at hand, because metal was scarce in those times of wars and massacres. They used it for martial spears and darts rather than peaceful ploughshares. Therefore Gudrun had agreed that instead the nearest monastery be asked for some bone of St. Sebastian.

As we have said, Gudrun was a descendant of pagan Basques and not very long ago had become a Christian – converted by love for a young male Briton who had just arrived from the other side of the Channel. Therefore she clung to their ancient beliefs and at the bottom of her heart refused to abandon them completely. And despite the announcement - about which I will tell you later - she still believed that somehow ancestors were involved in the begetting of children. In the same way that the bones of stone fruits are their seed, it was also suspected that human bones were equally human seed. Hence, it is hardly surprising that she would become infatuated with the bones of the holy legionnaire.

But it is unclear whether because of professional jealousy or because the import of what was about to happen was attributed only to her, or for other unknown reasons, that it was that the midwife helping Gudrun give birth had deterred her from her first initiative. The project had remained just that, a project, which is to say only an idea, and no longer was it carried to conclusion.

Hence the midwife did not fail to warn the others about the desirability of preserving the still bleeding umbilical cord whose stem cells - were they available - could cure in the future the malignant diseases that by chance may affect women or children.

It was better to prevent now than to regret later.

Once the time that Fate had marked elapsed, Joan was born. According to what her mother later told someone, it was a fast enough delivery. The women had called the father, who waited patiently in the next room, and had offered him the opportunity to cut the umbilical cord personally. Without needing be asked twice and with rare skill (despite being inexperienced in such tasks), he had carried it out happily. He managed to do it the first time, no need to try again. He had used for the task the disinfected tool he had been offered. He was such a father as to boast of being more skillful than others at doing what needed to be done; he wanted to show his responsibility in the face of History.

Then, to prevent infection, the midwife rinsed the cut with a blotting anti-bacterial sponge that she had brought for the occasion and, after leaving the cord securely tied up with a new sailor's knot that some Rhine rowers had devised, she administered the girl with an infusion of the freshly harvested leaves of Brussels sprouts, rich in vitamin K, intended to control blood clotting; also some eye drops, to give her clear view of the state of world affairs. Then, before the first five minutes after the birth had elapsed, she had been made to undergo a test then in vogue, to measure her five basic characteristics, namely heart-rate, strength of lungs, tone of muscle, the reflex response of her joints and the reaction of her tiny pupils to various colors, in order to discover if she saw everything in grey or whether she saw in Technicolor - in which case, an optimistic mood in life might be expected from her.

After having weighed and measured her, the midwife had written the data in a tumbo, or record book made of parchment, which she herself retained and that had been given to her, in exchange for an effective aphrodisiac, by the subchanter of the choir of the nearest the Episcopal church. This man had been temporarily afflicted by what doctors eventually called SIS, or sexual inappetence syndrome. In that unusual original book, bound in the hide of a Christian martyr, the midwife used to write down the births that occurred in the region. Thanks to such early registration, it is now known that at that time the population decreased steadily. This was due to hunger and the glorious wars that the emperor liked to make, because "his greatest ambition was to see the nation in its rightful place in the concert of countries". It was feared that if things kept going on as they were, a time would arrive when the hands to farm fields and conquer more land would be scarce, the same as the fruit of looting with which the wealthy classes of the time, namely bishops, earls and dukes, used to give themselves the life of kings.

All these precautions were common since they had been taken on the occasion of the birth of the Infanta Leonor, daughter of the first emperor, which had just occurred near that time in nearby Mainz, where the imperial court resided.

Joan left the test with a score close to ten, enough for her to be deemed healthy and robust. And then, without further ado or initiation ceremony, she was placed in the manger that had been placed in the room for the comfort of the mule and the ox, the place that was, for the moment, the driest and warmest available.

Gunilda the midwife

The midwife who attended Gudrun was not a vulgar woman. Besides assisting those who were on the verge of giving birth, she healed with plants all kinds of diseases such as tuberculosis and that other one called blood cholerine or black cholerine, in addition to the plague of Lazarus and what was then called the morbo Gallico.

It seems that the Gallic disease had come from the east, carried by Huns who, brought up in the vast grasslands of Asian Mongolia, had invaded not many centuries ago the already civilized and Christian Europe. Everybody in those plains and open spaces, women and men alike, rode at will whenever they could, and as among them reigned unfettered the freedom of morals, they did it since the cradle, and henceforth the fair God inflicted on them that frightening illness.

The Lazarus plague used to begin in the skin, and like the Gallic illness, the patient's flesh dropped in pieces. Both diseases were called pasizas, because anyone who arrived to drink from the same glass used by a patient caught them, and if he was sitting, anyone else who sat in the same place would contract them. Minimal contact was enough to transmit it.

Gunilda was already fifty-four years old, and from her mother and grandmother she had learned the skills of her profession. They too were midwives and healers and had passed on their knowledge, in addition to teaching her how to "conjure" by means of shrubs and herbs.

She cured with plants, and by observing the urine of the person suffering the disease she diagnosed as leprosy – the Lazarus illness - and many others. With concoctions that she herself made, she helped with childbirth. The "water of pigs or piglets" contributed to alleviating the birth, that is, hastened it, because having taken the potion the mother needed an hour exactly to start contractions. Once the fetus had been expelled, but the placenta was delayed in coming out, some roasted onion poultice placed over the stomach was the remedy, a truly wondrous cure that never failed. A basic requirement for feeding the new mother was neither to cure with smoke nor burn the quail or goose cooked for her, nor let her food be contaminated by ash from the fire, since in that case the woman was at risk of serious illness in her puerperium or postpartum time.

Disinterested and simple, she provided her services in exchange of what each family would like to offer, whether in cash or in kind - food, a forest deer, a woodcock or a duck from a pond nearby, and any produce from the last harvest or livestock. In this way, she had aroused against her the ill will of many and especially the enmity of the clergy who, jealous of the powers of this illiterate thaumaturgic woman, accused her of meddling and conducting her pagan activities without the requisite monastic license, besides having a pact with the devil, Beelzebub, and others of minor importance to carry out her nefarious arts. But since by means of her concoctions and filters she had cured the bleeding fluxions of the venerable Casilda, abbess of a famous convent, no one dared to oppose her, and for the time being they left her in peace and did not denounce her to the real powers then reigning.

Being a midwife and the only doctor who attended to the community, she was accepted and respected by many, so much so that in a dying trance (and ignoring the fact that that woman was illiterate), the count Ekkehard, a Burgundy noble, had left her by special legacy a book about gynecology written in Latin. The true reason for such a strange bequest has never been known, but the fact was recorded, to the wonder of some and the conjectures of others during the times that were to come.

Some shepherds worship her

Just as at the birth of Jesus, the savior of mankind, some shepherds had come to see him in the manger, in Joan's case too something similar happened, with the difference that instead of male shepherds coming to adore her, some female ones had come. Already women boasted of being able to do anything that the most virile man might do, even if it was something uncomfortable and unpleasant, in this case spend the night outdoors while looking after the animals that the landowner had trusted to them.

In that same area, called the tower of the flock, there were some female shepherds who, despite the unpredictable weather, spent the night in the open and were awake by turns to keep their livestock, mainly sheep and goats, safe, when suddenly, without anything having forecasted it, an angel of the Lord stood before them, and the glory of the Lord in its brilliance wrapped them and they were seized with mighty fear, because they were concerned about the unexpected visit of some alien being. And the angel said to them, in a language that everyone, even the most rustic, could understand:

Do not fear, nor be unduly alarmed, for behold I bring you good news, which will be of great joy for everyone who becomes aware of it: that today in the city of Carl the Great is born to you a female savior, who is the one sent by God, the anointed. And this will be a sign: you will find the child wrapped in swaddling clothes and lying in a manger in the company of her parents and the midwife and a cow and a mule that warm the air with their breath.

And suddenly there was with the angel a great multitude of the heavenly host, who in a rhythmical chorus of voices sang the following carol praising God: Glory to God in the highest, and on earth let there be peace among men and women by divine pleasure, not only among those of the flesh or those who boast of abiding the laws better than others, but also among those of the spirit and promise.

The angel did not bother to clarify such sibylline words, and it happened that as the angels departed from them into heaven, the women shepherds, without regard to the hidden meaning that maybe concealed those words, simply said to one another: come, let's go to Ingelheim and see this event which the Lord has manifested to us.

They arrived there in a hurry, and immediately found Gudrun accompanied by John, and the child in the manger. And having seen this scene, they made known that they had been told about it. And all who heard them wondered at the things which those uncouth ones had told them. But Gudrun heard, saw and was silent, and kept all these words in her heart, which reflected the attentive and thoughtful spirit with which God had endowed her. And the women shepherds returned to their herds glorifying Him and praising Him for all the things they had heard and seen, as had been announced to them.

The prophetess sorceress

JOAN - After my having been born without further mishap, and because of a sudden inappropriate whim, as cravings usually accompany pregnancy and do not happen after it, my mother had wanted to summon to her headboard the most famous of haruspex witches who had a shop open in the surroundings. In the fortune-telling art of reading the cards and other no less esoteric and magical tricks, none could match her. Without being difficult, she hastened to oblige. She put aside the useless stuff spread on the carpet of raffia that protected those who entered into that chilly room with bare feet from catching cold. She traced in the clay soil a magic circle, and there surrounded by the rare tools of her strange undertaking locked herself in it. With her ascetic fingers she smoothed out her hollow skirt whose false wrinkles could put at risk the transparency and smoothness of the predictions she was about to make. She uttered and muttered the incantations and abracadabra that the case demanded, and went into a trance divine in which she predicted for me countless successes and happy and unusual love affairs, in addition to a long life full of events and adventures.

And to underpin these new and joyous revelations, and to continue to increase her standing with the family, she pointed out that as soon as I had emerged unscathed from the womb that more than 8 ½ months had sustained me and given me loving shelter, I weighed 9 Roman pounds, which was a remarkable fact, because on average children born at that epoch failed even to reach six. Certainly, it was foreshadowed in such happy circumstances the special weight that eventually I would have in History. Later, when rhetoric knew a time of renewed splendor, it was said that the Roman goddess of fortune had destined me to be a woman of great value and an outstanding person.

My father was called Joannes Anglicus, blond and from the island of Albion. The Angles had populated the island three centuries before and in the word 'Albion' some saw a reference to the clear or pure white hair of its inhabitants. However I was a brunette, plump, round and cute, if somewhat tearful, and according to one of my relatives, just after leaving the cozy nest that for nine scarce months my mother's womb had been to me, I had yawned to the point of my little jaws being almost disconnected. Again the authoress of horoscopes and other fortunes saw reflected in it the tedium aroused in me towards the appalling vulgarity of the world to which indifferent fate had doomed me.

From the very moment of my birth I showed self-assurance and my IQ was high. A pioneer in her time and surely endowed with a precognitive ability that skeptics refused to acknowledge in her, the seer caught in me a glimpse of a queen whom her people would call Victory; an Englishwoman who centuries later was to reign endless and happy years in the westerly islands originally peopled by the British nation, also called Britons.

My mother was pleased by what such a kind fairy godmother had told her, and giving the flatteries and gifts imposed by custom, she bid farewell to the midwife and the soothsayer. A male after all and therefore less sensitive than the gullible females, my father was not so confident. However, and as I'll remark below, his astrological sign had predicted him to be a feminine and meek person.

With that, everybody got ready to make room in the already malnourished family for the new member that had so unexpectedly come. In case of things happening as predicted, such newcomer would have brought a loaf of bread under her arm, as the well-known fable demanded. For the time being it was purely metaphorical bread and not one of vulgar cereal, because the glory to come had been promised her only when the fated years had passed.

Two saints announce to Gudrun the birth of Joan

THE AUTHOR - Joan was born in a humble home, to artisan or lower middle class parents. They were industrious people, which is to say, hard-working, and they were not landowners, they had no property or any of the things that others called goods or wealth. Her father was an evangelist of the new Christian doctrine, while her mother was a newly-converted housekeeper, not yet entirely free of the beliefs of her pagan Basque people.

In the eyes of their neighbors, whose purity of blood was clearly beyond doubt, having been converted more than a century ago, her parents loved the Lord and professed earnestly the Christian faith. Before the birth of the baby, the heavens had given them three more children, two boys and a girl, hence now older than her. She came to the world when her mother, already worn by hard work and the unpleasant tasks proper to her subordinate female status, was nearing the end of her fertile period.

One night, nine months ago, just before the break of dawn, when darkness is about to dissolve and goes through the atmosphere like a soft and subtle breath that makes shudder the people's flesh, a time of magic, mystery and the Galician Holy Parade (la Santa compaña), St. Ramon Nonato and St. Ulrich of Augsburg had appeared to her in dreams. The first of these had been named Nonato, meaning 'unborn', because he was not born, but instead extracted by caesarean from the womb of his mother already dead. The second saint was only a casual acquaintance of the first, because at that time he just happened to pass along and the Almighty had made them the requisite pair. Later also Mormons would go by pairs, like the members of the Spanish Civil Guard. Previously a Pope had appointed them both patrons of those who were to give birth. The first, due to the circumstance of his unique birth; the other, because he had been accused of making pregnant an honest young girl who, ashamed of her unspeakable act, had concealed it from her parents and put all the blame on that holy man who meekly had not objected.

Despite the distrust of the good lady and her desire not to suffer again the discomfort of the painful gestation; despite her mature age that had hardened her arteries and given stiffness to her joints, and despite the fact that she was narrow-hipped and lean of flesh, which increased the risk of difficulties and dystocic delivery, the celestial duo had announced to her that by a higher and divine disposition she should reconcile herself to the idea that she would give birth to a daughter who with time and AMGD -to the greater glory of God- would become famous and live in people's memory for countless centuries to come.

Nonato ruled the roost and left the other in the secondary role of assistant, and to liven up a little the long and prosaic paragraph, and give it more poetic tints that would help the poor wretch to sweeten the bitter pill being offered her, after cleaning his throat and taking the pose that best suited the new role, he had recited in, the High German Gothic language instead of the Latin that was the norm among the wealthy classes, and with the accompaniment of the chords of a heavenly song strangely reminiscent of what later would be called gorigori, (funeral dirge) the following greeting:

Hail, Gudrun, you will be blessed among all women, because out of your body at the point of menopause will be born, as a phoenix that from its ashes revives, one that will organize on new foundations the world, so you will have to call her Joanna Petra, firm as stone and immovable rock on which everything else will rest, an example to the many nations that are to benefit from her empire and a true guide to the people who fill the orb of the earth.

I will point out that by citing the phoenix who revives from its ashes the person echoed St. Ambrose, for as is well-know, that ancient archbishop of Milan had tried to explain the Bible through metaphors, because if it was taken literally, no living thing would ever understand what was told there.

Here the saint stopped and put an end to his speech, for despite his blessed status as pure spirit, safe from the contingencies of the flesh, rendering him immune to the lack of breath, according to many, he had felt nothing other than breathless and had to pause the necessary time to recover his lost breath.

And then, once recovered, nothing else coming to his mind that might add or round and complete what he had said with such fervor and momentum, or perhaps because the chorus of singers of the musical accompaniment had reached the limit of the canonical verse, he coughed again, and without taking leave or in some other way showing a change of scene, he was gone as he had come, which is the same as saying by the forum.

Then, when such a miracle had just taken place, my father, John Anglicus, was absent, for according to the demands of his mechanical art, he went to convert to Christianity the few remaining Saxons who, after the thirty-three years of bloody war by means of which Charlemagne had endeavored to lure them gently into the fold of Christ, remained still unconverted. So Gudrun would have no one to tell about it, if it were not for the fact that Camille, her cousin, had not long ago gone through an experience that could match the one just recounted. The two women shared confidences, and, satisfied of their similar fate, they had returned calmly to their respective homes.

Her father suspects

JOAN - Now my father came back to spend at home the leisure time that the State of that time allowed him, since in the early summer the emperor decreed a truce in the war he happened at that moment to be waging, and in the forests of the Bulge devoted himself to hunting. Finding my mother pregnant, my father had his doubts, so that, pensive at first and more curious later, fearing himself unable to carry on his head the infamous sign of deceived husbands, one morning, after the last nap that precedes the new day, he questioned his wife about the interesting condition already quite obvious to everybody.

Demure and modest at first, and then, finally, once the scruples that made her wonder if it would be right to disclose what privately the two holy men had warned her had been defeated, that worn woman told the honest husband who lay beside her about the unusual experience that she had had some months before, and the words that she had heard, good news that the patient male, skeptical as I have said, and tired of the effort and anguish that feeding their copious offspring cost him, took it badly at first. Then, like the good Christian he was, he tried to get used to the idea and accept with exemplary resignation the burden the Lord had imposed on him.

Be done the Lord's will! It seems he said, at least to himself and to his sweater or vest, because he who reigns in heaven hears without listening and knows things before they have been told.

However, this stubborn and suspicious representative of male brotherhood knew no rest and was tortured with the desire to flee from that bed, perhaps tainted, to seek solace in another one and to renew his pristine confidence in the feminine gender.

Then, torn in his soul by such opposed doubts, there appeared to him in dreams the holy Bathilde, who admonished him by saying:

John, son of John, do not be afraid to have sexual intercourse with Gudrun, your wife, who is faithful to you, even though appearances seem to condemn her, because the shoot she awaits is the work of the spirit or wind that blows from the north and made her pregnant. She will give birth to a daughter, and you shall call her Joan Petra, the first name so she will appear as your legitimate child, although strictly speaking the name means '"God is merciful', the latter name for the fate that the Lord reserves her; because she will show the Christian people a new path.

All this took place to fulfill what, according the Holy Scriptures, the Virgin Mary had announced through the mouth of the well-known Sibyl of Samos: behold a Basque woman will conceive and give birth to a daughter, who will be named Joan Petra, meaning that by the mercy of God she will be a rock on which will rest the Church.

On waking from sleep, John felt relieved, like a bitter weight had been removed from him, and doing as the blessed one had told him, continued to live with my mother, and when she gave birth, agreed to give me the prescribed name.

My father's character

It should be noted that this fortunate man, who only in words and not in the usual manner had begotten me, was born on the other side of the channel that separates the islands of tin or British Islands that the Roman emperor Claudius had conquered some centuries before from the continental mainland. After being an oblate in a monastery for a time and having professed like the monks that had kindly welcomed him in their flock, he had felt himself inclined to a life of adventure and picaresque rather than to a strictly monastic one. So he asked his superior for permission to travel and make his way in the world and be a missionary, a permit that, given his docility and readiness for possible martyrdom, had willingly been granted him.

He had then migrated to the lands next to those of the Saxons, since at that time those obstinate pagans refused stubbornly to exchange for new gods those sufficiently effective old ones, and thus refused to convert to the one true faith. This caused many headaches for those ruling at that time, who longed for one only flock under one and the same shepherd, a flock whose head might be severed if needed by a single stroke of the sword, as Caligula had dreamed - that ancient Roman emperor who had appointed his horse consul and allowed it to eat alone, away from vulgar and vile company, in a manger of ivory and precious stones inlaid with ebony. The government of the masses is after all a risky business, and uniformity is a promise if not a guarantee that the wayward herd will not stray from the flock.

I must point out here that the name of that oblate came from what was then a common practice, namely that parents being generally poor and prolific could not sustain their numerous children, so that even when they were as young as five years old, they used to deliver or offer them to a monastery nearby, to serve the Lord and the monks and thus earn a living. Such a practice was called handing them over to God for life. John's father had done this; when the boy was not even ten years of age, he had delivered him to the abbot to be brought up in the sciences and the arts in which at that time and in such places boys used to be formed.

But back to my father. John (or Joannes) Anglicus - that was the name of the man who now began to be a missionary - made an ascetic bundle and after crossing the Channel -the one that separates Europe from the Island of Britons- travelled to Mainz, a continental city of the Carolingian Empire in which reigned the emperor called Louis the Pious, or by another name Ludovicus Pio. Besides being the son of Charles the Great, he was an exemplary man in whom were happily gathered all the virtues of such an eventful period.

Before proceeding I must record his sign and character. At that time in the British Isles there was not yet any population register; therefore according to probable calculation my father had been born in the month ruled by the sign of the twins, Gemini, an air sign despite its name, because at first sight no relationship seems to exist between air and twins.

Externally obedient and responsible, but capricious and volatile inside, those born under such a sign were also very romantic people who needed emotional bonds to guide them in life.

So say the knowledgeable ones, and they add that those graced with this sign are often tender in excess, so they need a firm hand, preferably a feminine one, to drive them on the right path. Therefore some considered them particularly prone to a vice that took its perverse name from Von Sacher Masoch. It is well known that the crooked ways are numerous, and many people weaker than him and left to their own devices would run a blatant risk of straying off course with no possibility of return.

Joan's father meets her mother for the first time

THE AUTHOR - Arrived the one who was to be the putative father of Joan (considered to be her father, even he was not) to that wild and uncouth land, he had zealously preached the good news he had brought with him, and as he was a good looking man and in the prime of his age -*dans la force de l'age*- without too much effort had right away convinced Gudrun, then a fresh young girl, of the excellence of what he preached with impetuous verb; and to beat the iron while it was hot and not lose the opportunity to offer the divine herd a new and docile sheep, had agreed to do marital life with her and in their leisure time, to teach her what perhaps she did not yet knew about of the new doctrine and pious exercises.

They had not needed a marriage according to the Christian rite. The still uncouth laws of those times put no objection to mistresses and concubines of lay and clergy, and the emperor himself had set an example by living with one of them since at his young 16 years and -according to ancient chronicles- in order to "protect him from debauchery and the ardent impulses of the flesh" and to prevent his falling into askew paths by offering natural comfort to his young desires, his prudent and foresighted parents had pushed him gently to live in concubinage with the young heiress Ermengarda, daughter of the Earl Ingmar Hesbaye, coming from an ancestry of pure and old nobility, and with her he had enjoyed and lived with in holy peace and harmony until the Lord of heavens, in whose arcane hands lies the fate of all, had disposed to take her away to a better life where are unknown the petty miseries and anxieties of this one.

The Briton missionary and his German sentimental female partner had spent several years living together, of which, as already said, had sprouted the blessed fruit of two strong young men and a virgin honest, teenagers all when Joan came into scene.

Some heavenly signs announce the birth of Joan

On the first of November, simple souls were at home ready to celebrate all the saints of the Julian calendar. That Gregory who would exchange it for the Gregorian one had not yet intervened. That night a girl was born in heroic circumstances. Her birth had been preceded by rare signs in heaven and on earth. Occasionally some comets held back their course, as if, by slowing down transitorily their mad dash, they were meaning to say that they did not want to miss an event that future historians would write about on golden letters on those marble friezes where outstanding facts are remembered. The planet Mars seemed to draw to the attention of the Christian population such a glorious event by an unusual spark; and at midmorning there was a partial eclipse of the sun so that for a few minutes it lost its accustomed brightness and looked dark in the skies. With polite deference it allowed itself to be hidden by the moon, a female star; it too announced thereby that in a short period the nascitura, the one who is about to come into the world, would usurp from its privileged position the ruling male star. All these were events presaging the future greatness of the girl to be born.

As for the popular Abenamar Romance - read by those aspiring to a high school degree - it might have been sung on her behalf:

Petra Joan, Petra Joan,

a girl who into the world was coming,

the day you were born

there were great signs on the sky,

the moon had concealed the sun,

a star was wandering on its path,

a star glowed unusually,

some others had fallen like rain...

a child born under such a sign,

would never lack a lover.

JOAN - As was later said, two days after my happy birth, my father had stated that his daughter Joan was beautiful, though he had to declare himself partial and admit that the little one changed overnight. Due to his sheer pride at seeing himself so potent and able to continue begetting terrestrial life, he did not fit into his robe.

He also devoted a few words to my mother, who was recovering quickly and soon would regain the necessary energy to resume the work appropriate to her sex.

The little Joan, he added, behaves well; she eats, burps and sleeps like the baby she is, though we, her parents, with the novelty, do not rest or relax as much as would be needed. We sleep much less than her, which is normal, I suppose -he pointed out for those who had perhaps not understood.

However he was bursting with joy at his recent condition of fatherhood and with legitimate enthusiasm referred to his offspring.

How do you manage to take her in your arms, more used to rising up in the air and invoking the Most High, than folding her on your lap and then rocking her? Thus a curious indiscreet voice had questioned him.

Phenomenally, but with tact and proper precautions, he had replied laconically, and without wanting to either get into more depth or commit himself, with the following:

I still do not find she resembles anyone, nor could I say whether she is more alike me than her mother.

And he had put it even more clearly: she does not cry any longer, it was only at the beginning.

To which someone, apparently subservient, had warned him: wait and see when she gets gas!

And for a while thereafter, he had had recommended to him some rare well- proven wild herbs.

With special prayers appropriate to the case, my parents thanked God for the gift that at such an advanced age as theirs He had offered them, and got ready to baptize their new daughter. Without any unnecessary delay, they wished to bring her immediately into the community of faithful believers. They promised themselves that early in the morning they would go to beg Don Aquilino to carry out the ceremony at the shrine of holy Hildegunda, whose unparalleled life was known in all pious tongues. The appropriate hierarchical authority had entrusted to the zeal and care of such a priest the flock and the parish of the hamlet and neighborhood in which they all lived.

THE AUTHOR - Because the family was poor, a cheaper priest had proposed to give her a most common name and to baptize her in a brick basin. She was not to be given any recent fashionable name nor a long roll of them, as those modern names would detract from the sacred ritual. Common salt was employed, and of tergal was her little cap. The water came from the river nearest to hand, vulgar words were the 'I baptize you', and four squalid coins were the godfather's gift.

Joan was baptised

JOAN - It fell to Licentiate Don Aquilino, the parish priest of Ingelheim, to baptize me. Customs were different then; a hunk of a man was he, big; he walked firm and straight on tracks and roads, with his stick making noise on turnstiles. It was said that on one occasion, when he was going to say mass, he had treated immoderately and squashed and bashed by the peasants who instead of taking orderly seats in the benches were seen obstructing the aisle to the altar.

He lived with his mother, whose name was Amiable, and two sisters. They used to go for water at the source, with buckets on their heads. It was common to have the bucket rings bright as mirrors. They were thoroughly cleaned and glistened. On one of them was an "A" for Amiable. When this lady died, the daughters took her away in a bullock cart, tied with rope so she could not move, for burial in her home town. Because she was a priest's mother, many parishioners attended her funeral. As far as the outskirts, they had carried her on their shoulders and from there by cart.

He was an excellent man, Don Aquilino, but because of the political instability of the last years of Louis, between 830 and 840, his flock became increasingly restless, as elsewhere, and did not stop harassing him and bothering him until his Bishop finally pulled him out of there and sent him to another place, near Mannheim.

His parishioners set him some traps, but he did not let himself be caught. Once on the road they had insulted him, but he, as usual, did not pay attention. Tired at last, he had to leave.

He did not take long to die. Mortally ill, despite the war, he found someone to administer him the sacraments. Once dead, his sisters had seated him on a cart, both dressed in light-colored clothes. They had promised themselves not to mourn. They prepared what they would say if somebody causally crossed their path or caused them to pause: they would say that there they were carrying a sick man, very sick.

Nothing unusual happened and they arrived safely at the village of his birth, where they buried him as was fitting. Despite the four scoundrels who teased him, he had left in the parish with some good friends.

Three wise women worship her

THE AUTHOR - But fortune, which the village witch had predicted would be good for the one born with such signs of divine preference, made the news of the happy birth and the foreseen auspicious destiny reach the ears of three ladies. Three holy women, as holy were those three who at the sacrifice of Golgotha had attended the Lord Jesus Christ, Mary, his mother, the repentant Magdalene and the compassionate Veronica.

The first was the abbess Edelvita, a Catholic and a cultivated woman who used to read Latin fluently. She was a new Hypatia, who had once been the head of the famed library of Alexandria. The second one was Nantilde, also an Abbess, although in her early youth she had been known as the desirable Nantilde, skillful in the arts of Venus and rival of Phryne, who in times gone by had left without speaking the wise men of the Areopagus of Athens, who had tried to reprimand her and asked her to give an account of the lascivious behavior of which some citizens had accused her. The third was Hilda of Whitby, the administrator of the monastery that bears her name and who, as Martha, the sister of Mary and Lazarus, felt comfortable when dealing with the prose of this rogue world.

Besides the three holy Catholic figures to which I have referred, you might see them also as representatives of three other ancient goddesses: Athena, experienced in science and letters; Aphrodite, expert in the affairs of love as nobody else and Hebe, who on Mount Olympus was in charge of the housework.

And it happened that these three pious women, who in the long nights of vigil and the prayer of their holy ministry had raised up their eyes to heaven and seen in it the strange signals announcing to the world the arrival of the prodigious child, had put themselves in motion to go to worship and pay her the proper respects.

Just as three Magi from the East had visited the child Jesus.

Those three holy women came from three different directions of the compass. They came from three notable cities, Aachen, Erfurt and Worms, to the north, east and south respectively of that humble Ingelheim. This was symbolically honored by the lunar triad, the three distinct phases of the nocturnal star which shows itself as a new moon, a nubile maiden untouched, a full moon, a woman fulfilled and in the fullness of life, and a waning moon, decadent old and worn. These are also the three faces of the ancestral goddess who had been mother goddess and wife, until the male God Jehovah had supplanted her in worship.

This God had been compared to the number four, since that was a complete number, round and full, just as the number three, lacking and scarce, had been attributed to women.

Once they arrived at Mainz the three ladies asked the first passer-by they saw:

Where is the child just born who comes to bring order to the land which at present is misruled by men? Having seen the signs in heaven we come to see it.

Upon hearing those words the Emperor Louis was startled and with him all his court. Then he summoned the chief priests of his realm and the most knowledgeable scholars of the sayings and deeds of the holy apostles and doctors of the Church and asked them where it was predicted the child would be born. To which they had responded: in Ingelheim, as it was written by the prophetess:

And you, Ingelheim, land of Austrasia, you are not in the least the lowest among the major cities Mainz governs, because out of you will come one who will lead the Christian flock. She will distinguish herself by her academic knowledge and her memory will last countless centuries.

Then Louis, remembering the signals with which the Highest had wanted to mark the descent into the world of His beloved daughter, determined to send someone to verify in place what was being told him. He called aside the three ladies who in the palace had surprised him when he was fully unaware of the matter. He made them report to him the exact dates when the celestial wonders mentioned had taken place and dispatched them to Ingelheim with this message:

Go and ascertain everything about this girl; once you have found her, let me know, so that I too can acknowledge her supremacy.

Having heard the king and the empress, who was named Judith Von Altdorf, daughter of Count Welf of Andech and Bavaria, whom Louis the Pious had married for the second time in the year 817 when Ermengarda, of Haspengau, was dead, the women set off. They took a path parallel to the river, thus shortening the route as well as avoiding other annoyances, because the dreaded winter was approaching. The rains being torrential that year, the oxen pulling the vehicle got caught in the mud, and asking when necessary, they reached the humble abode of John Anglicus and his wife Gudrun.

Filled with immense joy because they had already arrived safely without noteworthy drawbacks the long road, they entered the rustic house, saw the child with her mother, and after hearing from those present all the things concerning the case, they prostrated themselves on the ground and revered the little girl.

Then they opened their treasures and offered her as a gift the only extant copy of the Song of Bilitis, which on that Aegean Sea island and in her leisure time had been composed by the poetess Sappho; the shirt that in the last Olympic games had been worn by the female champion of throwing the Greek javelin; an effigy of the Venus from Wollendorf to remind her of the fertility attached to her human female condition; a little basket full of balls of wool of different colors, to point out the tasks of a good housekeeper; a basket in which the attentive eye could glimpse of a cover for the nursing bottle, then also called a rubber nipple; a bib, to prevent staining the blouse that she would undoubtedly wear; a bath towel and a pair of small socks called patucos, which with devout love and tender care had been made by the penitent women who with labor and hardship were purging their faults in a nearby retirement home; and a cornucopia or horn of plenty filled with cakes, honey and dates, a symbol of Pandora's box and the Mediterranean diet so conducive to living a long life.

Pandora was that unfortunate woman who let free evil into the world. In addition those women had offered the little baby a Barbie doll wearing the Swiss Red Cross on her nurse's attire and some little jerseys, Pierrots and a papal skullcap and sandals.

Switzerland did not yet exist, but they were already anticipating what in the future would come to be. And they were warned in a dream not to go back to where Louis lay in wait, so they took a detour and returned by another route to their homes, which is to say their places of origin.

A queen favours her

Meanwhile, the Empress Judith, brooding about the child prodigy meant for her, to err on the side of caution and not lose the train of History, nor risk being considered by the future generations a woman shamefully in the grips of male power, suddenly wanted to honor in person the new-born. Therefore aft the aforementioned ladies had gone away, she sent emissaries to Gudrun and John to inform them that in deference to the invulgar girl, she had arranged for her to be baptized not in the peasant church where for administrative reasons she ought to be, but in the capital city, with the pomp and pageantry that the occasion called for. For the occasion she would dust off the pan or bowl of porphyry and onyx inlaid with agate and other gemstones that for the edification of strangers and the admiration of future generations the monastery of the Servants of Jesus Adoratrices (nuns belonging to a religious order that endeavors to reform fallen women) had kept close to the city. This was a domestic container that according to centuries-old tradition was the same in which Jesus had washed the sweaty and tired feet of His disciples the original Holy Thursday night, before anyone could take his place at the table where everyone was about to receive the first communion that has been reported.

Many events had seen that container, basin or bowl. The apostles had guarded it amidst great hardship; because by its exquisite cast and rare gems it was an object which many poor devotees coveted. To begin with, it had first been kept safe against the iconoclastic fury of the priests of the Temple of Jerusalem, who tried to delete from people's mind anything related to the unfortunate prisoner dead on Golgotha, and then Saint Tecla, the favorite disciple of the Apostle of the Gentile Paul, had brought it secretly to Ephesus, where for three hundred or more years it had been kept away from Armenian and Persian barbarian invasions. At last, God willing it, the Emperor Constantine, and Helena, his mother, saw for the greater honor and glory of the Divine Master the flourishing to maturity of his one true Church. Then, until recently, it had been kept by the friars of St. Peter Regalado; and finally, as an especial gift, Charlemagne had given it to the monastery mentioned above, where the serfs, earlier called Sisters of the Nails of Christ, had preserved it with religious zeal and commitment until those days when this story begins.

We should note in this connection that originally the holy sisters were not called Adoratrices, Sisters of Adoration, but divine meretrices, ones who deserve something, in recognition of the merits they had earned in the face of the majesty of the divine Lamb. Until a new governess arrived at the Abbey, who was richer in the romance vocabulary that at the time was emerging as a corruption of the original Latin than the innocent devotees who had preceded her in office, had proposed to change the original name to a new name that, without entirely losing its prior connotations, better matched the respective positions of server and served.

A new occurrence had recently added to the reputation and renown of the wash bowl or pail. For the first time, and offering a precedent of such pious use, one had been christened in it who in time would be raised to the altar with the nickname of holy Hildebrand, a grandmother of Pippin the Short and hence great-grandmother of Charlemagne. And the infant Leonor, a recently born daughter of the king, had been christened in it too, as I have already told.

Coming back to the girl destined to be a hero, she would not be baptized with the common water, though blessed for the event, that flowed freely at hand, clear water as yet uncontaminated by the discharges to come, water in which once arrived the breeding season you could see swimming pleasurably the fish that the neighboring peasantry used to catch. Instead, she would be baptized with the liquid lymph brought for the purpose from the River Jordan itself, that sacred current at whose banks the Savior of men, first, and of all mankind, including females after, had taken an afternoon nap and where in turn he had been baptized on a May morning by his cousin named John the Baptist. A sample of the holy liquid having been taken, once the chronicles and cartularies had been duly consulted it was decided to seek the same place where according to tradition the wondrous event had happened, in order to wash the tender little head with the very water in which the Divine Master's symbolic sins had been washed, because it was felt that by dint of being a natural product, it had not yet lost its original virtue.

But whether due to incipient climate change or to some other factors of which ordinary people of the time were unaware, now the water was clouded with mud and unholy silt and needed to be purified and filtered to make it condign of the solemn function intended.

As will have already been noted by the keen reader, those who had wanted the thing to be this way had not thought about the saying of Heraclitus, according to whom "no one bathes twice in the same river," so the water with which the girl was about to be baptized would never be the same water in which our Savior had been baptized. Paraphrasing the philosopher above, you could say: it is impossible to baptize two babies in the same Jordan.

Joan's parents were dazzled and felt flattered because the mighty of the earth had put their eyes on them, so they complied with what the empress had ordered and prepared themselves to decently christen the child thus pampered. It was first necessary to appoint the godparents, for which the closest relatives of the happy family had been envisaged, but by due deference they consulted the views of the empress, and giving precedence to her judgment and wise decisions, as befits anyone born in the purple - in Constantinople called Porphyrogenitus - or at least dressed with it, they agreed to let the holy brethren Justine and Pastora, two people of high lineage then visiting the imperial court, bring the child to the baptismal font

The date having arrived, with pomp and pageantry the girl was carried to the main church of the capital Mainz. Then with such pomp and devotion as the case required, the bishop Hilduin, primate of office, undertook the task of snatching her from the hands of the devil, and delivering her instead to the blessed ones of the Archangel Michael. Attending him was the acolyte Incmaro, whom recently he had brought to his side because of his knowledge of Latin that among his contemporaries already commanded attention despite his still-young age. There was also the apostolic nuncio there, whom the reigning pope Paschal had sent in his place.

But instead of crying, as was usual among those who suffered at such a ritual at a young age, perhaps because of the sudden impression of cold water, the baby laughed joyfully, and after raising up her tender little hands and grabbing from the old prelate's gnarled ones the silver trimmed seashell with which, without losing a moment, he was about to baptize her, a shell which before had baptized plenty of other famous characters, poured straight into her hair the lustral water, but without uttering the words that accompany the ritual, because apparently the divine master had not seen fit to grant her then the gift of tongues that in the Upper Room of the holy city (I speak here of ancient Jerusalem) had He given graciously to the apostles - I mean without them having to earn it by good deeds.

I say that the tender girl had baptized herself without the aid of anyone, as if she had known that the reigning emperor, Louis the Pious, already mentioned in this story, had preceded her in the arrogant gesture. For he too at the right moment had taken from the anointed hands of the celebrant of the crown of king and had pulled it down cleanly and without assistance on his own brachycephalic skull. After doing this the girl had let out a loud sneeze, a healthy achoo that the audience unanimously considered a favorable sign and an omen of foolproof robustness, without blemish or stain.

For those who chance to ignore it, I clarify here that the term brachycephalic, i.e., broad and rather rude, describes the skull of those who by birth were inclined to weapons rather than to letters, which in short means that instead of making love they preferred to make war.

Before leaving for Mainz, the mother of the girl, who as mentioned above, had only recently abandoned in favor of the true faith the satanic vanities and pomp of the idolatry of her heritage, without having wholly detached herself from them, had wanted to carry out at home the ceremony called the washing of hands, an ancient religious ceremony in which the so-called 'grandmother', the midwife, before the godparents of the christening put their hands on her, washed those of all who attended the rite, who had previously been crowned with colorful garlands of flowers, with water mixed with various and scented petals, contained in a cup of onyx or agate, while with oboes, lutes and theorbos of old, the musicians convened for this purpose played special melodies composed for the occasion.

To baptize the baby the mid-afternoon was chosen, five o'clock sharp, at which time traditionally the most important events used to happen. At such a precise moment the bishop of Mainz, outdoors in the square in front of what with time would become the temple primate and was then being repaired, had stretched his hands out to pour on her head the water of the river Jordan that as I have already said had been brought from the Holy Land for the sacrament. The multitudinous ceremony had been attended by the imperial family in full, who during the ritual had disposed itself by alphabetical order on the Gospel side, while opposite them, on the Epistle side, the other dignitaries and their respective spouses placed themselves.

Following a family tradition and to avoid arrogance, no distinction was made and the godmother held in her arms the child wrapped in a white arrullo, so it was called, the same christening skirt that on like occasions had been worn by her brothers and sister, her maternal aunts and uncles, and no further back because they were recent Christian converts and the baptism was still something new. It is to be noted that the skirt was adorned with some Camariñas lace, from a remote region of Hispania at that time, that until recently had been held by the barbarian Swabians. At the time of the liturgy of the word, Pastora, the godmother herself, who meanwhile had handed over the girl to the godfather, had read full of unction a passage by the prophet Ezekiel who speaks of the sacrament that just then was administered, namely, to shed "upon you (the one who is baptized) a pure water that will purify you."

John, the girl's father, offered himself to the prying eyes in dark blue tunic, with fitted sleeves, long to the foot and fringed with sacred signs at the edges or hem, and he wore a pair of mules, those kinds of slippers whose tip was folded upwards, worn by the Romans. His neck was wrapped in a scarf of Croatian origin and almond color, while under a duffle coat the mother wore a tailored suit, the color of cocoa and peanuts, cream with a breath of milk.

Once the baby had become a member of the Christian community, the delegate of the Pope also a military, the Archbishop of Austrasia, had pronounced some words upon the case, recalling the duty of all, both clergy and laity, to contribute to the armed defense of the homeland.

An outstanding role was also taken by both the secretary of the nuncio and the archbishopric's master of ceremonies, besides a very skilled female painter, a remarkable woman now forgotten, whose name unfortunately History did not register, and thanks to whom we now know the most salient features of the lucky child

It seems she (the little girl) was plump and dark, but had blue eyes and her thin hair was the color of the minted gold. On one thing everybody agreed, that the baby was "cute and beautiful" as well as lovely and quiet, and her father was proud because in his words, "the emotion of being a father could not be described, you have to live it".

To the stupendous baptismal font in which had also been baptized some other celebrities, I have already referred. And in the course of the celebration, the Sisters of St. Cecilia, belonging to the choir of the monastery of Corbie, had sung in unison the appropriate songs. In that renowned convent many widowed queens had sought shelter and taken the veil.

In addition to the countless members of the folk and lower classes, over three hundred and fifty authors and story tellers had witnessed the rare function, who came even from the farthest reaches of the empire and bordering territories to attend such a great event. Among these Eginardo stood out, a famous chronicler of those far away times, a polygraph and stenographer, who in anticipation of what would be current in future centuries, was ahead of his time and objective and dispassionate wrote down everything that he saw. On behalf of blind people and agnostics, then abundant, because as has been said faith is blind and does not see where it is going, that astonishing man had also written in Braille.

Presentation in the Temple. The Mass at birth. The purification

Once the child was christened and returned to home, it had to be presented at the temple. According to the Law of Moses, this should be accomplished forty days after birth. Thus, once the prescribed days of purification had passed, the parents wanted to take her back to Mainz to fulfill the rite. It was customary to deliver to the priest at the time of the offertory of the birth Mass a pair of doves or virgin pigeons, i.e., those that had not yet reached the age of procreation. When the parents went about doing what was commanded, they were warned that the law only prescribed to present in the temple the first-born males in order to consecrate them to God, and nothing was said of children of some other sex.

That discrimination by gender much surprised the parents. Ignorant of the new legislation, they had not heard of it, the more so given the fact that among the Saxons and the Treviri, until recently overlords of those pagan regions, deities of both sexes were equally revered.

After thinking about it calmly in the company of friends and relatives, they agreed to perform the ancestral rite and present the baby on a Saturday in a glade of the sacred wood in which, until Charlemagne had felled it, grew Irminsul, the magic tree or column that supported the world, where on the night that the ancients called Walpurgis Night, devotees gathered to give due worship to the gods and goddesses of old.

So they did. And it happened that in Mainz there was then a straight man named Emmeran. A newcomer to the imperial court and a fellow diner at the table of the Pious, a just and exemplary man, he deplored the corrupt customs of the time and prayed to God for the golden age of primitive matriarchal rule to return.

All the female saints in heaven were with him and had revealed to him that he would not die before seeing the infant who the Blessed Virgin had sent to earth to regenerate it.

Moved by her, of whom he was an extraordinary devotee, on the appointed evening he came to the meadow, and when the parents advanced holding the baby in their arms to carry out the ceremonies of the pagan cult, Emmeran begged them to be allowed to take her in his own, which given his stern countenance free from viciousness was immediately granted him. So he took her with infinite care and as soon as he had her in his arms, he blessed the Virgin Mary, saying:

Now, my Lady, according to your word, you can let your servant die in peace. My eyes have seen the one that by your sublime decision will make men do right and in the Earth there will be such light as to show nations the glory of your gender.

The girl did not come to redeem humanity, which some other, a male, had already redeemed, but to spur and route them on a new path, where once and for all the hateful discrimination by gender would be abolished. Indeed, the Virgin Mary, just for being the mother of God, was granted only the so-called hyperdulia cult, clearly lower than the latria one, she who received his only begotten Son. The latter cult is one of the homage of love, respect and submission which humans offer to supreme beings and in general to some others equally supernatural.

The father and mother were amazed at what they heard about her baby. Facing successively three times the three cardinal points that he had to hand, Emmeran drew in the air the sacred sign of the cross and said to Gudrun:

Look at it, oh, mother, this child will cause scandal and turmoil in many nations. She will be a sign of contradiction, and you yourself will pierce your heart with a sword; so everybody's prejudices will be exposed.

At the meadow had also arrived the aged Veleda, a prophetess, daughter of Aurinia and descendant of a famous tribe of seers and soothsayers. Still very young, betrothed at twelve, she had lived in marriage for seven. Then, because of his immoderation at the table and excesses in the art of Venus her husband died early, a man of intemperate character and rude ways, and after reading what St. Ambrose had preached to the widows in the Italian city of Milan, until the age of eighty-four she had kept herself as such (i.e., a widow) in a convent. She never left it and with continued fasting and prayer, without rest even at night, she worshipped the Lord. With no other nourishment but the sacred form of buckwheat in her daily communion, she had lived three years in a row in a manner that had aroused admiration and attention among people. She arrived at this moment, and with neither pause nor rest, she glorified the Virgin and talked about the girl to everyone who eagerly waited for their gender to be recognized with the same respect and status granted to the other.

Some strange signs frighten everybody

The scene being finished, the people returned home, and within just one year, the heavens were once again dissatisfied with humans and some strange signals frightened everyone's mind, commoners and nobles alike. At night cats and dogs had fallen, and in a nearby pool frogs had become hairy.

A universal deluge fell on Austrasia. Rain and wind swept entire farms. Hundreds of villages turned into lakes. The river Main overflowed and invaded the streets of Mainz, where only the church of St. Stephen miraculously escaped the fury of the elements. Despite waves of up to ten meters storming its walls, not even a drop entered the enclosure, because the bones of St. Walburga lined the walls making them impermeable. The river flooded the slums. From the giant waves emerged a multitude of snakes and a huge dragon never seen before which after crossing the streets without being bothered disappeared into the Rhine. The terrified people ran for shelter.

The bones of the saint had been so effective because, as a result of a miracle performed by her, she had been appointed protector in incidents involving lightning, thunder and unleashed winds, and also sailors entrusted themselves to her.

When she was coming from the Britain at that time to preach the gospel to the surly Germans of Central Europe, during the crossing the North Sea had unleashed a terrible storm that had endangered the lives of everyone. But she had not let herself become intimidated, and by a demonstration of male initiative when the others did not know what to do but whine and despair, she had kneeled on the deck of the frail craft bringing her to the mainland and had prayed to God to appease the unleashed elements, a request which without delay was granted to her.

As a result of this early miracle and many others that throughout her long life she kept performing, her fame grew and so did the devotion that her death inspired. It is told that when some workers were restoring the church in which she had been buried, they had found her bones, but not knowing who it was, they had not given them due consideration. She had then appeared in dreams to the bishop of the time and had remonstrated with him for neglecting his duties. As a result he had ordered the transfer of the remains to a safer place and once there that the sarcophagus be opened. When this was done St Walburga was found there bathed in a sweet smelling oil, an oil that since then has continued to flow and has been used to address different occurrences. It stopped flowing only once when some robbers killed the bellman in the temple, and again when the Church launched an interdict against the reigning emperor. By interdict it was meant that Church authorities forbade the priests to hold liturgical services, closed the temples and sacraments were not administered; a kind of sit-down strike that lasted as long as the ruler in charge refused to apologize for their misdeeds and did not reform himself.

Back to the story: the ruler of the Franks also reacted when, together with the catastrophe above, some strange signs troubled his already pusillanimous mind. He worried a lot about them, as chroniclers said. The stars in the sky moved in a strange way, fearful unexpected comets appeared, there were earthquakes and interlunations or lunar eclipses, rotten grain fell from the sky, in the evening they heard unusual terrible sounds, stones and ice chunks rained, lightning was incessant, and unknown avian plagues killed countless people and beasts.

No less affected than him was a twelve year old girl from near Hildesheim, in the surroundings of Frankfurt, who like the prophetess to whom I have already referred, after having received from the hands of a priest the sacraments, ate nor drank, and persisted in her fasting without being anorexic. For countless months she had not taken a single calorie nor felt hunger or thirst or the urge to eat something.

Such things deprived the emperor of already scant sleep; he did not sleep a wink all night long and with songs of praise and prayers to God waited for dawn. Such ominous signs announced for the kingdom and the human race some terrible misfortune. The divinity was angered by the unabashed sinners who, proud of their bad habits, instead of reforming themselves and returning to the straight path, did not repent or impose penance on themselves.

To placate the divinity, Louis ordered that the people should abstain from meat on days of obligation, not to mention some other duties that on their own initiative the most compliant ones would like to add, as well as incessant prayers and abundant alms.

Everybody should give generously of what they possessed, not just to the poor, but to God's servants also, to priests and monks. He did not request it because he feared the wrath of God, but because it was his duty to be solicitous towards the Church entrusted to him; and despite so many signs that, as was well known, pointed to a radical change in the empire and the death of a prince, he ordered all those authorized to do it to celebrate Mass.

Louis orders the death of newly born children

In the south of Aquitaine, Louis had just lost his war with the Moors, despite the fact that before undertaking it his advisers and top priests had predicted that with the help of the god of battles, he would achieve a speedy and complete victory. But either those soothsayers were wrong or the god of victories denied one to him. Thus, after adding to the above-mentioned signs the embarrassing defeat, he mused about the causes of the calamity that hung over the empire. And it came to his mind what he had been told of that wondrous girl, namely that a midwife had attended her birth without papers, and also that, at the bedside of the new mother, a witch had told her fortune. All of that smelled a mile off of superstitious heresy, so he felt he had found who was to blame for the bad events that lay ahead and by a decree ordered all soothsayers and similar people dwelling in his land to be pursued.

By attributing his own crimes to a scapegoat, he copied Nero. Nero had put on Christians the blame for the burning of Rome, so that by following his orders Tigellinus had done his dirty work for him. Like that ancient Roman emperor, Louis sparked a chase in which many Franks died or were forced to live in bitter exile.

But it was not enough, and of that girl born among such wonders he feared the worst. So after consulting his advisers, who gave him carte blanche in the matter and urged him not to lose heart and continue the effort, he ordered that all the children under one year in Ingelheim and its outskirts, according to what the three holy women had told him, be killed. Thus it was accomplished that which another prophetess, the sorceress of Oz, had predicted:

"Saxony has heard the clamour of much weeping and lamentation: it is the Germanic Gertrude, weeping for her children and refusing to be comforted, because they are not longer alive ".

But such a scheme was of no avail to that ruler, because again in a dream there appeared to John the blessed Bathilde:

John, get up and do not be lazy as usual. Do not delay, take the girl and her mother and travel to neighboring Aachen, in the kingdom of Neustria, and stay there until I tell you, because Louis is going to seek the girl to kill her.

Bathilde had been a Saxon slave girl whose extreme charm had seduced Clovis II, a Merovingian king. Once married to him, she had given him three children. Later, her husband having been killed in battle, she had ruled the kingdom on behalf of Clothario III, then a minor. She had founded and endowed many monasteries. But the butler Ebroin snatched power away from her and she retired to the monastery of Chelles, where she soon died a malignant death in the odor of sanctity.

The Pope then in charge raised her to the altars.

John rose quickly, took the girl and her mother, and although it was a moonless night went swiftly to Aachen, first via Aix, then on to Aachen by land and on foot.

At that hour the Rhine boatmen were still asleep and John would not wake them because they were against starting the journey earlier than usual and would complain to their labor union. There he stayed until the emperor, urged by his young wife Judith, who asserted her credit before him, repented of his past cruelty, did public penance, and after confessing his sins and covering his head with the ashes of an early unpruned oak, revoked the order with which he had banished the hated subjects.

Thus was fulfilled what the Virgin had announced in one of the Marian apparitions of the past: *From Aachen I called my beloved daughter, on whom I have put all my hopes.*

My parents offer me to the Holy Virgin Mary

JOAN – Following an old tradition, princes used to offer to the Holy Virgin Mary in a famous basilica of the capital city their newborn children. I say an old tradition, but it was not centuries old, because uses take centuries to become traditional, and Charlemagne's royal family was scarcely one century old.

Therefore Judith and Louis were planning to present to that popular Virgin their most recently born child, a girl too, whom they had given the name of Leonor. As I had been chosen for a sublime future, my mother would not allow us to be inferior to those blue-blooded people, so she plotted to take me without much fuss to that same basilica and present me secretly to the Virgin, in order that I too would profit from the opportunity offered.

Hence when I was scarcely seven months old, early in the morning of the day chosen for the celebration she took me and carried me to the famed temple, where the archbishop of the diocese and his acolytes welcomed at that very moment the little princess. With them were the Dominican friars of the neighboring convent and numerous other high-status people who wanted not to miss the intimate event.

Carried in the arms of her mother Judith, the little princess went wide awake into the house. She wore a white apron and matching ties and around her neck a chain of beads from which hung a little Latin cross, a symbol of the scaffold on which the only-begotten male son of our supreme Creator had died. The baby wore neither earrings nor any other profane dressing which might detract from the solemnity of the ceremony, and was apparently entirely self-possessed, as befitted the height of her crib. She kept her composure and did not cry, limiting herself, with the bewilderment and interest of her young age, to just looking at her parents, those priests present and the two hundred or so idle nobodies who attended the happy event captivated by the singular atmosphere. She did not miss any detail.

The ceremony did not last very long; after saying one Hail Mary, the heirs of the kings had taken up in their arms their daughter, offering her to the holy Mother of our main divinity. In that precise instance and out of the depths of their diaphragms, or according to the more spiritual, their souls, those attending the event had exhaled in unison a sigh of wonder and relief which stirred emotion in anyone who later had of it any news.

In a corner of the temple, trying to go unnoticed behind a column, my mother did not miss a detail of the ceremony and tried to copy the gestures and attitudes of the illustrious royal personages; at the appropriate time she raised me sneakily in her arms, and facing the image of the Virgin, she pronounced in pectore, that is to say, to herself and without anybody hearing her, a prayer appropriate to the case.

In this way, and with the royal princess, I too was left under protection of that popular Virgin Mary.

CHAPTER 2 - The early childhood of Joan

Joan's father was an oblate in England

JOAN - In what precedes, I have already spoken of my father. He was born in England, in the vicinity of York, the same place of origin as Alcuin, one of Charlemagne's intellectuals, and had been offered to the Church as an oblate.

At that time, oblates had a bad reputation. According to the documents that record it, delivering the boys to the monks had led to bad practices later to be outright rejected, but at those times were looked at if not with condescension, at least with odd indulgence.

Sharing the straw mattress or the poor bed at night with minors was a deeply-rooted habit; pedophilia was something accepted and very few were against it. Pedophilia was then what later would be called sexual abuse. Apparently the practice of handing over the children as oblates only made it easier for the monks to violate them and increased their helplessness. Those holy men or those training to become such were unwilling to reproduce, to beget offspring, as they only wanted to have fun, to enjoy what they called carnal pleasure. And therefore they had no qualms about the hole they used.

About one of those boys whose father had given to the Church, an abbot had written: *the man handed me his son and it pleased me and I was happy with all my heart. But when the boy turned ten years old, obscene wishes tormented me and the beast of lust and pleasure dominated me, I wanted to possess him carnally.*

Nothing obsessed monks as much as having sex with children; in the desert the Blessed Macarius had seen so many hermits sexually abusing young people that he pressed them to give up the practice and not to take the little ones to the desert to do penance. But with the passage of time, nothing changed, the urge was still too strong, and even if monastic rules were imposed to escort children when going to the toilet to satisfy their natural needs, this did not prevent the monks continuing to abuse them.

They said: With wine and boys available, monks do not need the devil to tempt them.

Usually the priests sexually seduced young people in the confessional; but the so-called early penitential books, which detailed the penance to be applied to each of the many possible sins, only penalized those violated, not the rapists, blaming those who suffered the rape for having let it happen. They condemned the victim rather than condemning the executioner. A progressive saint had said that in monasteries sex with boys was like a bloodthirsty beast loose at will in the midst of a flock of sheep of the Lord, and therefore advised that because it was a sin against nature, the abused and abuser should be alike punished as accomplices. It was a comment that had stirred up the wrath of many. How dared somebody, and even in the same profession, criticize a centuries-old practice? It was scandalous.

The strictest ones held that a man copulating with another, also expressed as lying in bed with another, even more so if with one younger than him and therefore less able to resist, was something contrary to nature, something unholy, nefarious, and to be condemned.

I've never known what fate befell my father as oblate at that particular monastery of his native England. Many apostles, like St. Walburga, St. Boniface, her uncle, and her brothers Saints Winibald and Wilibald, had come from there, Ireland and Great Britain, to convert continental pagans, and many of them had also been an oblates, because in those iron times most parents begat numerous children they were unable to properly feed, so they gave them to the friars, to ensure they had at least a pittance and a bed.

In convents monks ate and drank hard, and the rule ora et labora, that is, pray and work, attributed to the reformer Benedict of Aniane, was yet to come.

Back to my father: when he met Gudrun, he was young and handsome and full of life. As was earlier said of the chaste Joseph, foster father of Jesus, our savior, it was unimaginable that God would give a as mate and companion to the mother of a girl whom He had reserved an sacred destiny a rude and vulgar man, whose task would be protecting, helping and nourishing me with the work of his hands until I came of age.

My parents' characters

My father, John Anglicus, son of John, was born in the year 784, on the 30th of May. He was blond and blue-eyed, tall and slightly awkward; on arriving to Ingelheim he was six feet six inches tall, which amounts to about today 1.98 m, and for having had a good start in life, wore oversized sandals. On turning sixteen years he was 1.80 m tall, so that in the abbey classrooms his classmates taunted him and called him a resuscitated Goliath and "big man without measure." Very fond of reading dusty old manuscripts, the prior and the prefect supposed him to possess passable intelligence and expected great things from him.

In fact if not by law, Gudrun, my mother, and John Anglicus, my father, had come to live together and share their common vicissitudes. He was born in the sign of Gemini, born almost in June, while she was a Capricorn, born on December 24: a curious astrological relationship theirs, an air sign and an earth one, from which had sprouted a Scorpio, me, a water sign that predestined me to show practicality, tenacity and energy in whatever I did.

Given their different respective signs, perhaps my parents should have foreseen the fact that, regarding my education, they were necessarily going to disagree.

While according to experts in the matter, those born in Gemini tend to be good fathers, if maybe a bit too lenient, especially with daughters, as Charlemagne apparently had been, those of the sign of Capricorn never forgave anyone anything, and in training issues they left no loopholes in which to move freely.

Many of the governesses who would populate the gallant and scandalous stories of later centuries had belonged to my mother's astrological sign, and all of them had considered a severe and uncompromising education as the fundamental basis of a balanced development. However, those Gemini not had it so easy because they liked children as they were and, rather than intervene and mold them, they preferred to let them grow freely, as they thought that in time they would see.

Probably some would have said my father was a bit naive.

Again according to experts, the astrological conjunction of my father and my mother, an air sign with an earth one, did not presage an eternal honeymoon, a happy life without clashes and conflicts. On the surface manageable and docile, as well as responsible, at heart those Gemini were very capricious and volatile, maintained the experts. Also very romantic and idealistic and easily prey of emotion, they were thought over-sentimental, that is, sensitive to the atrocities that plagued the era. Strong-willed but also very loving and tender, to remain faithful to a relationship they would need a lot of slyness to deal with them, which very few can show when needed.

But in the Capricorn sign of their partner resided perhaps the way to overcome the problems of chemistry between them. Capricorn was a constant sign, and those born in it pursue relentlessly their goals and once they reached them, would hold and defend them tooth and nail, including to immolate themselves on the altar of sacrifice if required. They could become incredibly loyal, but their perfectionism would generate some distance around them.

As a typical Capricorn, my mother was clever and bright and therefore was good at starring in any situation. But she also tended to be somewhat bossy. She tolerated it badly when someone called into question what she said.

Maniacal about timeliness, although in her, being a woman, the feature was more flexible than it would have been in a male, at the moment of truth, she was equal to the occasion. For that reason, although my father's wife, she could give him at least some guarantees of responsibility.

Despite their differences, something united them, namely, their awareness of the place they would occupy in any story. Irresponsible at first, my father knew that important things are not to be taken lightly, while my mother, obsessed with projecting herself in space and time was able to do anything to get them.

In any case my parents' life was in their own hands –pointed out those pundits, because astrology only shows trends.

My mother used to say that the story with my father had emerged from love at first sight. His sense of humor, wit and talent had been aphrodisiac factors which had led her to fall in love and let him make her four children. "I first saw him when bare-chested he preached to the pagans and that was already a great attraction; then at a banquet, luck seated me beside him and I found him incredibly witty, which put the icing on the cake", confided my mother, who, at forty-seven, admitted that sometimes even she had a tantrum, but with age she had learned to manage her big ego much more than before.

This was what she told us.

When they met, my mother was twenty-eight years old, my father twenty-one. He was an Angle, she was a Saxon, or rather a Frank of Basque origin; he seduced her, promised her who knows what, she believed him or let herself be fooled. He was an apostle, inexperienced and still a virgin, at least in dealing with women. He had left the convent, immigrated to Germany, met my mother and she met him, made a married life, had three children and produced me.

My fate written in the stars

Those who made horoscopes and disclosed our way of being written in the stars, at the time of my coming into the world had forecast that I would be an active and determined person on one hand, and a calculating and cautious one on the other, that is, able to swim and eat at the same time. Besides this I would be easily irritated but nonetheless also gentle, strong-willed and soft at times and reluctant at first to marry. I would need to think twice, to the point that I would never do it or would decide only after reaching maturity.

They would also warn their listeners that in dealing with those born under this sign of mine, never to oppose them and shy away from any discussion or confrontation, because they risked leaving scalded and with their tail between their legs.

I was a Scorpio, a water sign crossed by the sun and ruled by the planets Pluto and Mars. Therefore I was predicted to be very active, thirsting to possess and dominate and endowed with an uncommon willpower. Although a fighter already since birth, I would also be quiet and very jealous of my privacy.

I was going to mature very early, would be very fond of studying and would like especially to excel over others and distinguish myself. I also would play with children of the opposite sex, and in our mutual relations I would be the boss, because my inclination would be to not tolerate imposition from anyone and to leave scratching fleas alone, as they say. First of all I would always rule the roost, and not just in the bedroom, so I would never let anyone force me to make me the bed. (Mind the joke).

It was also predicted that I would show greed, eat with appetite and sleep soundly. I had been marked as a great personality. I would be a woman blind, drunk and tough, a tenacious Scorpio, vital and prudent. Born under such a sign, I would not stop at anything or anyone and would get anything that I had proposed myself. Volcanic, feverish, vital, energetic, active, calculating, cautious, vain, jealous, a great lover, though potentially unfaithful, such would I be with the years.

Like all those born between 19th October and 20th November, I would be intuitive, passionate, strongly magnetic and very committed to always holding the reins myself. I could be jealous, resentful, spiteful, compulsive, obsessive, stubborn, vindictive and very quiet. In my professional life, nobody would be more respected than me or more feared, not because of my cruelty, a trait mistakenly attributed to my sign, but because of my strength and preparation.

Those who would eventually plan to present me with a pet should take into account that I would prefer over any other animal insects and invertebrate creatures, because in general the bony spine and roughly speaking everything hard and meaty would make me nervous; my symbol would be cod, or better yet maybe eels and mackerel. My favorite organs would be the sexual organs, and my capital motto, "I want."

I would impose by my physique and my mere presence would suffice to captivate others; by my enviable vitality; all the good and bad of the other zodiacal signs would meet in me. According to my astrological chart, nothing would stop me and from the very beginning I would be a winner, never a loser ready to sacrifice and die for the cause. Though irascible, quarrelsome and vain, generosity would overcome me, so I would not misuse the power that I would win by my own effort; thus protecting the weak ones would obsess me.

As a mate, I would not be surpassed by anyone, since my ability to love would know no limits and I would be always able to cherish with unbeatable force the choice of my heart, (as Hildegard had loved Charlemagne, to the point of giving him ten children), though at the same time I would be potentially jealous if not in action.

I was not going to take anything lightly; hence to make me happy would be a very difficult endeavor. From my earliest childhood I would be considered a devotee of family, and if one day I held a prominent position, I would care first of all about my closest relatives. I would even die for them. Therefore I risked falling into the unseemly nepotism that would push me to grant the best positions to my dependents and kin.

Of my same sign had been Godesvinda of Anheim, an excellent woman in the arts and letters; the female painter Sofonisba Angustiola, who with rare skill had recreated the Roman frescoes; the Princess of Éboli, at first an intriguer and later a devout; a future president of the American States and a mayor of a suburb of the outskirts of Paris.

My parents were not quite happy with what the Western horoscope foretold, so they wanted to know the Chinese one too, according to which I belonged to the sign of the rooster and that farm animal would represent me better than anything else.

I was therefore neat, precise, organized, honest and direct and very fond of eggs, that I would easily put upstanding (like Christopher Columbus had done according to legend).

Of an extroverted personality and because those of my sign tend to be fun and silly, I would be inclined to large meetings and telling dubious jokes; very able in addition to express myself orally and in writing, I would quickly learn to pronounce with dignity and aplomb words frowned upon. And where wise maidens would think twice, I would throw myself head first into the craziest situations. I would be a whirlwind.

Like my mother, Gudrun, I would be weak on the side of egotism: I would have a tremendous, though well deserved, ego. Sometimes I would be a little uncertain, especially when blows the Swiss south wind, the foehn for some, the north wind to others, and sensitive to flattery as much as to the delusions of grandeur. Work would fill me with enthusiasm, though not so much housework or the construction kind.

My early education

Comforted by such forebodings, my parents promised themselves happiness. There was no time to lose; my education should start at once, above all to prevent being thwarted from such a happy promise of future triumphs.

Clearly I was bound for glory, so it was better not to take unnecessary risks. First of all I had to be educated in the fear of God's, as on Him depends even the slightest trembling in the wind of a blade of grass.

As aforesaid, my mother's zodiacal sign pushed her to be stern; she was not in favor of indulgence but instead she intended to make a show of firmness from the very cradle and not to spoil me. By educating my body, punishing it, she would teach me to behave, while my father, professionally dedicated to others' salvation, or to put it another way to teaching them the right path to heaven, would be responsible for my soul, which he would educate by means of pertinent examples.

To educate someone was the same as to teach him to obey. A novice in the Christian faith, my mother Gudrun showed herself a fervent adept and boasted that no one surpassed her in devotion, so she was more Catholic than the very Pope. She liked to memorize the biblical statements heard in the church and that her husband often repeated, and mainly paid heed to those regarding the education of children – such as those of King Solomon, whose wisdom she admired, and who recommended educating them without any compunction.

Beat him with the rod, had said in his "proverbs" that wise man, for surely thou wilt not kill him. Nor deprive yourself of hard spanking him, because if you do not know why you hit him, surely he knows. And he added: a good spanking on time will save much future hard punishment.

Gudrun heard that advice and was prompt to follow it to the letter without deviating from it one iota. Nobody could accuse her of not being a good mother and not knowing how to raise her children. In that, nobody would give her any lessons.

Unfortunately, her innate inclination had been compounded by the fact that at the time it was customary to spank without compassion one's own children, everyone did, so much so that busy mothers who had no time to deal with such lowly work employed the services of a strict housekeeper, schooled in the art of corporally punishing naughty children. Ladies who offered their good services and promised to support them with good references and qualifications were employed for the purpose.

I was not spared that kind of early training.

Solomon had stated: Who spares the cane, hates his son, but who loves him, soon applies the punishment. Discipline your son, because there is still hope, and don't let his pain to soft you. Folly is housed in the heart of a child; the rod of correction shall drive it far from him.

My mother was persuaded -a Christian mother of then- that "deep inside, children were inclined to indulge in adultery, fornication, impure wishes, lust, anger, fighting, gluttony and hatred "; she was convinced that for me to not grow crooked and given to evil, I had to be firmly held. Failing to do so, I would pluck myself the ears, with my own nails I would pull out my eyes, break my arms and legs or touch myself; I would certainly reduce myself to pieces and like an animal would walk on all fours. And what was worse, if she did not hold me, I would rebel and discharge upon her the rage that possessed me, because I was so evil that if she spoiled me too much, I would soon become a master of my own parents.

Such was the usual thinking when I was a child. In everybody's opinion, children were so violent that you even had to hold their head firmly so that they did not rip it. You should also not let them stare idly into space; because idleness was the mother of all evils and fantasy the source of countless aberrations.

Mothers and wet nurses of the time wrapped the child in cloths and tied him so tightly that it was a wonder that, left by the hearth, swaddled and wrapped, the child did not choke or suffocate. All the time it was the same: my mother laid me on a board, put on me a shirt or a rough and crumpled diaper, and over them she wrapped the girdle. She immobilized against my chest my little arms, and then fastened under my armpits the strip of cloth, down to the buttocks, to the feet, covered my head with a cap and secured everything with needles. She tied me so that I could not move, and I think that by God's mercy she did not oppress me until the point that I could not breathe and I drown, and I even believe that the same God inspired her to put me on one side so that my spittle poured out of my mouth and I did not choke on it.

I screamed with all my strength and kicked against that bondage, and to silence me my mother could not think of anything better to do than to catch me in her arms and cuddle me without ceremony, with violent shaking, which most of the time was of no use because I kept screaming. Then to quell my howls she put in my mouth a piece of cloth she had to hand made into a ball, on which I almost choked and was about to suffocate and drown. With the other hand, she fastened with pins my diapers and the idea did not occur to her that I might well be complaining because some of them, misplaced, had punctured me.

In addition she believed in the evil eye and the envy of evil spirits and malicious neighbors. Therefore, she locked me all day long in the dark in a secluded room, and, so that nobody saw me, she covered my face with a cloth. Then, to counter the possible ill will of others, she put inside my clothing sharp metal objects, without considering the risk that all this meant for my welfare.

In those days, everyone was afraid of everything and everybody. Also, for the reasons already given, to avoid ill will and envy, my mother drove away evil spirits by rubbing with salt my skin, which irritated me terribly, and smeared my nipples with excrement, forced me to drink my own urine and asked visitors to spit on me and say, ah, the ugly and horrible girl!

She fed me without taking off the diaper and never bathed me, so that I spent days wrapped in my stool, and if I cried, she did not care and let me cry lying on my straw bed, left me in a corner or swaddled and hung from a nail in the wall for hours while she attended to her work.

Of no avail were the recommendations of those who were more sensitive or knowledgeable and insisted that we children should be bathed and not left in our stool, so that for the first year of my life I was mostly covered in shit from head to foot, stinking, swollen and my skin full of ulcers to the point that just by touching me they made me scream in pain.

It could have been worse, because in many places to combat the supposedly violent innate inclinations of children, they were kept tied to a board even until they were three years old.

My mother wrapped me conscientiously, so that when no one looked at me I could not do bad things, any mischief, as all children by nature did, because it was taken for granted that we were all possessed by the devil. She used to go out and forget about me after hanging me, bound and abject, from a nail on the wall. That way, I guess, I knew from a very early hour what it meant to suffer in silence, as quietly and without complaint as our divine Redeemer had suffered on the cross; and there, motionless and silent, from early on I began to pray without tiring of the sorrowful mysteries of rosary, so that soon I had learned them by heart, barely moving my lips and just muttering the prayers of the rite, so as not to bother with unwelcome noise and childish babbling my mother or anyone else who by chance was at home.

My parents had the habit of reciting the rosary with the family at nightfall. We all gathered together in the main room of the house that served as living room and recited the Our Father and Hail Mary, ending it all with the litany.

My mother chastens me

My mother hit me at least twice as often as my father did, and when they thought I should be punished, she did it much more often than him. Later I knew about some girls who in middle age had written some diaries or confessions where they recounted their first few years of life.

"She was a curious woman, my mother!" described one of them. "Children seemed to inspire her with a vindictive animosity, with a fury for beating and banging them, against walls, against chairs, upon the ground".

"My mother followed to the letter the advice of educators, in never sparing the rod, insomuch that I have frequently been whipped for looking blue on a frosty morning; and, whether I deserved it or not, I could be sure that every day, without missing one, I would be corrected".

"Mom hit us for the slightest reason. Not merely she gave us a spanking on the ass, but sometimes she flogged us with a whip. Our bruises lasted several days".

"Mom hit me often. To not spoil me, she whipped me every morning; if she didn't have time in the morning, she hit me at noon, rarely later than four o'clock".

"Sometimes my mother had no time to beat me; others she complained that at morning on giving me a beating, she had hurt her back, because I had kicked and she had got a wrench, so that she had recourse to a professional who for a reasonable price offered herself for beating children; or she arranged with a street guard she had met, to punish me once a week, whether I had deserved it or not."

Those skilled in the matter advised mothers, "once turned one year and even before, we must teach children to fear the rod and cry softly; accustom him to do without a murmur what he is bid by hitting him all the times needed. God himself has ordained it so by giving the mother the power and placing in her hands the helpless babe. If a child disobeys, you must cause him such steadily and unwavering bodily pain that disobedience and suffering shall be indissolubly connected in his mind for ever" -said another one. "And since the child is necessarily dependent on their parents, he will not bear a grudge against those who have hurt him… However much his mother hits him, the child looks for her and values her above all others."

Children began being beaten in the womb. My father did not used to beat my mother, but usually husbands hit at will their wife, and over a third of all were so battered, physical assault increasing during pregnancy. The only law on the subject put in the books referred to the maximum allowed size of the staff employed.

Half or more of the mothers began hitting their infants even before they had completed a year. A mother declared in respect of hers:

"Before he had learnt to speak … I ended up with his whims. He was not yet a year and already feared the rod. In the house was rarely heard that hateful noise of a child crying and the family usually lived in as much quietness as if there had not been a child among them".

"Even if the child do not cry and for him to obey a mother's merest glance will suffice, you should not give up beating him willingly, and you never would start too early, as in the case of this mother and her 4 months old child:

"I hit him until he had purple the whole body and I could not more, and he did not budge one iota".

Even if the child was crying because he felt ill, he should be whipped:

"Before one year old and when she cried, we began to correct our daughter. We have taught her a command over her feelings. Even if she cries because she feels ill, we hit her with the stick until she dominates and calms down".

"Children must always show submissive and obedient; it has to be done soon, as later it will be very difficult"

And another mother added:

"You have to begin spanking them when they are still too young to remember and hold it against you."

Those were hard times. Children could be stoned to death if uncontrollable. An author had written:

"It is only reasonable for parents to scold their children ... hit them, cause them pain, sent them to prison ... if nevertheless they still rebel, law allows to punish them even by killing them.

Ancient Romans flogged in public their children, in Sparta it was not uncommon for older people to hit children and even kill them. In the "confessions" that as those of St. Augustine had reached us, things like this were read:

"The whip to train the dogs was by the door; the leather strap to sharpen razor blades was hanging from a nail in the wall of the kitchen; and in one corner, the paddle to drain laundry. If we showed mischievous my mother no longer had to use it; she had only to look to the corner for us to quiet."

As to me, probably to relieve her guilt, my mother often made me praise God aloud while she whipped me. She enjoyed making me show her my bare ass and ask her to punish me by whipping.

One theologian felt enraptured before the divine wisdom "which had given buttocks to children so that they could be beaten without irreparable hurt."

After the beating my mother forced me to thank her for having corrected me, and to kiss the hand that had punished me, or the stick or baker's peel, or the rod and the whip used instead.

My father let my mother do and sometimes if his conscience pricked him too much, he reminded us of the treatment he himself had undergone at first in his home and later at the monastery to which he had been delivered:

"I also was educated in that harsh way", he confessed; "our mother obliged us to stop crying and to thank the rod with which she tried to bend our will."

An episode among many

I'll tell of an episode among many. I was still too young, around six years old. One morning my brother and I played without care, thinking of nothing in particular, when one of us two -I have forgotten who- suggested we exchange clothing: he would dress in my shirt and skirt and I his pullover and pants. And without thinking twice we did so.

We sauntered around a little and everything would have gone well, without further consequences, were it not that it occurred to us to show off in public. We went out in the street and let passers-by see us. Some laughed; some just smiled and kept moving.

Attracted by the uproar, my mother came to the door and saw us. I can see her reaction even today. She didn't laugh or smile. Suddenly I saw on her face that expression of harsh rigidity that sometimes she showed, an air of grim determination, as if she clenched her teeth and promised herself she would rather die than give up. She took us by our arms and wordlessly dragged us back into home. My brother managed to slip away. As for me, she took me into the kitchen.

Once there, without even raising her voice she said, "Get off those trousers you seem to feel so comfortable." I stood still, as if I had not heard or had not understood what she was saying. She pulled up a chair and sat on it, and after looking at me calmly repeated, "your trousers down! I will not tell you again! I'll not repeat it twice."

Without taking my eyes from her face, I started to undress. I had the impression that it never ended, as if I contemplate myself doing it, I lowered my trousers and took them off. I left them lying on the ground.

She looked at me and grinned: "Not like that, little girl," she told me, her voice sharpened by a slight bit of anger and annoyance. "Neatly; hang them up neatly."

I picked them up and smoothed the fabric. I laid them over the back of a chair.

"Good, I see you are learning". Then she paused: "Now those panties too." I did not hesitate. My fingers stretched the elastic of the waistband and, without thinking; I pulled my panties down and over my feet.

Then I stood there, feeling silly, and waiting for her next order. She smiled at me and left the room. When she returned there was a wooden hairbrush in her right hand. Moving deliberately she took from the dining area an armless wooden chair. She placed it carefully in the centre of the room and, hiking up her skirt, sat facing me. I stood there and felt a mixture of apprehension and embarrassment.

She shifted slightly in the chair, settling back into a comfortable position and beckoned me to get over her lap.

I reached her side and looked down at her white and full legs. I knew what was about to happen and a shiver of anxiety ran down my back.

As I hesitated, she impatiently tapped the hairbrush on her thigh, as if to remind me of her previous warning.

I swallowed again as I bent at the waist and allowed my knees to buckle. I knew that as soon as I was over her lap she would feel my fear. I lowered myself over her lap as gently as possible. Then I was in position. Her hand moved slowly across my buttocks, creating chills of excitement that made my body shudder from the crown of my head to the tip of my toes, with a mixture of pleasure and panic. "Well, little girl," she said as her fingers danced across my bottom, "you are now comfortable."

She was right. My position was humiliating. I was being treated like if my feelings did not matter in the least. She did not care about my dignity, my confusion and shame. I was, nevertheless, comfortable.

Then I felt her fingers on my legs and the tail of my shirt being folded over my back. My rear end was exposed to the air and to whatever she wanted to do with her wicked hairbrush.

"Little girls are not supposed to be comfortable when they are being corrected" -she told me. I could almost hear her chuckle as she spoke to me. "Little girls are supposed to be very sorry when they are naughty. You are not sorry now. You will be sorry very soon".

I did not respond. I expected her to say something else. She didn't. She had a more effective way to communicate with me. The back of the hairbrush crashed into my backside with a sound like a book being dropped from a great height and landing flat on a wooden floor. I felt myself being pushed against her legs by the force of the blow. Then my vision went white as the pain flashed across one side of my rear end. She did not even pause to take back her breath. Splat! Before I could even catch my breath from the first swat, the hairbrush landed on the opposite buttock creating a new insufferable fire. I was surprised at how much just two spanks had hurt. And worse, I knew the thing had only begun.

"Ouch!" I cried. "That hurts". This time I heard her low, throaty laugh. "My little girl is no longer comfortable." she said. "Now you are starting to learn how to be sorry."

She said nothing else. The hairbrush clutched in her long fingers spoke for her. Its electric message came through loud and clear. I didn't even have a chance to catch my breath; the paddle began to land on my bottom an instant after she spoke. It stung.

It was even worse than that. It felt like someone had taken a burning torch and dropped it on the soft flesh of my bottom.

It didn't take long for me to start to cry out. By the time she had given me a dozen hard swats my whole bottom felt like it was on fire. I gripped the legs of the chair to keep from reaching back. I kicked my legs in the air. Then it got worse. The hairbrush started to revisit spots that it had already set on fire. The stinging got worse. Between each spank I could think only of the pain in my bottom. Then the hairbrush would crash down again and the fire would burn even hotter. My rear was so sore that even a light tap would have created waves of pain. She didn't give me any light taps. She didn't stop just because I was yelling and kicking and wriggling. She continued to swat my buns with that evil paddle until my eyes clouded over and, unable to stand any more. I could feel tears in my eyes as I reached back with one hand and tried to cover my bottom.

Please, I cried out. "No more. I'm burning up. I can't stand any more. My mother stopped then. When she stopped paddling me, I thought she was finished. I took a deep breath and told her how sorry I was. I was wrong. "Stand up." she ordered. I almost jumped to my feet. My hands flew back and tried to comfort my throbbing buttocks. I was so intent on rubbing my bottom that I did not notice her manoeuvre me between her legs. I was not aware of what was happening until she started to pull me down again.

"What?" I exclaimed. She did not pause until I was draped over one of her legs. I was bent at a very acute angle with my nose almost on the floor. Then I felt her other leg push against the back of my legs, pinning me in position. "I am not done yet, little girl." she said. "You are just starting to learn your lesson." I could almost hear the chuckle in her voice.

"No." I cried. "No more," and reached back again to protect my rear. She grabbed my wrist and pushed it up into my back. My nose bumped against the carpet and the back of the hairbrush fell again on my bottom. Her strong leg and hand firmly immobilized me. I could not move as my sore heinie stuck up as a perfect target for her hairbrush.

I have never felt so helpless in my life. I struggled and wiggled but my bottom stayed in position and the hairbrush continued to fall. All I could think about was my bottom. The rest of my body seemed to become nothing more than dead attachments to a spot of pain. My buns seemed to swell and pulsate as she continued to spank me. Finally I realized that I was no longer kicking or struggling. I was crying; I knew that because I could feel the tears rolling down my cheeks and I could taste the salty drops as they dripped into my mouth. I was begging; I knew that because I could hear incoherent pleas pass my lips between my sobs. Otherwise I was just laying there absorbing each swat. My bottom no longer throbbed. All I could feel was a deep ache that seemed to penetrate even deeper with each of her regular spanks. I thought that I had been over her lap forever. She stopped then.

She stopped spanking me and laid the back of the hairbrush on my back. She held me tightly in position as her hand played with the sore flesh of my bottom.

"I think you are sorry now" -she told me.

"Waah." I cried like a small child. "I'm sorry. I'm sorry" -I said in a voice choked with sobs. I bubbled like a naughty child trying to appease an angry parent. "I think you have learned a lesson." -my mother said to me.

I sobbed again and gasped as I tried to talk. "Yes," I told her between sobs. "I have. I have."

"Good," she told me. "When you get up, kneel and thank me. Then you can kiss the hairbrush and thank it for helping to teach the lesson."

Even though the fire was still raging in my bottom I realized what a humiliating ritual she was ordering me to perform. I balked. "No." I said. "Don't embarrass me like that."

"I see I was wrong." she said. "I see that you have not learned your lesson."

She did not use the hairbrush now. Her hand was sufficient. She slapped one buttock and then the other. There was not much force behind the blows. There did not have to be. Even the light slaps made the stinging worse.

"No." I cried. "I'll do it. I'll do it."

She paid no attention. As I cried and protested, she slapped me a dozen times before she stopped again. She held me in place for a few seconds.

"I will release you now." she told me and, as she spoke, I felt her hands leave my wrist and the pressure depart from my legs.

Free at last, I rolled onto the floor. I stood, stumbling as I got to my feet. My hands were on my bottom as I hopped and danced around the room. Nothing helped. The pain continued. The throbbing continued. I could stand it no more.

She allowed me to bounce around the room for a moment before she issued a sharp command to get my attention. "You were not told you could do that." she said sharply. "You were told what you had to do. Do you wish to be spanked again tomorrow?"

I ignored her.

The pain in my rear was too great. I continued to caper around the chair rubbing at my sore bottom.

She spoke again. "If you do not stop that right now, I will put you back over my knee."

This got my attention. I did not question her right or ability to do so. I forced myself to stand still and then walk over to her. She spread her legs to provide me with a place to kneel.

I forced my knees to bend until they touched the floor. I could feel her knees close against my sides. They touched me and held me in place. I looked and saw the hairbrush extended to me, hanging in the air just inches from my lips.

I tried to talk but could not. I swallowed and looked up at her. There was a stern expression on her face and I knew what I had to do.

"Thank you," I choked out. "Thank you for correcting me."

I stopped talking.

"Kiss the hairbrush too." I shivered at the commanding tone in her voice.

I put out a hand to steady the brush and bring it to my lips. It felt warm as though heated by the exercise of beating my behind.

"Thank you," I told the inanimate object. "Thank you for the lesson you taught me."

I looked up again. There was a smile on her face now. It was a smile of amusement and of pleasure. It was a smile that said that she now owned me and that this scene would be repeated whenever she thought it necessary. Her hand stretched out and patted my back. With gentle pressure she helped me up. "Come," he said. "I'll put a cream, I will heal the blisters." She gently touched my aching back and taking my hand led me out of the room.

After punishment, all praise seems to double, especially when both come from the same person.

She owned me. I was painfully aware that it would be very difficult for me to forget what had happened, and what was even sadder, that I would miss her beatings.

We love with horror and hate with inexplicable love what gave us the maximum sorrows and hardships.

Corporal punishment is effective

For teaching virtue, nothing was equal to punishment in effectiveness. Of St. Romuald it was said that he had looked for a teacher to lead him on the path of goodness, and having found one in the hermit Marine, this teacher forced him to recite psalms as the recitation called the Donatus was done in schools, a kind of reading primer or catechism of questions and answers from years past.

Often the young Romuald mixed up words and when trying to say one thing, he uttered something else that was not effective. Then the teacher Marine, with the ruler he always carried, gave him a blow on the left ear.

So the days passed, the student learning, his master teaching. Until one day that meek Romuald, whose readiness to endure without protest this treatment would today have drawn attention as unusual, said to Merino: master, in this left ear I cannot hear any longer; from now on, hit me on the right side, I pray.

Whether that teacher made a reply, nobody knows.

Coming back to my mother, she lost control when hitting me, her eyes sparkled with anger, and she used to hit me in the head with her knuckles between which the thumb hovered so that the blow would hurt me more. And sometimes she hit me in the ears with both hands at the same time, which caused me excruciating pain in them. Or she grabbed my ears and twisted them until I was screaming in pain.

She did not like it when I went away without crying or complaining. She kept on hitting me until I mourned. Although she boasted of being good and that in comparison with her there were some much worse, she pointed out the need to punish me "until the correction ploughshare had opened deep cuts in my back."

She was skilled in cruel metaphors.

Whenever my mother hired professional flagellants, they enjoyed preparing the scene.

They assembled a narrow board, long and strong, belts, pillows and a good, long flexible rod of birch, and then bid me to undress. If I cried, they would hit me more. If I struggled to endure without complaint, perhaps I was rewarded by receiving ten strokes instead of twelve.

The law did not punish cruelty against children unless it caused their death. A mother clarified:

"If you flog a child to make it bleed, it will be forgotten, but if you hit him to death, authority will become involved."

We were punished with the same tools with which criminals and slaves were whipped: you could use whips, paddles, bamboo sticks, iron bars, the cat-of-nine-tails, bundles of sticks -whatever you had on hand.

Parents were warned they could beat their children without the risk of death if they avoided hitting the head or face or kicking them as if they were sacks of potatoes; it was enough to hit them with the rod on the buttocks or flanks; they certainly would not die.

Some other ways of educating children

In our lives, torture was an everyday occurrence. Many acts that no longer strike us as strange were just torture. Almost from the moment I was born, my mother bathed me in icy water. She did not think that freezing was torture. In the depths of winter she carried me to nearby icy Rhine and forced me to immerse myself in it, she did it in the name of tradition, it was a party. She made a large hole in the ice and plunged me in the resulting pool. Adults around were laughing in revelry. No one would take into account my tears and my protests. Nobody noticed the pain reflected on my face.

Bathing children in ice water was a common practice, the colder the bath the better.

"The mother took into the courtyard the naked baby and a pot of hot water, poured the water on the snow to melt it and created a puddle which could serve as a bath container for several days; all she had to do the next day was to break the crust of ice" -recounted an uncaring witness.

The shock was brutal. In the morning, the horrible screams of the little ones awakened to bathe in that icy water were heard in all the houses. Just like hot red steel is tempered by immersing it in cold water, it was said that the child bathed in cold water hardens. When my mother bathed me, she covered her ears with whatever was at hand, not to hear my cries; she was preparing me for the harshness of life.

A clergyman recommended parents to wash daily in cold water the feet of their children; otherwise the excessive softness of the treatment would surely destroy them. He recommended making them wear shoes so thin as to be always drenched in water, besides tunics and robes that would make them continually feel cold.

Everybody was adept at these supposed hardening practices. To harden their children, people living farther east often used to send them to bed wrapped in wet cold cloths; in other places they were made to sit for hours with their feet wet.

Mothers were insensitive to the suffering of their children and in some places often bathed them in water so hot they were badly burned.

It also was common for parents to toss their infants through the air like a ball, and it was said that a brother of the emperor, while being passed jokingly from one window to another, slipped out of the hands of those who held him and hit the ground.

In many places children were baptized by putting them in icewater. It was usual, it was a virtue. On one occasion the child slipped through the hands of the priest. The water dragged him down and the boy drowned: Give me another, shouted the man of God, while the father and mother could not quite contain their joy... because their baby had gone straight to heaven.

My mother made me sleep with my hands tied, and to teach me self-control forced me to wear fish bone corsets, iron collars and steel pajamas, and to sit for hours in the stocks, fastened to a board.

When I grew a little older, she wanted to accustom me to always walk with my head high. She thought it fit for people of high birth. With ropes and sticks she made a kind of harness and forced me to wear it, so that if, sloppily, I let drop my head, my hair felt a painful jerk.

It also was a common thing to lock us up for hours in a closet or alone in a dark dingy room, sometimes to get us out of the way and to not disturb anyone, sometimes to punish us for some wrong, real or only imagined, or just for pure discipline.

Often we were purged with daily enemas just before eating so that the new food did not get mixed with previous feces.

My mother never sent me to bed without encouraging me to think about death and the eternal torments of hell. More than once my parents took me to witness public executions, and back home they used to hit me to record firmly in my mind what I had seen.

We got scared and fear was put in our bodies by threatening us with monsters that would take us away if we misbehaved: the bogeyman, perverse imps, birds that would rip off our flesh into strips and so forth.

Usually my caregivers intimidated me by masquerading as wild beasts and shouting and pretending they would eat me.

A tale was told of a mother who had four daughters and all four had committed suicide. They were called the suicide virgins. Then the mother would say to anyone who wanted to hear: "I do not understand why they have killed themselves, my daughters; I gave them lots of love, and our home was full of love."

I was my mother's favorite, she beat me daily.

I grew up in virtue and grace in the eyes of God

God causes most pain to those He most loves.

With the Christian and severe education that my mother gave me, to which my father added, I grew up in virtue and grace in the eyes of God.

Like Jesus Christ in Nazareth, in my humble place I grew and strengthened and the grace of God was with me.

So my parents laid the foundations of my later virtue. It was said that very soon I would learn to suffer in silence and pray with my mouth shut. My parents did not like to hear me scream, it exasperated them.

In any other person, such an education would have caused havoc, but by special divine deference, from the very moment I was born, God deigned to show me his love. I soon showed signs of having been elected to an uncommon destiny. God preferred me and very early manifested Himself in me. Newborn and delivered to the care of a wet nurse, I refused to suckle her breasts because she was a woman of a messy and mundane life. Instead I took very well to the breast of my mother and to other honest women. And when I started to crawl, I used to praise God. In my diapers I did some miracles, as it was not necessary to wash them; as soon as my mother took them off me, magically they appeared properly ironed and clean. Also I performed some wonders through the water in which I was bathed; the plants watered with it in the garden grew fruit twice the normal size. And my poop exhaled a sweet smell like that emanating from the corpse of many serfs of God.

As they later told me, when I had not yet turned three years old I spoke Latin with perfect clarity and correctness, like a learned person, and my goodness and devotion at such a young age drew the attention of everybody.

Things did not end there. On one occasion, when I was about two and a half years old, my mother told the neighbors how proud she was of me and added, "Joan is very active and moves all the time, she behaves like an older girl. She cleans the house, dusts my room, sweeps the floor of her own; she even wants to help me in the kitchen, but I think she is still too young for such a task.

"Sometimes you would think that she is a little too helpful. Rather than playing in the street with other children, she prefers to help. Thanks to her I'm not bored. Other children sit in a corner and stay there doing nothing, like a fool or an idiot. Although at night she likes to hear stories, often staying awake until two or three in the morning to help me out in what must be done. And the next day she gets up at half past seven or eight. She just takes a nap every two or three days. If I order her to do something, she does it immediately. She makes her bed herself, when I say to do it. If some day she is not in the mood, I offer her some sweet, and then she agrees. And if by chance she resists and sulks, I command her to go to her room and do not let her out until she changes her mood. Even more, if she sees me tired and I need to lay down a moment, she thinks that it is her fault I am sick, and then she brings me a pillow and clean sheets, and a glass of water: she is very considerate, regarding others too.

Recently a woman had a baby and Joan helps her bathing him and puts on the talcum powder. If she hears him cry, she looks at once for the bottle.

On one occasion, when she could not find it, she took a pot of milk that I had saved and tried to have him to drink from it. Sometimes she rocks the cradle and sings a lullaby. She is very protective of the child. If the other children ask her about him, she replies that he is asleep, because she is afraid they do not know how to handle him gently, and pushes away those most rough. She collects dirty diapers and brings clean ones. She once wanted to change the baby, but she was mistaken and did it badly. I hardly scold her. However, yesterday I gave her a good reproach because something annoyed me; just by the tone of my voice, she knows if I'm angry. If I want her to see reason, I point out a strap that hangs from a nail and she calms. Although on one occasion, I was out and she wanted to bathe the baby, but the water was too hot and she burned him. Also my other little son, the younger of the two, is very willing, although not as much as Joan. At only twenty months, he has already picked up the cloth and dusted the furniture. I was lucky; thanks to them, I have gotten rid of a great load."

Such my mother thought of us. And it has been said that when I turned four years, my eyes smiled continuously, tirelessly, and in them could be read a cordial hello.

My early rebellion

If I listen to those who claim to remember it, from the beginning, everything in me was privileged, miraculous and supernatural. To purify the water from a polluted stream I could utter a single word. I made clay figures of birds that once released into the air, went flying, and it was even said that I had resurrected a child who had fallen from the roof onto which he had climbed and had smashed his head against the floor causing his death. But I had called him by name and he had stood up unharmed as if nothing had happened. And again, in the shop of a neighbor who was a dyer (in the village many people practiced that craft) I put my hands in a tank indigo blue dye. The angry owner scolded me, but to compensate him for the damage, I kept pulling out of the tub one by one the fabric he told me and the colors he wished. Astonished, that man finished thanking God for bringing me there.

One afternoon when we were playing in the square, I wanted to represent scenes from scripture with a boy of my age. The boy told me that he would like to set sail with me and other animals, a pair of each species in the Ark of Noah. To please him, after modeling the Ark from clay I asked him to close his eyes and, hand in hand, the two of us would enter the boat. He did so and he felt so keenly that the game had become reality that he released a cry and looked at me as someone who sees visions. The charm was broken, and then we were once again only a pair of kids who have fun and make noise on the street.

But when I was six years, I went through a crisis that threatened to derail the omens. Apparently I had committed the mischief that the wisest ones say is inevitable in children. So our neighbors gossiped, more or less angry according to category and size of my latest stunt. I did not much like a friend of mine, so I made him wither like a dry bush, and another one suddenly dropped dead because he had pushed me carelessly from behind. The less benevolent ones accused me of being possessed by the devil. My parents were not pleased on hearing it. Apparently on one occasion my mother had started crying disconsolately because a neighbor had told her that I was very bad, the very flesh of the devil. This did not prevent on another occasion an unexpected visitor catching her whipping my innocent ass with a wooden board.

But I, so cute with my sweet eyes, my tight braids and my perfect nose, was a healthy girl, lush and ready to have fun and, above all, to impose on those around me. Pert and pretty and the youngest of four brethren, people blamed me for being dominant and fickle. At the same time, even if it may seem contradictory, my also piety drew attention, which can be explained if one considers that with my brothers I was educated in a devout environment.

Once, hidden in a corner, I was examining my conscience and accounting for my behavior during the week. It had not been the worst one: I had been stubbornly determined to be taken to a charity raffle during the Carnival and they had taken me, I got my way. Later, as my brothers refused to attend some worship that I had devised (a few litanies sung to a fragile red clay figurine of the Virgin), I had given them a violent shove. When I learned that one of my cousins was going to have fun too in the festivities of that day, I invited him to play with a knife and wounded him slightly in the thigh, so that he had no choice but to go to bed and miss his fun. Throughout the carnival he would not be able to go to the carrousel or any other amusements. But I had done it for his good.

Sometimes I headed the family prayers. One day my sister did not want to go, because she was busy with her lace-making cushion; then by a kick I sent rolling down the stairs her lace and spools, bobbins and shuttles...

I had a bad temper.

During winter I was skating with my friends and by crossing intentionally in the way of one of them I made him fall. He hit the ice with such a force that he broke a rib on the right side.

There his martyrdom began. Nobody was able to heal him. His wound festered and it affected his whole body. What to everyone had seemed an unfortunate accident eventually was found to be one of the unfathomable plans of the Most High, because out of that injured boy came someone who by his unparalleled meekness before suffering would set an example to all.

He spent years lying in bed and his persistent pain seemed to increase steadily. Some suspected that he pretended and wanted to be interesting. Also it was thought that perhaps the devil possessed him. To test him, a priest tried to give him communion with an unconsecrated host, but he saw the deception and made him feel ashamed of his lack of faith.

God rewarded him by making him feel in prayer great pleasure accompanied by visions. Many miraculous events occurred by the side of his bed. When he was reciting the Marian Psalter, the precedent of the Holy Rosary of the Virgin, it could be seen how with the Hail Mary roses sprung from his mouth. A famous preacher saw him in spirit and went to visit him. The pious Arnold, Abbot of Fulda, treated him as a friend.

From fifteen years old until his death, he knew all sorts of pains; he suffered from head to foot and was very emaciated. The morning of Easter Day he was in deep contemplation and saw that Christ was preparing for him the last rites.

He died in an atmosphere of great sanctity. It was then demonstrated that God wrote straight with crooked lines. And that not even a blade of grass moves in the wind without his consent. This does not prevent me ignoring it when my childish malice had caused the disaster.

By his activity as an evangelist my dad was making himself known and we settled more comfortably. Sometimes we received guests, and I always deemed excessive those big dishes of meats offered to those guests at our home. Before the party and without thinking twice, I used to collect for the poor as much as I could. The others were piqued and did not look well on what they called my hobby, because it mortified them to see diminished their own magnanimity and generosity.

I had so much pride and conceit.

By special mercy of God, that early rebellion, if it can be so called, gradually disappeared and now my greatest pleasure was to listen to my mom and to have my dad read me some lives of saints.

My first devotions

As soon as I turned six years, the Holy Virgin invited me to live by pleasing God. At seven, I promised to pray in all my free time, without games or frivolous amusements, and I saw the Queen of Heaven. And as St. Rose had done prior to me, at eight I no longer indulged in the pleasures of my age, but prayed before every pious image, though I preferred the Virgin. I also fasted, and just after meals I used to chase the poor to give them some alms. Not in vain and according the Holy Book, Tobit had told Tobias his son before sending him to collect an overdue debt, "alms deliver from sin and death and do not leave the soul in darkness."

At that age I preached a homily and everyone present was touched. The rector of the diocesan seminary did not approve of a girl giving doctrine lessons to professionals, so he chided my parents for not keeping me on a short leash and not teaching me due respect for superiors by giving a good spanking more often. I stared at him fixedly and though he was healthy, that same night he fell down dead. The rumor spread that I had supernatural powers and that everybody should beware of me. I flatly denied it. I have said before how a child of the neighborhood pretending to be a camel had rammed me on the shoulder and there, a moment later, he died by the kick of a feral donkey bitten by a horsefly.

It seemed I showed myself vindictive in excess.

I was overwhelmed with a great fervor and desire for spiritual absorption. I spoke to an image of the Virgin and child, but they did not respond. I complained to them. One day the Lord agreed to my wishes, the image became alive and the Holy Virgin put in my hands the child Jesus. I asked them: "Why did you not pay attention to my pleas?" To which they quietly smiled.

At ten, I attended a Lenten sermon preached by a popular missionary. With such ardor and eloquence that holy priest spoke of the passion and death of Christ, and did it with such sweeping emotion that all attendees broke into tears and some of them even fainted. But they were given immediate relief. Such were the groans and so great the clamor that there was no choice but to interrupt the function.

As far as I am concerned, I fell in love with our Redeemer. From then on my favorite target of devotion would be Jesus Christ crucified. One day, before a crucifix dripping with blood, I heard our Lord say to me, "Look at this state I am in, my dear." "Who put you in this state?" I asked, and he replied, "Those that belittle my love and make fun of it." Since that day I decided to love Jesus Christ more than anybody else.

Martyrs impressed me a lot and the blood spilled by St. Andrew, St. Sebastian, and St. Ursula and her 11,000 virgins clouded my mind. I saw everything in red, and, as later in Hungary the Countess Bathory would bathe three times a week in the blood of prepubescent handmaidens, I too wanted to swim in blood - at least in spirit, because to do it in the flesh would perhaps have been a bit too much.

Such horrid tortures as those caused by heathens to so many male and female servants of God captivated me.

From their pulpits preachers thundered against the odious doctrines defended by heretics. They railed against Gotescalco, who needed no intermediary in his dealings with God, and against Arians, who, stubborn in their infamies, refused to give up and recognize in Him three persons on an equal footing. These they painted as so many damned; that is, reprobate or condemned to the torments of hell.

Three centuries earlier and in more than two hundred homilies, St. Caesarius of Arles had distinguished himself in Gaul by terrifying the faithful with the final trial. With thundering eloquence he evoked before them the tribunal of Christ, an eternal and severe judge, and his harsh terminal sentence. He was an intellectual terrorist.

Even when I was asleep, and though I did not quite understand the precise meaning of "eternal", to my mind those unfortunates who in the flames of hell writhed with unspeakable pain. I asked my mother and she said that "eternal" meant "forever."

Everything I read played stubbornly in the same key, the key of eternal punishment, and with difficulty I attempted to remove from my mind the thought that pain and glory were forever. I pondered a great deal about it and I liked telling myself often: "forever, forever, forever." Later I thought it pleased the Lord my repeating this a long time, because that way was imprinted on my soul since childhood the way of holiness.

According to a book of godly examples that my father used to read to us, at one time a soul from purgatory had appeared to a devout, and when the visited devout wanted to know about the tortures suffered in that place, the banshee had asked him to stretch out his hand; he did so, and the tormented one poured on it a drop of sweat that, as if it were cast iron or lead, had drilled through it from side to side.

Even though we knew well that other kids our age did not behave like us, my brother and I liked to hide in a corner and talk about God and the salvation of souls. Among other things, we said to each other that the martyrs "bought very cheap the pleasures of the paradise" and wanted to be like them, not because we especially loved God, but to enjoy as soon as possible such celestial glory as they enjoyed.

Though modest and unassuming, our parish church abounded with altarpieces and pictures depicting in detail the torments of hell and purgatory, besides those sufferings of many Christian martyrs. Lying on a grid-iron, St. Lawrence was roasted, flames came out from under him and licked his body, the coals seemed alive, dark red tongues of fire rose, so well painted that even just seeing them scared me, the heat burned the generous flesh and roasted it, the entrails of the saint opened and the innards shone in the glare, the melted fat fell into the glowing embers and dimmed them.

In another picture, St. Bartholomew, naked and tied to a table, was flayed alive. After that, St. Stephen was stoned with the gravel of a rocky ground; his face was bleeding; he was wounded in his head, he moved to pity whoever looked at him. He was kneeling and, without losing his composure, he prayed for his executioners. There was also a Christ on the cross, naked, in a sea of blood, his body marked by the whippings, with a swollen grey face, disfigured; cloudy his eyes, twisted his mouth, speared his side.

In a dark corner, tied to a pole, there was also the Roman legionary St. Sebastian. He writhed and contorted himself, pierced by the sharp arrows that his comrades had shot at him to punish his treason. He had become a Christian and had refused to go on slaying and terrorizing in the name of civilization so many neighboring countries and people. It was hard to discern whether his expression at the stake was one of pure delight or sheer pain.

Fascinated, I used to halt to contemplate such a bloody scene, and if in the first few days the spectacle caused me chills and horror, little by little I became accustomed to it and, back at home, I missed it; and when for a while I had not pleased myself in those devout representations, I felt that something was missing. I even think that my young flesh quivered with a mixture of fear, disgust and some odd and unknown delight.

My imagination would not let me sleep. Before my eyes was a pious altarpiece depicting Purgatory that was in one of the side chapels of the small local church. Those naked men and women immersed to their waist in a lake of fire impressed me beyond words. The holy Virgin and the angels, bending towards them and offering them a holy scapular of our Lady of Mount Carmel, rescued only a few.

Many nights I've stirred the house with my screams after waking from a nightmare in which I believed myself in hell. My parents and my brothers had to run to calm me down. The whole matter made me so anxious that, though still a child, I offered for the suffering souls many sacrifices, alms and rosaries. I used to say my prayers kneeling on a little gravel that I had spread on the floor to mortify myself. At night the bells of the many churches of the place seemed to toll: forever, forever, forever, and I reached to find peace only when, forgetting myself, I offered myself as hostage to the Holy Virgin and asked her to take out of the abyss the neediest.

CHAPTER 3. From childhood to adolescence

They educate me in suffering

My mother was the one who educated me. But Joannes Anglicus, John the Englishman, my father, did not lag behind: he too educated me; his method was less harsh and painful than Gudrun's, but equally effective.

At night, sitting by the head of my bed before I fell asleep, he used to read to me the life of those countless saints who by God's special mercy fill the heavenly mansions. He took them from St. Bede's martyrology, very popular at the time. There were then plenty of such martyrologies, booklets or catalogues of saints, confessors, martyrs and virgins whose virtues had been edifying examples in the past. With patience, perseverance and painstaking calligraphy, they were copied on the desks of the abbeys.

By dint of being an austere and penitent man, my father had a special predilection for martyrs, those saints who on the book were called confessors, and for all those who by renouncing the world had lived away from its vanities and pomp.

Starting from the beginning, because as said St. John the Evangelist had said, "In the beginning was the Word," and because he was skilled in doing things as they must be done, that is, in the right order, my father began to edify me by reading about the hermits who had once populated the Egyptian desert.

They were called hermits, those who lived secluded in isolation and were given to contemplation and penance. Unable to withstand the harsh conditions of life in cities, they had fled into the wilderness, where they lived and punished themselves, until as to everybody else the fatal hour arrived to them.

The first night, at the side of the straw bundles of my mattress, he started telling me the following: "For you to see how this life is no bed of roses, but a valley of tears, listen, my dear, to the examples offered by so many blessed men and women; look then how St. Sisin lived three years in a tomb without sitting or lying down or taking a single step. And oh wonder! His circulation did not weaken in the least. He did not feel pins and needles in his legs or anything of the kind. Neither did his heart suffer later from the lack of exercise. Perhaps it was because he ate little, and only natural foods, raw or barely cooked. This once more proves that, contrary to what many ignorant people, you must address before all the health of your soul and let God care for that of the body. Because, what does the whole world serve to gain, if in the end we lose the soul? It serves it nothing, obviously.

Behind him was not Saint Maron, who vegetated eleven years in a hollow tree trunk, perhaps an oak tree a few years old, and out of whose interior sprouted some huge spines that prevented him any movement, on pain of prick and bleed, annoyed by the stones that hung down his forehead; the same way that, among some primitive peoples, women use to hang silver coins from different countries. But they adorn themselves to enhance their beauty in front of the young men of the tribe, and not by mortification, as that saint did. Probably from him would come eventually the iron maiden -that damned contraption consisting of a hollow female effigy internally lined by very sharp metal needles and inside which inquisitors used to torment heretics. Later, madams of brothels or sado-masochistic pimpings would adopt it as part of their professional furniture. In the past the practice of asking on behalf of the predilections of someone else for a woman or man for lewd purposes relating to the bed and erotic games was used to be called pandering.

Saint Marana and saint Zita loaded themselves with so many chains that they only could advance crushed under the weight, without anyone knowing where they had taken them, or whether they were made of metal or something else, because by then iron was scarce, there were no blast furnaces, and it tended to be used for practical purposes such as keeping slaves in their place. So they lived, those saints, for forty and two years without their backbones suffering or their joints being afflicted by the osteoarthritis of the elderly.

St. Acépsimo meanwhile took upon himself such a load of discarded scrap iron, that when he went out of his cave to drink, he had to walk on all fours, like other four-legged animals, and never lifted his head. St. Eusebius lived three years in a pond that because of heat remained dry for long periods, and he used to drag the weight of twenty pounds of brass oxidized chains; he had got them almost for nothing, because, being ahead of his time, he preferred to recycle rather than throw them away; then he added initially the fifty carried by the divine Agapito and then eighty more that the great Martian had dragged.

Oh, male and female specimens, worthy of such wonder and amazement as they cause in those who in our times are unable to show a similar heroism! Thus they pointed to us the right path that leads to the eternal imperishable glory, that is, that never fades", muttered that loving father. And he went on reading:

"All his life St. Sisoe was exercised in the love of holy scorn, so he walked on the trails and side-walks in search of those who would insult him and spit on his face, in which he was not always successful, because he used to live in the wilderness. Also holy Isadora, in the first female monastery founded in the desert, sought only one thing: to be despised unabated. She hated self-love, which others call self-esteem. Covered in wretched rags and without ever wearing shoes, she spent her life in the kitchen of the monastery, and was nourished by the bread crumbs that she collected in the floor with a sponge and she drank the water used to scrub the pans.

All his life exercised in the love of holy scorn Saint Sisoe, so he walked on the trails and side-walks in search of those who would insult him and spit on his face, in which he was not always successful, because he used to live in the wilderness. Also holy Isadora, in the first female monastery founded in the desert, sought only one thing: to be despised unabated. She hated self-love, others call self-esteem. Covered of wretched rags and without ever wearing shoes, she spent her life in the kitchen of the monastery, and nourished of the bread crumbs that she collected in the floor with a sponge, and drank the water to scrub the pans.

"Note, my dear", my father then said, "that at the end of the fourth century in the desert regions of Egypt lived twenty-four thousand ascetics. They were like a divine army whose ranks they filled and whose battles they fought. Like the dead in their graves, they lived in underground places, dwelt in huts made of branches, in cavities without any opening but a hole to crawl out of, so small that they could not even stretch their legs.

"Like so many troglodytes, they crouched on large rocks, steep slopes, caves, tiny cells, cages, dens of wild beasts and trunks of dead trees, or perched on columns. They lived like wild beasts, because St. Anton, the first Christian monk, had thus decreed. Given that according ancient ascetics, real fasting is permanent hunger, and the more nourished is the body, the more exiguous is the soul, with their fingers they culled out from camel dung a grain of barley, and for days or even weeks they refrained from any food, without being affected by scurvy, nor suffering anemia or weakness.

"Since I went to the desert, I have not eaten any lettuce nor other vegetables or fruits, nor grapes or meat, much less any fish and I have never taken a bath - confessed proudly the monk Evagrio Pontic - because hunger, dirt and tears lead to God. God does not appear susceptible regarding his worshippers.

"One Onofre said of himself: "For seven years I have been sleeping in the mountains, I feed myself of lolium and leaves of the trees and have never seen anybody." Paul Tamueh lived among buffaloes: "I live with them, and like them I eat the grass of the field. In winter I lie down beside them and they warm me with their breath; in the summer they crowd and shade me."

"John the Egyptian lived fifty years in a hut and he ate grains and drank only water, as birds do. John the Exiguous watered for two years a stick planted in the desert, but he had to bring the water from a spring more than an hour away from the place. Finally the miraculous stick sprouted and it is said that it can still be seen by all those who seek it with faith.

"Generally it was stated that a monk should be an obedient animal endowed with reason. The itinerant hermit Besarión never entered into a settlement, and as a Flying Dutchman or Yankee globetrotter wandered without goal, crying day and night. Nothing hurt him, nor did he moan about the evils of the world for original sin and the guilt of our first parents."

Here, with compassionate eyes full of tears, John, my father found that I was asleep, and even as Jesus Christ had rebuked his disciples in Gethsemane for not having stayed all night in holy prayer like him, I might have been criticized that I had not endured to the final reading. But by dint of being a good father he decided to let me sleep and leave for another of the many nights yet to come to read what was left to read of the lives of saints.

He extinguished the light of the oil lamp and after depositing on my pure forehead a candid kiss he retired to bed with Gudrun.

The following night, again he set out to educate me in the fear of God, so he continued where he left off.

"A different path to winning the kingdom of heavens followed in Syria and other regions for the pascolants, from pasco, the Latin term meaning to graze, to pasture", my father read in a calm voice. "St.

Ephraim, he continued, "Doctor of the Church, also called the zither of the Holy Spirit, used to say about them: "in the company of wild animals, as if they themselves were such, they aimlessly roam the desert. They graze like horses". Almost naked, as they came into the world, men and women grazed like animals. Even their external demeanor had much of the beast, because as soon as they saw a person, they fled, and if they were pursued, fled with incredible speed and hid in inaccessible places. They could very well spend an entire Christian life eating grass on all fours. On the shores of the Dead Sea and all nude, the venerable Apa Sophronias grazed for seventy years. Grazing became a pious profession, a vocation. A hermit introduced himself with these words: "I am Peter, who grazes on the banks of the River Jordan." In the region of Chimezana, nothing was left for animals to eat, because the pascolant hermits had left the ground bare, so that farmers pursued them to the caves and, not letting them out, they made them starve.

"A special example was given by the Abbot St. Shenute, who along with famed St. Anton was one of the first in gathering under one roof and governing by the same rule those ascetics, whose offences were countered by flogging. It has been told that at night the screams of those punished did not let anyone sleep."

My father tells me about martyrs

And so night after night my father bore out his pious work. Finally, when he felt me ready to assimilate more substantial food, he began reading to me some lives of martyrs, those heroic people who had not hesitated to give their lives for the faith rather than have their arm twisted. To start with, he spoke to me of the three saints called Faith, Hope and Charity.

Wisdom, a Roman matron, had three daughters, who had been baptized with the names of Faith, Hope, and Charity respectively. In Greek the mother was called Sophia, and Pistis, Elpis and Agape her three daughters. Under the Emperor Hadrian, all three had been martyred. The eldest daughter, holy Faith, then twelve years old, had been beheaded; her sisters, holy Hope, ten years, and holy Charity, nine, had come out unscathed from a fiery furnace and that is why they had their heads cut off.

Also worthy of my deep admiration was holy Epiphany, a Sicilian maiden of the second century, born in Morocco, where she won the destiny of martyrdom because in the circus a raging bull had torn her in pieces.

In northern Africa meanwhile holy Marcia had retired to live in peace in the jungle, but the infidel pagans, irritated by the exemplary humility she showed in front of their abuse, did not want to leave her alone, and in the circus had delivered her to the lions. But nobody knows if it was because they were fed up with Christian flesh or for some other reasons that those beasts refused to do her any harm. She was exposed to the rush of a sexually excited bull, which merely gave her with its horns a bad bump; in the end, she had been cast to a leopard that without turning up his nose at her, as the others had done, ate her in one mouthful and so sent her to heaven, where no one suffers any more.

At Nicaea, in Bithynia, back in Asia Minor, holy Teodota had been the mother of St. Evodio, whom the governor Nicecio had condemned to be beaten to death. The prefect Lucacio had asked for her in legitimate marriage, but returning from mundane love affairs, she rejected him and he denounced her, so that she was martyred, along with three of her children. They were thrown into a fiery furnace, from where, unlike that which happened to Daniel and his companions, according to the biblical story, nobody escaped alive.

On another occasion, the priest Fructuosus and his deacons who were in prison and had been sentenced to die in the amphitheater were burned like conifer torches.

At ten o'clock in the morning of their last day, the prisoners had been offered food, but the priest had answered, on behalf of himself and the others, that they were accustomed not to break the fast before three o'clock in the afternoon, and anyway, even expressing gratitude for the generous attention, that same day they would have in heavens a tasty feast.

Without further incident, they were led to the pyre, which was already on. But in their torment, the Holy Trinity was with them: the Father did not abandon them, the Son aided them and the Holy Spirit accompanied them in the midst of the flames.

The fire had burnt the cords that fastened their arms, and as if it under a strange spell, they lifted their arms up in a cross. Therefore many of those present, more superstitious than average, feared some harm would befall them, but nothing occurred, and thus the burned saints went up straight to heaven.

In another place, they threw into the darkest corner of a dark dungeon Vincent the Martyr too, and tied him with some old, used and very unclean chains. But suddenly, at midnight, a heavenly monochrome light illuminated the cell, the floor was full of spring flowers, the saint was lying on a soft bed and the angels descended from high to his side and recreated him with celestial harmonies, while one of them gave him courage telling him: "Arise, illustrious martyr, and join us in the heavenly choir!"

This he did without even the shortest hesitation, and although without uttering a complaint he had endured the torments inflicted upon him by the executioners, he could not resist the foretaste of heavenly happiness that thus was offered to him, and at that moment he breathed his last and returned to God.

The following morning, when his executioners found him dead, they felt disappointed because they had expected having some fun at his expense; so as revenge, he was exposed naked to the mob on the Gemonian Stairs in Rome, where usually the corpses of those who had been punished with death for conspiring against the state were tossed.

But the Lord, who looks after his own, did not allow the holy body of his servant to be desecrated, and sent a most black raven that, by pecking fiercely anyone who dared to approach, defended him against the voracity of dogs and other nasty beasts who wanted to feast on the remains. Then those thugs tied the body to a heavy stone and threw it into the river, but instead of sinking to the bottom, as all had expected and usually happens if a miracle does not intervene, he floated on the water and a wave that arose just at that moment carried him gently down to deposit him on the banks. Then his brothers in the Lord came to pick it up and give him a Christian burial in the catacombs.

And what to say about the three young martyrs, Lawrencium and his sisters Cristeta and Sabina, who had refused to burn incense before the bronze and marble statues of the Roman emperors regarded as gods? They were whipped, they were tortured, they were subjected to unspeakable brutality, which is to say an excessive cruelty and maltreatment, but they persevered in their songs of praise to Jesus Christ until, exasperated, the gross minions of those evil authorities broke their heads by banging them against the hard stones and scattering on the ground their whitish brains.

Pagan judges had prohibited them Christian burial, but a monstrous serpent, which for some time and with its demonic activities had frightened the entire region, had become the guardian of the innocent dead. Not only did it frighten the birds of prey, which promised themselves a happy feast of the carrion that the incipient corruption presented them with, but also the profaners with bad intentions. It even frightened a Jew, who risked himself by getting closer to the snake than the limits of decency allowed, by invoking the name of Jesus and promising the monster that he would become thereby a Christian; he escaped, avoiding by moments being swallowed by that snake that the Lord had sent.

The idealism of puberty

The days passed and by special allowance of the true God the frequent fasting did not do any harm to me nor mortify my body, so that I grew and strengthened, I climbed trees, rode a tiny pony, a lovely one, and I shot with a bow those targets I saw, bathed naked in a nearby stream and at the same time by listening to my father and watching him and experiencing the education that my mother gave me, I absorbed the rudiments of the art of converting the heathen to the true faith.

But I am anticipating to events. In those years, when I was barely ten, the craving for martyrdom took me over; I wanted to go to the land of the Moors to preach to them the holy gospel and there be persecuted and insulted, to have thrown at my face some rotten cabbages and similar vegetables and if necessary even stools, to suffer for the love of God and then even die.

But God had otherwise provided.

As soon as I realized that because of my tender age it was difficult if not impossible to go where I would be killed for God's love, I decided to abandon for the time being that idea and replace it with that of being a hermit. Therefore in a vegetable orchard at home, following the instructions of a manual that, by trial and error I myself had composed, I endeavored as best as I could to build, with pebbles and some branches of trees, some hermits that usually ended up by falling apart, so that in no way was I achieving what I wanted.

Would it be so difficult to reach the glory of St. Mary of Egypt, whose dreadful penance in the wilderness was everywhere spoken about, as well as those of St. Cecilia, St. Agnes and many others that it would be tedious to enumerate?

Following in my endeavor, I appropriated all the rags that I found at home and founded a religious order whose name I forgot. Disguised as a nun, I forced my brothers to follow a rule that I myself had devised. I appointed myself prioress. With a clap of my hands, I made kneel the other "brothers and sisters", their arms crossed, or to lie prostrate with their head on the floor, like Muslims, which they did, uncertain of whether to make fun of me or follow me in the strange hobby. And I forced them also to say my many prayers, especially the Litany of the Holy Rosary, in which my father was very devout, and so we all had to be, and I tried to hide behind walls and hedges and in secret places, and hide all of them with me.

My amusements were somewhat peculiar.

Some members of the Imperial Family came to Ingelheim to spend the summer vacation. Thanks to them I had been baptized with pomp and circumstance in the primatial church, and so they now often invited me to their summer cottage on an island of the Rhine. There I met Bilequilda, eleven years older than me and the daughter of the Countess of Main; there was also Matilda, twenty-two years older than me, daughter of Louis the Pious, and her daughter Nantilde, fourteen, her brother Rannoux, nineteen, Luitgarda, Cunigunda's daughter, also nineteen, and her brothers, older than her, and Otto of Lorraine, younger than me by only one year, and Ode, who only was three and still a baby, and Hildegard, only seven, and Ermengarda, who had already turned six.

The fact is that I had become fond of building little altars and of doing before them what the priests of the Lord did, namely, sing hymns, bless the faithful, intone the divine psalms, incense the place and even preach the doctrine. I loved the role and everybody, including the elderly, let me do: the elderly ones, with condescension, as if it were only a bizarre quirk; the youngest submitting to me as I showed more determined than them.

Once, on a Sunday, all afternoon we had played. We were a group, and when it grew dark, I called everybody to give them the usual snack, consisting of almonds and figs and in the relevant season an apple of the pippin kind, grown in neighboring orchards. Like a queen on her throne, imitating the one whom some centuries later would be called Emmanuelle, sitting on a high back wicker chair, I put them in a row and required them to parade one by one before me. I remember myself smiling, not in any way threatening, nor grim, just smiling, and as a condition of receiving that friendly gift, I demanded them that when they came up to me, in thanksgiving for the food that was given to them, without them having especially deserved it, they prayed a Hail Mary.

Some refused, wanting only to take the snack and run away to eat it reservedly in a secluded place, and not wanting to yield willingly to what I required from them, they would not please me. But calmly and sure of myself I stuck to my task and refused them the snack if they did not compromise. I do not remember if eventually they surrendered or if they were firm in their refusal. Maybe in the end they gave in and did what I asked, because I always ended up imposing my will.

I was but a child.

Lost and found in the temple

Every year my parents went to Mainz to the October fair.

I had only just turned twelve when they were ready as usual and heading to the capital to celebrate the anniversary. After the feast, when they were preparing to start back home, they misplaced me, because I had stayed in the imperial city. I had not asked their permission nor was old enough to spend the night outside home, as laws did not yet consider me emancipated from their loving care. They thought I was at the party back home and by the end of the first day they searched for me among relatives and acquaintances. As they did not find me, they turned around and went back to look in the city. After three days they found me at the school of the Archbishop. Sitting amidst the prelates and abbots there assembled, I listened attentively and asked a few questions. My intelligence and my thoughtful answers charmed all those who heard me. My parents were amazed and my mother told me:

—Daughter, why have you done this? Your father and I have looked for thee distressed because in these uncertain times we feared the worst.

To which I answered them sententiously:

"Why have you sought me? Did you not know that I have to take care of myself and from now on to make my own future, the sooner the better? It is obvious you are not at my level."

But they did not understand anything I told them, so that I went with them back to Ingelheim and lived under their tutelage.

My mother kept in her heart these memories and I guess today she would have liked to have a graphic record of my development.

When my parents had done all the things prescribed by the religious law of the time, they returned to their modest abode at Ingelheim.

My school years

All this happened in my first few years. Then I began school.

During childhood I lived in two environments: the religious environment of home, with Gudrun and my father, where the Holy Virgin, Jesus Christ and all saints dominated the scene, and the school environment, not a secular one, strictly speaking, but at least a bit more mundane and less narrow than the other one. Later I was hardly able to reconcile the two opposing world-views.

My mother was ambitious; she boasted of her Basque ancestors and wanted to be among high-placed people. I learned at home my first letters, and from her pious books she specially taught me, but after reaching the required age she thought of sending me to the palace school that at in imitation of his father Charlemagne, Louis had kept open in Mainz. The cathedral canons ruled it. For me entry was not difficult, because as I have mentioned, the Empress Judith had taken me under her august protection. Due to her influence I was admitted to the classrooms. The Emperor Charlemagne had endeavored at first to make women receive education, but now it all came down to teaching them how to spin wool and do other domestic-type activities. But my father had kept busy giving me some knowledge. Reaching school age, I was reading fluently. I spoke Latin and the vernacular and even had some notions of theology, as my father saw me as a future deacon or at least a continuation of his apostolic work. Therefore I was admitted in the school attached to the archbishop's palace in Mainz.

The canon prefect of the school argued that it was superfluous to teach women more than strictly necessary to be a future wife and mother, and with regard to my intellectual gifts, he did not expect much from me. Therefore on the first day, because the fame of my early studies had preceded me, he wanted to test me and put me on show in front of everyone. He asked me if I thought it was fair for me to compete in skills with men, because as everyone knew "women were by nature below them".

I could not restrain myself any longer and, more daring than was expected of my young age, I replied that in principle there was nothing contrary to both occupying the same place regarding the matter, since the inferiority above alleged was not an obvious thing.

Wanting to settle the matter once and for all to shut me up, that pedantic schoolmaster quoted then the authority of St. Paul, who apparently had surely said that women were innately inferior to men. Women are beneath men in conception, in place and in will – thus had asserted such a holy man. In conception, because Adam had been created first, and Eve afterward; in place, because Eve was created to serve Adam as companion and mate; in will, because Eve had put hers aside, and unable to resist the Devil's temptation, had eaten of the forbidden apple.

I did not want to accept this, nor had I been convinced by the arguments in support of the thesis, so I dared to answer that, far from meekly accepting what was attributed to St. Paul, it would be better to understand the whole thing upside down. Regarding conception, Eve surpassed Adam because though she had been created second, she was made from one of his ribs, while he had been made of vulgar clay soil. As to the second point, God had created Eve inside paradise, while he had created Adam outside it. And finally, Eve had eaten of the apple for love of knowledge and learning, while Adam had eaten it merely to please her and because she asked him. As was evident, Eva surpassed Adam in all three aspects, despite St. Paul having said otherwise.

My response had not pleased him and we became enemies. I was called a pundit and presumptuous.

I went to school, along with my contemporaries and acquaintances. I liked to mix with the Imperial Family.

In those days school life was hard. We left our beds at dawn and after folding our bunk mats, wetting our face and neck with cold water and saying the prescribed prayers, we took a frugal breakfast in silence and then learned to use all kinds of utensils and tools. We were taught to till the land and care for a farm, as well as music and mathematics. We learned to answer the questions from the Donatus and to erect buildings. To the Donatus, a booklet of questions and answers that we had to know by heart, I have already referred. Until the time of Emperor Charlemagne, the education of male children had been simpler: they were taught to ride on horseback, archery and telling the truth, and that was all, but then things changed. As I have pointed out, I had learned my first letters at home. Perhaps because she was a recent convert, at first my mother was very religious. She had filled our house with holy images, always wore a scapular of Jesus Christ or the Virgin - I do not remember her removing it even to sleep - and she had prints, she had books, she had all that was religious, but later, after I was born, she renounced religion. She had asked God for another husband, one not so long absent, God did not listened to her. From her I learned all the prayers that were in the world. She taught me a lot of religion!

Regular instruction was very rudimentary, much more if intended for girls. Those learning to read and write were very rare, let alone do accounts. In general the population was illiterate. I do not know whether it was fortunate or unfortunate that my case was different. My parents were themselves learned people. So I started too soon on the path of wisdom. I had not yet completed four years of life when my father made me memorize the entire Gospel of St. John, and more than once he punished me if I did not repeat quickly those rare words or did not understand them. I entered fearfully the palace school. We all feared it, it was common knowledge that usually teachers beat their pupils; although I arrived having been beaten, I went with a fear, a fear I do not know how to describe. My mother had taught me, she had warmed my ass more than enough, and she taught me the letters, and I read the primer, the so-called Cato. She taught me to read and she had spanked me

My mother had bought me two primers, the first to learn the letters of the alphabet and the syllables - the one that begins by saying my mom loves me and such stuff, and on the first page it had the figure of Jesus Christ. We used to call the syllabary the face of Christ. One day my mother and I went to cut rye and she, wanting me not to waste time by playing, took with her the booklet. I did not want to study and in order to go for a walk or conceal that I was not doing the labor, I left it over a compost pile that was there, and a loose goat, the wind having moved the pages, came and ate the face of Christ. But my cunning mother had bought me two of them. At that time it pleased me, the feat of the goat, but we came home and, ah, here's another one! I was happy because the goat had eaten the syllabary, but my smart mother had already bought me a copy!

It should not be thought that school life was easier than at home. Just entering the classroom, a small stone-walled chamber adjacent to the cathedral library, we were frightened by an enormous painting covering the wall at the front of the room. It was a picture of a woman dressed in the long, flowing robes of the Greeks. In her left hand she held a pair of shears; in her right, a whip. The woman represented Knowledge; her shears were to prune away error and false dogma. Her whip was to reprimand lazy students and encourage learning in those who resisted. She had thick eyebrows sharply drawn together, her dark eyes glared from the painted wall, seeming to focus on the observer, their look hard and commanding, and the corners of her mouth curved down, creating a stern expression, to make it understood that in no way would she tolerate jokes. She looked menacingly at those who dared to raise their eyes to see, and hers transmitted an urgent message of submission and obedience.

The first steps in the way of the letters were not easy, whether at home, as in my case, or in the various schools, mostly religious, because laity were not allowed to open any. Children were whipped, as it was assumed that no one could learn anything if not aided by beatings. As one educator said, "Fear is good for putting the child in the mood to hear and pay attention. A child cannot quickly forget what he has learned in fear." In his writings, St. Augustine recalled the beatings that regularly he was given at school and remembered the benches of torment and hooks and rings where the most unruly were hung, and other torture devices.

Children were beaten for any error, such as failing to distinguish the dative and ablative cases, and were often whipped, stripped in front of the whole community until they bled, and schoolmasters seemed to enjoy the punishment. Some of them used to take into their lodgings the most pretty and amorous boys, and after a blow with a rod or a whip used to meddle with their privates. No child understood why this abuse took place.

"Through the first five or six years we were taught to cover our nakedness and shameful parts, and suddenly... along comes a teacher who forces us to unbutton our trousers, push them down, lift our shirt, show everything and receive the whip in the middle of the class."

In her diary a school girl in a nunnery had written:

"Mother superior took my head tightly under her arm, and the brawny red-cheeked lay-sister scourged my back with a three pointed whip till the blood gushed from the long strips and I fainted".

At that time no child escaped being beaten, at home, at school, on the fields... from childhood to adolescence; all were suffering from battered child syndrome. The Old Testament endorses spanking children, and goes so far as to recommend punishing with the death penalty those who curse their father or mother.

In the eastern regions of the empire, parents punished their children with a hundred blows of a bamboo pole, strangulating them or having their flesh torn from their body with red-hot pincers. St. Ambrose praised parents who spared not the rod; St. Augustine lived in dread of the lash of his teacher, and the Latin poet Martial joked about the complaints of those living next to a schoolroom:

"The shouts of schoolchildren being whipped and hit with the rod awakens the neighbours annoyingly early in the morning."

Among the ancient Romans school education was typically brutal. The ferule was a bamboo cane. Sticks, whips, flogging, leather belts, bundles of dry branches and so on were also used. Children were beaten with the ruler, especially in the palm of the hand and sometimes on the back. They were beaten so severely that their limbs swelled to the point of disabling them from holding the book or notebook. Mothers themselves asked the teacher not have pity on the children.

Little by little some reformers began to question if the day and night hitting of children was right, and said that casting them on the ground and kicking them like dogs to correct them was at least questionable, if not abhorrent. Nevertheless, for most the situation barely changed.

The then prevailing ideas about education

By teaching it was meant to train children to obey, to submit to authority. Those who showed themselves strong willed and adhered to their own opinion were considered stubborn and rebellious, and therefore it was frowned upon. Given the punishment with which such traits were fought, an intelligent child would want to escape it and usually he or she could do so without any difficulty, as when adaptation imposes itself, intelligence helps find countless ways around. Educators have always known this and have exploited it for their own purposes as the following proverb suggests: "the clever person gives in, the stupid one baulks." An educator said: "I've never yet found wilfulness in an intellectually advanced or exceptionally gifted child." But the child in question does not perceive that in the end this advantage is going to cost him dear. In later life, as an adult, he would be able to exhibit extraordinary acuity in criticizing the ideologies of his opponents -and in puberty even the views by his own parents- but within a group that represents the early family situation, he would still display a naïve submissiveness and uncritical attitude that completely belie his brilliance in other situations.

Fathers received from God their own powers (and from their own parents). Teachers find the soil already prepared for obedience and political leaders had only to harvest what had been sown.

Corporal chastisement, the most forceful of punitive actions, was the main factor of education. Like at home the staff symbolized parental discipline, the fundamental emblem of school was the cane. The ferule was the universal panacea for all problems of the school as the staff was in the house. From a long time ago peoples knew all this "hidden form of talking to the soul." Nothing more obvious than the rule: "Whoever does not listen, must feel." The pedagogical spank was a strong action that accompanied words and intensified its effect. Direct and natural was the slap, which usually precedes the pulling of ears, which clearly carried the child to think of the organ of hearing and how he used it. Slap appealed to the organ of language and called for better use. Both types of punishment were the most simple and effective. The highly appreciated noogies and hair-pulling were also on the agenda and were equally significant.

Christian educators could not afford to give up any kind of corporal punishment; precisely the one most suited to certain crimes, as being humiliating and upsetting, attesting to the need to bow to a higher order and also showing how paternal love has to be energetic and not indolent or passive.

A conscientious teacher declared: "I would rather not be a teacher at all than have to relinquish my prerogative of reaching for the ultima ratio of the stick when necessary".

"A father punishes his child and himself feels the pain, hardness extols you if your heart is inclined to softness" -said one. "If to his students the teacher is a parent as he should be, he would also know how to love them with the ferule if necessary and with greater purity and depth that many natural parents".

"And although we call a sinful one the child's heart, we say: such heart understands this love, even if not always at the moment".

This internalized "love" would accompany "the youthful heart" until adulthood, and in many ways the already grown person will often allow himself to be led without resistance and readily accept various forms of propaganda, because accustomed to having his inclinations manipulated and has never known anything else.

And manuals that instructed on the proper formation went on to say: "first and foremost the educator shall ensure that the first education not wake hostile inclinations contrary to the higher will nor feed them; on the contrary, he must prevent them by all means when they arise, or at least eliminate them where possible. He should deter the child from resisting to be passively formed, and already on the first signs of opposition he should be accustomed deeply again and again to the contrary ".

In short, make him used to get annoyed, irritated or vexed and to not always get his own way.

Very early the teacher should encourage in the child these diverse and durable higher inclinations. Often and in various ways he should awaken in him merriment, joyfulness, excitement and hope, but also, rarely and briefly, sadness, fear and the like. He would seize the opportunity to do so when meeting the multiple needs of the child not only physical, but also and above all spiritual, sometimes when he had to deny them, and different combinations of the two states. However, he should arrange everything so that it be nature's doing and not his own, or at least so that this appear to be the case. In particular, he should disguise the origin of the unpleasant occurrences.

The person benefiting from this manipulation should not be detected. By intimidating him, the child's ability to discover falsehood in others would be destroyed or damaged. This would be also manipulation.

In the struggle against wilfulness, causing a child to feel shame could also be a stratagem. Thus connoisseurs recommended: "stubbornness should be broken at an early age by making the child feel the adult's unquestionable superiority." Subsequently, shaming the child would have a more lasting effect, especially in certain robust natures for which obstinacy is often allied with boldness and energy. Toward the end of his education, either a veiled or an open allusion to the ugly and immoral nature of the tare must convene in enlisting the reflection and the full force of the will against the last remnants of it. In the last of the above stages, conversation "alone" is to operate successfully. All these means will be used as soon as possible.

He went on: "if not yet achieved the desired end, intelligent parents should at least be reminded the need to make their child docile, malleable and obedient right from the start and accustom him to obey the orders given him. This is an essential aspect of moral education, and to disregard it would be a grave error. During early training, without forgetting the duty that forces parents to keep the child happy, the proper discharge of this one is the supreme art".

And to illustrate the principles defended, he cited among others the following passage:

"Until his fourth year of life I taught my son basically four things: to pay attention, obedience, good behaviour and to moderate his desires," said a fashion father.

"The first I accomplished by continually showing him all sorts of flowers, animals and other wonders of nature and by explaining the images; the second, by constantly making him, whenever he was by my side, do things at my bidding: the third, by inviting children to occasionally play with him in my presence and, when there was a confrontation, figuring out who was responsible and prohibiting the culprit to play for a while, the fourth I taught him by often denying him what he asked for too strongly. So one day I picked up some honey and brought to the room a jar full. "Honey, honey!" -he exclaimed very happy, "Father, give me honey," and, drawing a chair to the table, sat down to wait for me to spread a couple of rolls. Instead I put forward the bottle and said, "Not yet, first we will plant some peas in the garden, and then as soon as we have done it, we will eat a bagel with honey." He looked first at me, then looked at the honey, and finally went to the garden with me".

"Also, when serving food, I always arranged it so that he was the last one served".

"My parents and a little cousin were eating with us once and we had rice pudding, which he specially liked. 'Yes', I said,' it is rice pudding, and you'll have it. First the elderly shall have some, and afterwards the little ones. This is for grandma, this one for the grandfather. Now it's up to mom, now to dad and now your cousin. Whom do you think this is for?" "For me", he replied cheerfully. He did not find this arrangement unfair, and so I saved myself the annoyance parents have who give their children the first portion of whatever does come to the table".

We were educated by fighting our vitality.

I'll not close this chapter without referring to my parents ideas regarding sexual education of children. This is what they preached and believed.

"Because young people are curious and sometimes by strange paths and means they acquaint themselves with the physical differences between the sexes, every discovery they make will feed their already heated imagination and thus endanger their innocence. It would be advisable to anticipate. It would offend all modesty if one sex were permitted to disrobe freely in front of the other. And yet a boy should know how the female body is fashioned: otherwise their curiosity will know no bounds. Both sexes should learn about this in a solemn manner. Illustrations might give satisfaction in this matter, but they also inflame the imagination and awaken a wish for a comparison with the natural. All these worries disappear if for this purpose one makes use of a lifeless human body. The sight of a corpse evokes solemnity and reflection. By a natural association of ideas, in the future his memory of the scene will also produce a solemn frame of mind. The image imprinted in his soul will not have the seductive attractiveness of images freely engendered by the imagination or of those elicited by less solemn objects. Everything would be easier if young people could learn about human reproduction from an anatomical lecture, but as the opportunities are rare, anyone can impart in the way described the necessary instruction. The chances of seeing a dead body abound."

"Also fulfils this function the systematically induced disgust with one's own body".

"For them, instilling modesty was not as effective as teaching children to regard disrobing and all that goes with it as improper and offensive to others. For this reason it would be suggested that children be cleansed from head to foot every two to four weeks by an old, dirty and ugly woman, without anyone else being present, although care should be taken that even this old woman doesn't linger unnecessarily over any part of the body. This task should be depicted to children as a disgusting one, and they should be told that the old woman must be paid to undertake a task that, though necessary for purposes of health and cleanliness, is yet so disgusting that no human being would accept it."

As it happened, parents tried to protect the innocence of their children by fighting the sex drive with pictures of corpses, maybe without knowing that at the same time they planted future perversions in their souls.

I have often wondered about my reaction and behavior in situations such as these. I still cannot ascertain which the natural and spontaneous behavior is and which only learned.

A devout portrays me

After these unfortunate years, St. Epididymus of Arimathea had described me in these terms:

"The girl Joan was proud of her skill at washing dishes, and looked at glasses against the light to see if they had been thoroughly cleaned. She was particularly able at the precursor of the game of boules and more than once the ball got out of her hand and struck someone's head, though without serious consequences. She was always herself, that is to say, she showed herself continuously happy, noisy and unusually tender, and used to laugh nervously. She liked to sleep late; she made breakfast and used to go for a walk in the nearby woods along with a cat that she cherished.

She was concerned about the welfare of pets.

Once she had a dog that was contemplative by nature, but she maintained that the animal was depressed. She made every effort to force him to jump up as puppies of his own kind do, but only managed to make him even more depressed. On the rare occasions when the animal finally made a pirouette, Joan overflowed with joy and grabbing him frantically she hugged and kissed him passionately.

She was beautiful, much prettier than any of the other girls around. She was neither false or inflated. She was a girl of long legs, thin, flexible. She had a silky complexion, of a snow white shade, that the weak sun of the place was not enough to brown, wavy black hair, bright and lively eyes, olive-colored pupils, perfectly arched eyebrows, an aquiline nose, and very red and full lips. Her face was a beautiful oval, and her hands and fingers were long.

Her beauty had become a curse because many men who had known her wanted to woo her and marry later.

One such lover had confessed: "When I was still a child, I was fond of seeing her walk with other girls and something attracted me to her countenance. Sometimes I looked at her, angry with myself. Then she disappeared, until some years later I met her again. I could not speak, because her beauty left me baffled. She was neither tall nor short. Cinnamon was her color and her eyes were more expressive than can be imagined; she had a florid complexion, beautiful hair, somewhat curly, and perfect features. She was not in the least promiscuous. We became friends; I never introduced her to any of mine. Years have passed and I have never let her down off her pedestal. One day I found her somewhere and still she was just as beautiful as ever, her beauty had not ceased to fascinate me; by chance I saw her once at the graveyard, all dressed in red; she was a perfect child of dark eyes.

"I liked especially her personality, as she was very happy, she lived to make others happy, even though she had suffered. To me she was always the best, I have no words to describe her, really she helped me in one of those times I felt the blues, and she was one of the few people who left a mark on my heart."

It was not uncommon for someone to fall in love with a little girl. Some centuries later, Dante would fall in love with Beatrice when she was nine years old, a brilliant girl, charming and composed with rare mastery, adorned and wearing a crimson dress... in Florence in 1274, during a private party, in the merry month of May. And when Petrarch fell in love with Laura, she was a blonde nymphet of twelve years, running with the wind, with pollen, with dust, a golden flower fleeing by the beautiful plain at the foot of the Vaucluse.

According to my eulogist, I was beautiful, determined, intelligent, intuitive, passionate and always dignified. Further, I was a presence, ambiguous, a nymphet. Through every pore of my skin breathed the evil of nymphomania. I was the angel of sex and the angel dwelt in my detachment.

Because she was separate from what she offered; because there was no one like here, said another devotee, suggesting such a pure sexual pleasure.

The frankness with which I offered myself without ever being rude, my explicit sexuality from which, however, transpired an air of mystery and even reluctance, my voice, full of suggestions of erotic arousal and yet that of a quiet and shy girl, these were the elements of my allure. And they disclosed a young girl trapped in a fantasy land, unconscious of herself.

That holy man was a poet.

CHAPTER 4. Joan knows love

THE AUTHOR - Joan had turned 15.

Both her father and her mother had glorified the exalted life of those who by despising the world and its pomp had sought out the true path. She read or heard these stories with such ardor and avidity that she forgot almost everything about the other duties of her age and condition.

As she herself confessed, the free time left her after meeting the daily domestic duties and meeting the other devotions, she spent in exercises appropriate as much as necessary to maids, such as the needle and frame or canvas, and often the wheel. If to relax her mood, she left some of these exercises, she made use of the entertainment of reading some pious or frivolous book at hand, in any case something edifying and helpful, or playing with a stringed instrument, because music soothes the troubled mind and relieves weariness of spirit.

With such a life, which I describe here, her fancy grew full of everything that was in the books she read, of mystical fervors such as burning ardors, swooning, outbursts, ecstasies, raptures and transports, and so much was impressed on her imagination that the whole fabric of invention and fancy she read was true to her, so that there was not in the world any history which more deserved her faith.

In short, her wits being quite gone, by dint of reading and pondering and dreaming of adventures, she hit upon the strangest notion that ever a madwoman in this world descried. This was the notion that she fancied it was right and necessary, for the salvation of her own soul as well as for the service of others, to embark on the road in quest of adventures, roaming the world to preach the gospel and seeking martyrdom if the opportunity was offered, putting into practice herself all that she had read of and heard tell of as being the usual practices of servants of God. She would right every kind of wrong where she would find it, and expose herself to peril and danger from which, confessing her faith, she was to reap without excessive exertion eternal renown and fame.

The exemplary lives of saints moved me

JOAN - One afternoon, after eating and having given myself a treat of a river trout, I went for a walk along the shore of the water course that in the vicinity of my house flowed, and lo, a portly young man whose blond head framed a pearlescent glittering halo approached me and told me earnestly while showing me a papyrus in his outstretched hand: tolle, lege, tolle, lege. The words I initially did not understand, but a casual passerby, more knowledgeable in Latin letters than I, translated for me: you must take what he urgently offers and without any ceremony or fuss read it, take it and read it, take it and read it. So without any longer being a hypocrite, I held out my hand and took what that great man offered me in his, after which he vanished in the air and I no longer saw him. I figured that without doubt it was an angel who, as was then customary, was a chosen one sent from time to time by God sent to tell people what they ought to do. Therefore, once back home and having examined more closely that heavenly text, I saw it was an account of the life of St. Lucia, that virgin and martyr of Italian Syracuse who in the early centuries of our era had suffered martyrdom, so I sat, made myself comfortable and started to read what was written there which was as follows.

St. Lucia, Virgin of Syracuse, patron of opticians, photographers and dressmakers, protects the sight. In 304 she was martyred. The unfortunate girl died in the reign of evil Diocletian. Her pagan suitor requested entry to her virgin's chamber, to which she made it a condition sine qua non that before going ahead he should become an adept of the holy Christian faith. But the peeved boy would not hear of such fastidious obstacles, so he accused her of being ungodly and denounced her to the authorities, who doing their duty took hold of the lady and demanded her to consent without being obstructive. But as she refused, because she only obeyed the true God and nobody else, as the many others had evil and capricious intentions, they cruelly ripped out her delicate eyes. Because of that, she was piously represented with them on a plate and was appointed protector of those who devote themselves to issues regarding sight, either healing it or to losing it, or to exercising it to make a living.

Once read that divine text, I realized how much pampered I used to live, if I compared myself with that martyr, when virtue was still appreciated and young girls took pride in offering to the Lord of heavens not only their virginity, but also blood and life according to occasion.

Therefore I wanted to be myself a virgin and martyr, like her, like the sisters Justa and Rufine, and like so many others had been in that Golden Age already past and whose account would be endless if someone proposed to make it.

What courage and female determination was shown by those two holy virgins!

Saints Justa and Rufine used to sell on the streets pottery they themselves made. On one occasion they offered it to someone who passed by indolently, with the result that, turning the situation upside down, he had touted them by asking plaintively for a small donation for a clay idol that he himself carried.

Disappointed in their hopes by such a strange proceeding, and recovering from the surprise that had overcome them, they reproached him for his behavior. The complained that he continued cultish worship of tone and wood images, mute and inert, instead of worshipping the Lord God, who rules and reigns in heaven and earth forever and ever, amen. And after making clear that "they prostrated themselves only before an uncreated God and not in front of an idol that had no life", they knocked down to the ground that effigy, and with a holy stick reduced it to that very dust from whence it came.

At this, that wretched individual got angry over the fact that people of so little substance as two Sevillian saints made mockery and derision of that which he had for a God. Calling a guard who watched nearby, he denounced them. After reading them their rights and being accused of causing undue scandal on the street, they were arrested and taken to the nearest police station, where once their case was heard and they were sentenced to death, they were handed over to the so-called secular arm, that is to say, to the executioner.

Who, following orders, had them killed.

All this happened in Hispalis, a town in Roman Hispania, also named Seville.

No less admirable had been the case of holy Justine, also a virgin and a martyr, whom, in African Carthage, a sorcerer named Cyprian had wanted to convert to his evil arts. The result was that she, no doubt more eloquent in her faith than he had been in his, converted him, by expounding to him the gospel of sweet Jesus, because, as has been said, the ways of the Lord are inscrutable.

I decide to go and convert Muslims

With the recent example of the Sicilian saint, and by extension the others that might be added, I was excited and increasingly moved to bear witness to the true faith. In imitation of so many others who in the manner of that rare perfection had preceded me, I felt also intense desires to give my life for the Lord.

One of those whom tillers called serfs was in the town; a convert of my father and a young man who with repeated signs of pleasure and submission had shown beyond any reasonable doubt had caused me to not to be completely indifferent to him. Although at the moment I was not thinking about profane love and preferred the divine one, I offered to let him come closer to me if he was ready to live with me in the heroic purpose and passion that I was about to face. I disclosed to him my secret intentions and proposed he accompany me to where better I could accomplish my holy enterprise.

Him, as a wise man safe from female vagaries, after having rebuked my boldness and condemned my resolution, and yet seeing me bent upon my purpose, offered to keep me company "to the end of the world."

After having convinced him, the first priority was to decide the place most conducive to the goal pursued. As it were, I took a look around me. Where it was most likely that we would be beheaded for preaching the true faith?

Islam was conquering the world; its growing tide was unstoppable and only ten years after having conquered Italian Sicily, the Muslims dominated Palermo, where they had increased by an excessive amount the fees that prostitutes had to pay for exercising their unholy profession.

Some other customs belonging to those Arabian infidels were offensive too. On Thursday evenings they filled nightclubs, where, having arrived from India, Bayaderes performed their brazen belly dancing naked or wrapped in only seven veils. On weekday afternoons they gave themselves up to leisure, by taking baths in promiscuous public baths and attending cock fights in improvised pens or wrestling sessions in the ring. On holidays they liked to go hunting. Primarily they hunted the hare, partridge, wild geese and ducks that populated the fields around. After shooting them down and, as was mandatory according to the Koran, the hunters cut the neck of the prey, therefore making it fit to be eaten without any damage to the body's health or the soul's salvation.

The population idolized wrestling champions. They earned fabulous sums and were exempt from paying taxes. To preserve their physical strength, they must practice chastity, which clearly went against nature. Women covered their faces with a veil, wore the Muslim headscarf, lived secluded in the harem and those women's quarters called the gynaeceum and were only allowed dealings with eunuchs and other equally impotent males.

Arabs used to bring the eunuchs from the Greek monasteries they raided, because Greece had for a long time castrated its monks before them being allowed into the convent and many died in the operation; therefore the price was high.

And last but not least, parents used to marry to a close and known neighbour their yet prepubescent daughters, after checking the horoscope of both and the character of the respective mothers-in-law. They would also apply make-up to corpses, before delivering them to the pit.

Such unheard-of aberrations cried plainly in the eyes of God. Therefore I made up my mind to walk barefoot to the nearest place where such perverse customs prevailed and introduce myself to the authorities, to speak ill of their disorderly conduct and, in so doing, to become a candidate for martyrdom. At the same time I occupied myself solicitously in saving from the eternal flames of hell those many unhappy creatures who lived sunken in such supine ignorance as theirs.

Then I found out that recently a Muslim community had established at nearby Treveris, whose way of life and customs would certainly not be much better than those of their Palermitan brethren.

I was burning with the desire to preach the gospel and give my life for what I believed, hence without further delay I tried to put into practice what I had devised.

The minutes became hours and impatience gnawed me. But by then my zeal mitigate as I began to concentrate in what I had planned to do that same night; then promptly I gathered in a linen pillow a clean shirt, and some jewels and money, for what might happen.

And without giving anyone notice of my intention, let alone my brothers and parents, one morning on a cool July day, I dressed for the journey, put in a bundle the few items of food provisions I found at hand and through the door of the humble peasant house, ensuring that no one saw me, I started out with great joy and delight on seeing how easily I had made a beginning to my good purpose.

I left my house with many imaginings and the young man who was my servant, and set off, led in flight by my desire to convince of their wrong ways those who were in them. If such a thing was impossible, I would at least say in honest words the facts of the future life that after the madness of their earthly awaited them.

At noon we had already covered some leagues.

Those who followed our same path, we asked to let us ride to the rump of their mounts in God's name, but most of the time, because we were two, they passed by without hearing our prayers and with curiosity and puzzlement looked at us.

After toil and pains that I avoid describing here, we arrived at where I wanted to be, and entering the city I asked where the governor lived, and having been duly informed, I went to his mansion for an interview.

Meanwhile I had prayed Psalm 23 "The Lord is my shepherd", as the view of some sheep that grazed over there had reminded me of the words of Jesus: "I send you as sheep among wolves." And so it was that the Mohammedan sentries guarding the doors of the residence pounced on me like beasts and would have killed me, if it were not that I started screaming, "Governor! Prefect!" Thinking that I was carrying out some diplomatic task or wanted to become a Muslim, they stopped beating me and took me to the governor.

The prefect was called Abd-el-Gazar. He was the son of Ben-el-Guzzler and grandson of Abu-Saré-of-the-table. I explained to him that no one had sent me nor did I prefer the religion of Islam to my own.

"On behalf of my Lord Jesus I come before you," I said, "and on his part I bring a message to all of you, that you must believe in the gospel."

I also explained to him that, for the sake of his soul, I would prove, in the presence of the elders of his city, that their religion was false, not by the arguments of the Scriptures (because they do not believed in the Bible), or rational ones (because faith is above reason), but by me and their religious leaders entering a blazing fire. "And if the flames consume me," I concluded, "it would be imputable to my corrupted nature, otherwise, it will signal that your religion is false, and thou shalt become Christian and believe in Christ, strength and wisdom of God and Lord and Savior of all."

Those Muslim religious leaders there present were alarmed, but the prefect, with quiet voice replied as follows: "Oh, amazing young girl, I wonder how you show yourself so imprudent as to come and tell me to change my faith; if I did it, I would be stoned to death; better return to your home, where doubtless your worried parents await; go the same way you came, because you do not know what you are up to."

Then Abd-el-Gazar ordered the treatment of the bruises done to me in the arrest, and that I was treated with respect. And meanwhile I was allowed to freely proselytize the word of God to those who were there, but without success because they looked at me with hostility and distrust.

Not so much the prefect, who, having summoned to his presence some of their most important religious leaders, each day talked with me and tested my faith and knowledge.

"Let this young girl approach me", he said, "she seems a true Christian!". And I tried to talk him about Christ.

When Muslim leaders arrived and learned the reason for the call, they felt outraged and scolded the governor; because instead of the defending law against an opponent, he showed recklessness in giving audience to that infidel, who, according to convention, should be beheaded. But he reassured me with the following words: "This time I will go against the law. I'll not condemn to death one that, by risking her life, came to save my soul."

As I saw that my stay there did not make sense any longer I asked permission to return to my homeland. He then offered me precious gifts and jewels magnificent, but I did not accept, even for distribution to the poor, fearing bringing into question my good name.

The Mainz basilica keeps with other relics a carved ivory horn that the prefect had given me as a pass, so I could move freely in those places under his authority. When I left, he said to me privately: "Please, pray to God to deign to show me what law and religion pleases him most."

My pious attempt fails and I return home

I returned to my home a little chagrined, since I had not found what I was looking for, and while these things stirred in my fantasy, I consoled myself of my first failure. I pretended with faint and distant hopes to entertain a life that seemed useless and without purpose.

I had being absent from my parents' home and the city, for nowhere had they found me. As a result they almost went out of their minds and did not know what steps to take to find me.

Therefore not knowing what to do, there came to my ears a public proclamation, by which a prize was promised to whoever found me, and giving the particulars of age and the dress I wore. I heard it was said that the boy had taken me from my home, the one who touched my heart. This shows how my credit was fallen, as it was not enough to lose it by my returning, but also with whom I returned, a subject so low and so unworthy of me.

When I heard the announcement, I left the place with my companion, who was beginning to show signs of wavering in the fidelity he had promised me, and that night we entered the thick of the forest nearest, fearing being found. But as they say that the bad call another, and the end of a misfortune is often the beginning of a bigger other, so it happened to me. My good follower, loyal and safe so far, when he saw me in solitude, prompted by what I can but call his imbalance rather than any charms that by chance would adorn me, God willing it, took the occasion of the seclusion and distance in which we stood, and with little shame and less fear of God nor respect of me, wooed me.

And seeing that I with right and concerted reasons responded to the shameless words of his purposes, he laid aside the entreaties of which he intended to profit, and went beyond limits.

But just Heaven, that seldom or never stops seeing and helping just intentions, favored mine, so that with my little forces and little effort, I threw him to the ground with the blow of a stick that by chance I had found, and I left him there, not knowing whether dead or alive, lying at my feet.

My first impulse, carried by the shock and exhaustion was to run swiftly and go into the woods, with no other thought or plan than to hide in it and escape my parents and those who on their behalf were looking me for. But after more reflection and realizing in how very precarious situation I found myself, and how unwise it was for a girl to without guard nor any supporter to be exposed to the wiles of the world, I determined to reverse the situation and show myself imperious in front of the one who according to the metaphor of that time had wanted to attack the fortress instead of putting it patient siege. I was reminded of a saying taken from Philidor, a notorious chess player, that my father, also fond of this game of kings, used to repeat: "the best defense is attack."

The first love of Joan

As I said, at first in suspense, as the occasion was not the most appropriate for entertaining any love affairs, I realized that I did not think ill of the boy's kindness, nor had I too much insolence for his requests, because I felt pleased at seeing myself so valued and esteemed by a not bad looking boy in the prime of life, and it did not disgust me to hear in his mouth my praise. In this, even the most ugly women are glad to hear themselves called lovely.

On the other hand I remembered what I had learned about love in religious books. According to them, love is total rendition, obsequious submission. By the royal path of complete renunciation of oneself you achieve it. Carried away by his irresistible love, overwhelming, one delivers himself, surrenders; his love knows no bounds, nothing stands against it, scruples vanish, there is no more shame. By submitting, the lover consents to everything the beloved proposes, does everything that the beloved desires. The beloved punishes and humiliates him and his love for the abuser grows stronger. He treats him like a puppy and his love grows. And finally the ultimate prize comes, when the lover is allowed to bury his face in the cozy lap of the one who dominates him, who thus rewards him. Like a ship in the harbor, in the bosom of their lover those who so surrender to him, find themselves safe from the vagaries of the world. Those who know them appreciate these moments of complete surrender; because only those who let themselves be dominated without any reserve demonstrate the intensity of their love. And only the one who passes the test gets the absolute award.

I remembered what I had come to say, and once that young man had recovered his spirits, firm in myself I spoke to him plainly:

"You ought to quit me, but I prefer to interpret the requests of which you have made me the object by accepting that I am not indifferent to you. Maybe you would not dislike speaking of the love that it seems you profess. Then tell me about yourself."

Without being asked twice, he told me about his circumstances. His father practiced medicine in the country, straightened dislocated limbs and in cattle as much as in people, neutralized the evil eye and other ill will. He intended his son to join his medical practice and even surpass him, so that when the fatal hour arrived, he would inherit a ready-made clientele. Meanwhile he paid him a generous allowance as long as he continued with his studies.

But he wished to become a writer, and perhaps even a poet, an ambitious that can only be achieved with a sound apprenticeship in the literary craft. He would like to start by taking a position as a copyist in some monastery, like so many that in such places learned the clergy occupation, if such an anachronism is allowed to me. His father was wealthy enough to assist him in this plan, but would not hear of it. As a consequence that boy feared he had been weak in choosing medicine and a handsome allowance rather than penury in the uncertain literary world.

As may be expected, however, he did the least work necessary not to cause antagonism with his father and continue to receive income.

When I knew he had risked his safety and well being by agreeing to accompany me to seek martyrdom evangelizing the infidels, I watched him with interest.

Sir, I said, what you have just told me I do not think the most prudent in a situation like yours. It seems that only reluctantly you follow on the way you say.

He nodded.

And apparently your father does not take too much interest in your preferences regarding lifestyle, I said.

Again he nodded.

I have some experience in directing young persons that by their extreme youth are prone to take lost paths: a most rewarding exercise that I also do with pleasure -I said while holding up an arresting finger. If you were to submit yourself to me, I might stimulate you into greater application; you will see that in the end you will feel motivated to redouble the efforts on the path chosen. However, I am obliged to warn you that I require total submission to my methods, which include resort to drastic measures.

Mistress, I admire you so greatly that I cannot conceive of any measures which might be too drastic for me -he said hastily and with broken words.

Again I stared at him. And I wanted to test him.

Good heavens, sir, how very impertinent of you! Admire me, indeed! I do not know what entitles you to harbour such sentiments, let alone insult me with them, on so slight an acquaintance. Come here! On your knees before me! And submit yourself to my displeasure.

He stumbled to do as he was bid and with all my strength and an open hand I gave him a stunning box on the ear that sent him rolling a few steps.

I am most awfully sorry, Mistress, I could not control myself, he apologized.

That, I fear, is all too evident, but something which I shall shortly deal with. You will place yourself in my tutelage, then? You will submit, body and soul, to my commands?

Body and soul, Mistress.

Very well, then, I will take you on for a probationary period. If this proves satisfactory I may consider accepting your permanent submission.

I was reminded of the myth of Cybele and Attis as my mother had read it. I thought that somehow I was offered the chance to revive it. I, the goddess, he, my submissive slave. I could not resist the temptation.

I must acquaint you with some essential rules. All our conversations will, unless I direct otherwise, follow the present model, that is, with you kneeling at my feet. You will hold your hands behind your back and keep your gaze down at my feet except when I speak to you, at which times you will look me in the eye. And you will only speak when called upon. Is that understood?

Yes, Mistress.

Moreover, you will always tell me not merely the truth, but your innermost thoughts. This I shall test at once, requiring you to describe what sexual activities you practise.

I remembered that the devotees of the goddess Cybele had no qualms about sacrificing their manhood castrating themselves. It was not therefore too much that I should ask as much from who in such a way accepted adoring me.

At this he blushed and instinctively looked down at the ground, only to receive another swingeing blow from my open hand. As to his answer there was no doubt. Too short to seduce even the lowliest of the maidservants and too aware of the dangers of venereal infection to engage any of the many whores who thronged the land, he was obliged to confess that often sought satisfaction in himself.

Yes, hm. I am not surprised. It is a common predicament in young men. Masturbation is not the greatest of many potential evils; better by far than consorting with those vile prostitutes who dishonour our sex. You will henceforth desist from such practice except at my direction, for relief from tension and the sake of your general health, of the body as of soul.

I desire you begin at once. Depart to these rocks, bring yourself off into a handkerchief and bring it to me as proof. If you cannot reach a successful conclusion, you will report back to me.

In truth, I had all this time watched how he contorted himself in various ways trying to conceal his excited state as best as he could. In the event, therefore, he reached his successful conclusion all too soon and returning in a few minutes with his handkerchief, he fell once more to his knees -as I had told him to do- while holding his offering.

I took it wordlessly.

I was wondering which was to be the next step when he said fervently:

Oh, Mistress, I am at your disposal whenever you command it.

I gave him another painful blow.

I said very clearly that you are not allowed to talk to your pleasure, but only when I ordered you. Do you will have forgotten? You must remember.

He accepted the punishment silent and said nothing.

Now you may kiss the toes of my boot. Go! Do it! Do not procrastinate or I'll give your back what to feel.

I raised my hem fractionally to reveal the tip of a smart little black leather button-boot.

He bowed and kissed them devoutly, as was de rigueur that he did.

Well, now depart for a time where I do not see you.

I let pass several hours before calling him back.

Once again I had him before me, and without losing a moment I did him to fall at my feet and questioned him. I asked if he had relieved himself as he had said was his custom. As expected, he denied it, but probably lied, given the weakness of character that he himself had attributed. I let me not be deceived.

Look at me in the eye and answer me again.

I set him a trap. If he said no, he doubled the offence, and if he said yes, he looked a fool.

Feebly he responded yes.

Without a word, I got up and approached him.

You have committed two serious errors. I must punish you.

And without further ado I caught him excruciatingly by the ear and had him remove his jacket, waistcoat, trousers and drawers and stand naked in front of me.

I stood in front of him, flexing in my hands a long slim cane beforehand plucked from a bush that grew nearby.

I raised his shirt-tails and tucked them into his shirt collar.

I suppose you have not been flogged since you left school. As you are new to my discipline, six strokes will be sufficient, which represents extreme leniency on my part.

I saw curious that he was in a state of acute excitement, which inevitably became apparent to me. The ridiculous spectacle made me chuckle.

I grabbed him with force and still kneeling I had him to support his face on my lap. And while he remained firmly held and immobilized in that humiliating position, on the exposed rear I laid on six vicious strokes of the cane.

I had no pity. He had to learn one lesson.

When I let him go, tears were running down his cheeks.

It was a useful lesson to you, sir. Now kiss the cane which has punished you, gather your clothes and take them with you a few steps away. Then you are to relieve yourself as usual and when you are dressed, will bring me the result, as before.

It did not take him long. He returned quickly and presented me his love offering, as he had done the previous occasion.

To this episode followed similarly a few others. The last one I showed more severe. I announced calmly there was no occasion for unusual leniency, and I gave him twelve strokes with the cane.

Again he cried, paid me tribute and brought his offering.

I noticed that gradually he seemed to change. He appeared increasingly eager to repeat the experience. He was more lively and filled with vigour. He seemed himself to seek punishment. The repeated punishments became closer and closer.

Also I felt different. Even my face seemed changed. My normal calm was replaced by animation, my eyes flashed, and my voice was hoarse and charged with emotion. As if I was under the influence of some strange tonic, a powerful aphrodisiac.

The sixth day, I tried to get unusually dressed. I have said before that the day I left home, I had put in the bundle a spare shirt and some clothes. I received him as if it were a designated date and party. He knelt at my feet in the manner which had become a familiar custom.

You may look at me, sir. I am pleased with you, and will accept you as a humble servant. The ceremony which this entails, I must warn you, is not pleasant and, once you have agreed to undergo it, there will be no turning back. Once enrolled, you are bound to me for as long as we both may live, and obliged to perform whatever tasks I may impose on you.

He didn't answer and I accepted his silence as acquiescence

If you require some time to consider, you may leave now and reflect alone; if you return, it will be a sign of assent; otherwise you will never again bring the case to your mind.

While I was talking he did not stop looking at me. Pleased, I felt in his eyes his mute adoration of me. Being at my feet, I looked taller to him and if before my womanly figure had been magnificent at his eyes, it was now little less than divine, to that contributing our respective attitudes of mistress and slave. I had swept my mane of fair hair into a French twist, the better to reveal my delicate snow-white neck enhanced by a choker ribbon of black silk.

I noticed that the lust clouded his eyes.

The fire of love devoured both us. He flung himself at my feet and kissed the pointed toes of the delicate shoes peeping out from under the silk of my robe.

I need no time, Mistress. To be yours is what I most desire, and I will gladly pay whatever price is necessary.

Without a word I drew him to his feet, and pressed his head against my bosom. My scented skin felt burning hot. We remained thus for some time in silence, and then I said:

Ah! First you must undergo a painful ceremony, I fear. But then you will, in time, learn what delights I can offer you for your obedience!

And, with unusual gentleness, I added:

Now go over there to the cave that nearby we have discovered lately. Remove all your clothing in the entrance, go inside and totally naked, wait on your knees in the middle of the room, and concentrate your mind on the image of me, your absolute Mistress. Go!

He scurried down in a state of ecstasy.

Passed the threshold of the cave, he found himself in a great vaulted chamber illuminated only by the glow of a sunbeam coming through a hidden crack. He sank to his knees and, as his eyes became accustomed to the dark, he saw before him a kind of shrine and before it a stout wooden post, waist-high and covered with strange carved symbols.

On the creaking sand, he heard my footsteps approaching. Paralysed with terror he dared not turn round, but waited for me to come forward to the altar and stand at the centre of the illuminated area, as if I were on a stage and the light of a powerful spotlight wrapped me.

Stand facing me and repeat after me: you are my Mistress and I am your slave. I am here to become yours for ever.

He could hardly make his words audible.

I felt like transported. Just then were forged the deeds that some years later would inspire the Ring des Nibelungen story. My mother, Gudrun, a Saxon, had told me about the heroines, Brunhild and Kriemhild, the two Nordic Valkyries, and for a moment I identified with them. In front of me, kneeling at my feet was Siegfried, willing to suffer for my love.

In rapture it also came to my mind those Provençal Courts of Love, where knights like Lancelot had entirely given up their own will and were willing to worship for life their chosen lady. And overcome with inspiration I added:

Good. Now listen at what I say and repeat after me: you are my Walkyrie, my Boadicea, the warrior witch whom I obey as my Mistress.

I saw myself as if was seeing some other person, I no longer was the one I used to be. The young and fragile maiden scarcely formed had transformed into a wild and threatening figure clad in fur and iron. Like a glove has a hand, I was stringently sheathed in a many-buckled leather cuirass set with shining inch-long metal spikes, which made me terrifying and savage but in some strange way also sensuous.

I was the iron maiden, inside which heretics were tortured.

He did as he was bid.

I serve an ancient Goddess, and my mission on earth is to restore the dignity of womanhood. You are a man, but one who recognises our mastery over your sex, and therefore a fit ally in our design.

I began then to chant in Saxon tongue a great song I had learned from my mother, and turning to him I offered him the rag weed that a sparrow hawk had brought me in a cup of horn, the same as a pure white dove had brought down from heaven a vial containing the precious oil with which holy Remigious would baptise and crown Clovis, the pagan king of the Franks.

Drink this potion: it will help you through the ordeal, the painful experience which is now to come.

The draught tasted herbal. Though only faintly alcoholic, it made the head swim.

Now I stood with my back against the wooden post.

That sacred wood of which the tree Irminsul had been an exponent. At its turn it was an image of the phallus, of fertility, the tree at the base of the world.

According to my mother, back in Saxony, her host land, women used to request pregnancy in country orgiastic ceremonies. They danced around Irminsul, tree, pillar, column, betilo, and cipo sacred, that all these names were given to it, which in the woods sanctuary represented the supreme goddess of the primeval matriarchal cult. She dwelled in the sacred forest trees and governed fertility. Immortal souls, the seeds of life of those who were born, permeated the crowns of trees and their fruits. Those women who danced around it wearing on their head a wicker basket that contained symbolic phallus, would be pregnant.

In Caria, Laconia, at the parties called cariteias, women requested the goddess Artemis Cariatis their pregnancy. They danced in a grove of walnut trees and on their head they carried a calathus or basket of phalluses. In Lucania and the caryatids festivities, they called upon the goddess Aphrodite. In Sparta, they asked it at the Helenoforias celebrations; the goddess was Helena; they carried helene (pots) on their head and then held orgies in the nearby mount Taigeto.

Kneel before me, lower your head to my toes, and embrace both the sacred oak and me with your arms.

In a state of exaltation and excitement, he assumed the position. I began to chant again, and then giving a harsh cry discharged a ghastly blow across his back, with a coarsely knotted leather lash. Another cry and another blow. His pain was unbelievable. Yet in some strange way, it was not merely bearable, because at the same time I could see on his face an expression infinitely voluptuous.

Cry after cry, blow after blow, in a slow and cruel rhythm. While passionately he kissed my feet and tears ran down his cheeks on to them, he was screaming with the pain. The blows continued to fall with calculated ferocity.

Enough!-I cried triumphantly.

The chanting ceased and so did his ordeal. He felt exalted.

Stand up, and stand against the sacred oak!

He rose unsteadily, leaning against the post, and did what I told, as I did the same, so that we both stood in a tight circle around the pole blessed. With the sound of an iron blade being drawn from its sheath, I gently produced from a scabbard a long ivory-handled knife. I revealed naked my two breasts and with a slashing movement I made a cut on one of them, the breast nearest to him, just above the large brown nipple.

Our arms linked our bodies tightly together, while like in an intoxicating dream I saw how the spikes on my divine cuirass dug fiercely into his flesh.

Our bodies were pressed together, and I forced his head down on to two soft mounds of flesh, with blood running freely down both. I sang with vibrant voice:

My breasts give blood, not milk. Drink the blood, and you are mine.

He lapped deliriously and with ecstasy and I comforted him:

You have undergone a painful experience, I fear, but your services must not go unrewarded. Let me make it up to you. Taste the sweetness of victory.

I let him fell into my beckoning arms, and he passed a thrilling time lying in my bosom while I caressed him in many delightful ways.

All praise appears double after a beating, especially when administered by the same person.

He remained transfixed, filled with many pleasurable sensations and wondering if all had been but a dream.

When at last he came to his senses, he found himself in the bush; and everything was as if he had only dreamed of.

CHAPTER 5. The second departure and life in wilderness

> Simon Peter said to them: "Mary leave us, as women are not worthy of life." To which Jesus retorted, "Behold, I will lead her to make her a man, so like you, she too may become a living spirit. because every woman who becomes a male will enter the kingdom of heaven."
>
> From The Gospel of Thomas.

My conduct in the affair I have just narrated should surprise no one. I had learnt it from the martyrology from which my father used to take those lives of saints that he read to me every night. Thus, in the life of St. Ulrike, we are told that when she had been reformer in a convent, one of the novices showed slow progress in the path of perfection that the mother abbess encouraged her to follow, first she was admonished, then reproached, and at the third fault, she was made to come to reason by the lashes of a whip. This same blessed one never tired of warning her meek flock that the greatest virtue of a sister was holy obedience, also called self-sacrifice, selflessness and self-denial.

The case of a novice, Beatrice of the Mother of God, whom a prioress refused to admit in the newly founded convent, was also noteworthy. Apparently in her childhood she had been persecuted and even abused. She was only seven when her mother's sister, who was fond of her, promised to appoint her successor. This aunt was a single woman living alone without any relatives at her side to protect her and look after her interests, and her maids wanted her to leave them her possessions at her death. So they tried to sow enmity between the aunt and niece and her parents.

They accused the little one of having commissioned them to poison the good lady. From over-confidence or for some other obscure reason, the aunt believed them, and returned the girl to her parents. These, spiteful with the loss of what they had expected, blamed the girl, hit her daily for an entire year, punished her in some other ways and forced her to sleep on the floor. But God punished the slanderers. They contracted rabies, and before dying repentant they confessed what they had planned. Some years later, the father wanted Beatrice married, but she refused to please him and told him she had made a vow to enter the religious life.

Again her father thought she lied and was just trying to hide some sin of the flesh that interfered with the project. He once more subjected her to unspeakable abuse and was about to strangle her. She escaped death miraculously. Bedridden she spent three months recovering from her father's assault.

All this shows that to flog somebody because of his or her supposed misbehavior was common. No one lost his reputation by it.

The couple's relationship was fraught with uncertainties.

The pros and cons of blessed matrimony

Having now tasted profane love and not knowing what to do, I decided to go back home. I did not think it would be too difficult to get myself forgiven by my father, who though a severe man, nonetheless professed to me his unalloyed Christian love. I had realized that to travel the world dressed as a woman was full of inconveniences; it endangered my body and, what was worse, my immortal soul.

I was among my family once again, and after having heard what had happened to me during my absence, for the moment my father was silent, thinking what could be done to ensure that I abandoned those dreams that he judged childish fancies and did not return to run such risks as I had run.

It was then the case that he tried to find me a husband and therefore he promised me in marriage to a young neighbor of fairly good descent and outstanding personal qualities.

At first I did not object, but there in the depths of me, half consciously, I saw vaguely that by marrying and forming a family I rebelled against my deceased mother or in some way challenged her, because without knowing how, in the depths I felt that it was a supreme rebellion to get married and have children as she had had. It would amount to snatching from her the mother role and her youth, to rub in her face her age and ageing.

Then there came to mind everything that she had read to me about marriage and also the sovereign knowledge endorsed by the Church holy fathers. I thought first of Tertullian according to whom marriage was based on the very act of prostitution, so the best thing for any woman was not having a husband.

His opinion would lack any weight if isolated, but to corroborate it had come St. John Chrysostom, for whom death was where marriage was, and where there was no marriage, there was no death.

I have already mentioned St. Justin.

To Clement of Alexandria, another holy man, intercourse was a pernicious disease, "a little epilepsy." And Origen used to teach that during the usual sexual act, the Holy Spirit was absent. Perhaps because he could not stand it, he chose castration.

I remembered then a secret confidence that Bilequilda of Maine had once intimated to me: "Look, Joan", she had said to me, "I am some years older than you, and as you know, I have been educated in a monastery for noble youth; well, in the chapel I have often begged the

Holy Virgin: O Madam, you who conceived without sin, grant that I may sin without conceiving."

To this was added what my mother attributed to St. Augustine, namely, that a mother, given that she has been married, would have a lower position in heaven than her daughter who had remained a virgin.

That holy North African bishop "would have preferred that children were planted by hand, like cereal."

In Milan St. Ambrose had also spoken about that issue: "Marriage is honorable, but more so continence, because if those who surrender their virginity in marriage do right, those who do not surrender and keep it, do better.

But earlier he had said that "as a natural institution in accordance with the will of God, marriage's first and deepest purpose is not the mutual love of spouses, but the creation and formation of new lives." Words that seem to contradict what he had previously said, since they implied that to preserve one's virginity was better than to bring children into the world. This is something that according to the Bible the Lord would have disapproved of, because He had commanded our first parents to "be fruitful and multiply."

But no true Christian would dare criticize the holy fathers of the Church.

And to Pope Leo I, no earthly mother "conceived without sin."

Then St. Isadora of Seville had said that even if marriage was good "in itself", its "circumstances" were "bad" and you had to atone daily for the pleasure taken in it.

Most of the clergy who handled the case were consistent in considering sinful all sexual dealings. And according to Innocent III, "sexual intercourse was never consummated without the itch of the flesh, without the burn of lust, without the pain of libido. No one would dare to deny it."

Intercourse was a vicious act. This was a most surprising thing indeed, because no one could imagine breeding without the preceding sex. At least for the time being and as long as assisted reproduction was not yet devised.

The carnal act was supposedly always linked to sin, a grave sin, because "in nothing was it different from adultery or fornication, so long as it involved sensual passion and heinous pleasure," since, "Adam corrupted us, we were born and conceived in sin and nuptial debt is never satisfied without sin; the spouses are not free of sin."

At first the couple was not allowed a kiss with tongues. But when with the relaxation of customs it began to be seen as only a venial sin, ecclesiastical authorities would not permit it straightforwardly, but offered a casuistry in which they indicated exactly how far the tongue could penetrate into the mouth and the kiss still be honest, and where the dishonesty began.

To avoid pleasure charming the couple and trapping them in the misleading net of lust, the so-called "monk's shirt" (chemise cagoule) was recommended, which covered the body to the feet and laid bare only a narrow slit in the genital area.

All this was part of the so-called moral theology, which those responsible for guiding others must learn.

Leaving aside the obstacles that ecclesiastics put in marriage, other secular reasons advised you to prefer the eunuch. Eunuchs were plentiful; almost all of aristocratic and urban origin. All of them used to be castrated to prevent them wasting energy on anything other than serving the State. Usually they let it be done voluntarily, because it was an essential requirement for those who wanted a career in the world. Great patriarchs and prominent generals had been eunuchs. Their crippled and sterile status was considered a privilege.

Rather dead than married

So coupled with the practical considerations, the strong and holy sentences relating to the matter overwhelmed me. They did not put things easily. Thinking twice, I found myself unfit for marriage, and thought that, in heaven as much as on earth, I would profit more by surrendering myself to the Lord and being His alone.

I decided to be of one piece. Once I had taken a path, the point of honor would not let me turn back for anything in the world. And in imitation of the St. Joan whose adventures a popular playwright had recounted, I repeated to myself: They want me get married, my God, but to be twice married, because You are already my husband, would be a depraved thing. And I know Your jealousy, I don't want make You, my God, jealous; I want to leave my father, who out of human respect prevents me in the good I pursue, and on behalf of a mortal husband deprives me of a divine and powerful one, immortal and rich. Only Your love will fit me that if I leave my father, in You, my Christ, I shall find, king, lord, husband and father.

I could be rightly said of he who would court me, what Don Quixote would later say to Maritorna, the maid who, at the inn where the gentleman watches over his arms, pretends that the daughter of the innkeeper is in love with him: I pity you, fair sir, that you should have directed your thoughts of love to a quarter from whence it is impossible that such a return can be made to you as is due to your great merit and gentle birth, for which you must not blame this unhappy indecisive girl whom love renders incapable of submission to any other than Him, whom, the first moment her eyes beheld him, she made absolute master of her soul.

The environment in which my parents had brought me up resulted in the fact that all my life I felt alienated from others, while at the same time quite rare and precious.

To escape the fate for which against my wishes I was destined, at first I thought to copy St. Ode, who in circumstances similar to mine had cut off the tip of her nose scaring away the unwelcome pretender; but considering that the likely bleeding might attract attention and would lead me to boast of it, out of humility I rejected the idea.

I then thought about what had happened to another, St. Catherine, who one day, desperate because of the annoying harassment to which her stubborn suitor subjected her, who would not take notice of her again and again turning him down, attempted by a disgusting and poisonous ointment to damage the beauty of her face. But when in Rome, in the garden of the house where she lived with her mother, she tried to implement her heroic intention, there fell on her head a large stone from the wall that seriously injured her; no doubt, God, having made her so attractive, did not want to see thus destroyed the beauty of this mystical woman.

I also gave up that project.

In similar straits St. Suzanne had also found herself. Time and again the son of the prefect of the city proposed marriage to her and would not take a no for an answer. She, fed up by such importunate solicitation, told her uncle, Pope St. Caius, who did not object to such a wedding: "You know, dear uncle of mine, that having taken a vow of chastity I cannot give my hand to another husband but Christ, and here I declare that I never will give it to anyone but Him. Rather nun than wife. For all the traps that the judge could set to force me to change my purpose, for all the many torments with which he threatens to take me to the bedroom of his son, I hope that by the mercy of my Lord Jesus Christ, they will rip from my body a thousand souls before they take from my heart the faith that to my divine husband I have promised, and they will not even cause the determination of your humble niece to falter."

Moved by the eloquence of his holy relative, St. Caius insisted no longer that she change her intention.

Equally courageous, precocious and illustrious had been St. Ines. At age nine she made a vow of virginity and devoted herself to Jesus Christ. She was only thirteen and already many men wanted her to be their wife and sentimental companion, but she rejected them and to their requests responded with rare eloquence: a wife who wants to please others insults her husband. The one who first chose me is the only one who will own me.

Coming back from school on one occasion, the son of the prefect of Rome saw her and fell in love with her. He followed her and found out who she was. Back at home he communicated his sudden love to his father, who for the moment made him consider his youth and the many opportunities to succeed that his condition gave him in life. But the young man did not let himself be dissuaded. With his father's permission he proposed marriage to the girl and offered her great gifts. But regardless of his manly bearing and his good appearance, Ines refused him saying: "Depart from me, pabulum of corruption, because another lover has asked for me. With precious stones He has adorned my right hand and my neck; He has put priceless pearls on my ears, and marked my face to not accept another dear one but Him. I love Christ, I'll be the wife of Him who was born of a virgin and whose Father bore Him with no female concourse, and in my ears He has sounded harmonious chords. When I shall love Him, I will be chaste; when I'll touch Him I'll be pure; when I receive Him, I will be virgin."

Overwhelmed and perplexed by this series of words, and preferring love to slick speeches, he denounced her. To punish her arrogance she was exposed naked to the obscene eyes of the populace or mob, but suddenly she grew silky hair that covered her from head to toe, as later would cover Lady Godiva, and one who dared to be near her, fell dead on the spot. She pitied him and, not wanting him to suffer because of her, she prayed for him and raised him.

Condemned to die at the stake, the flames refused to burn her. They put themselves aside and formed like a chalice or cup in which she appeared as a gem in its case.

"Why are you so lazy and take so long to send me to glory?" The young girl rebuked her subtle executioners who showed unwillingness to do their job. "May this body perish as it is loved by eyes to which I do not want to give any pleasure" she added.

Finally they beheaded her. Rhetoric did her no good. And those pagan idolaters stoned to death a sister of hers who went to pray at her tomb.

St. Ambrose said about her: "She loved God from the moment she knew about Him, and new-born she met Him."

I finally thought to resort to that expedient that in a similar trance had been employed by the holy Portuguese Princess Wilgefortis. Having prayed to God for protection, there grew suddenly on her face a bushy beard like that of an energetic man, a sight before which the person who aspired to her hand felt the love he had promised her weaken. However, as the Lord did not come to my rescue as quickly as on behalf of Wilgefortis and was slow to address my prayers, I determined to the problem alone, with my own strength.

I was much impressed by such heroic examples and in no way felt I could aspire to ever reaching such sublime heights as theirs.

I decide to consecrate myself to God

I felt called to a higher life and to despise worldly matters. Once I had gathered a few ornaments and jewelry that hitherto I had worn, I gave them to the poor and no more had any dealings with people my age but only spent time older ones of recognized piety, because it was not in vain that St. Remigius had declared: "have fun with the young, but deal with the old." Finally, given that since my early years there was talk of "the sweetness, charm and irresistible sympathy" that radiated from me, so that I was considered beautiful, in order to lose my sex appeal I stopped washing my face, even with cold water.

My father did not seem to take offence at my new attitude, and without worrying about it, he left, intending to retire for three days to a monastery of his choice. As he walked away, I sent someone of my confidence to ask for an interview with a holy monk who carried on a virtuous life nearby. And in his presence, I disclosed to him the divine call that in my soul I felt, and the holy man replied with the words of the Lord: "One who is not willing to leave father, mother, brothers and all things for the Kingdom of Heaven is not my disciple."

And to top it off he read me the epistle that St. Jerome had written to Heliodor: "Your widowed sister will come and will open to you her arms; your servants will come; the nurse who nursed you and her husband, who are like second parents to you, will meet you and tell you: to whom would you entrust us in our old age and who will assist us in death? Who will bury us? Especially your father, a venerable old man whose forehead some wrinkles will furrow, limp and weak the once mighty chest, he also will block your path and will remind you of all your life, since the day he first received you into his arms until now."

Thus my father will evoke my childhood and my departure will dismay my family and servants. But the old man continued to read: "The whole house rests in you and is about to fall... What are you doing under the parental roof, cowardly soldier? Even if your mother, with flowing hair and robe in tatters, and even if your own father lies in the doorway, you should step over his body... here the piety of a son is to be pitiless."

Despite such concerted reasons I did not let myself be immediately convinced and told the monk that if I persisted in my purpose I feared incurring the wrath of my father, whose apple of his eye I was, to which, resorting to more drastic measures, he argued that without any doubt he would find comfort in my other brothers. Having overcome thus my resistance, I asked him to admit me into the religious life, which he did immediately.

But once we had finished the interview and I was alone, I reflected and reached the conclusion that my father would not turn back on his original intention of giving me away in marriage, and I would not be able to avoid his anger, because if I hid, he would doubtless discover me, and would drag me back to the home using force if necessary.

I prayed fervently to the Lord to deign to show me the path to follow at that crossroads of helplessness.

He heard me no doubt, the Almighty, because one of those mornings, when lying down on the grass of a nearby meadow I let the sun's rays warm my cold limbs, which moisture had somewhat stiffened, and suddenly the idea came to my mind that my many ills were due partly to my womanhood, my abundant and long golden hair, my roundness and generally everything that those who know about such matters have called female secondary characteristics; and if I managed to disguise them and make myself pass for a man, it would certainly ease my difficulties.

In this pious attempt women had preceded me in taking male personae, male clothing and male names and passing as monks; women such as St. Mary of Egypt, a woman of easy morals to whom, on the threshold of the Basilica of the Holy Sepulcher at Jerusalem, Jesus Christ appeared, so she withdrew from the bad life in which until then she had pleased herself and after dressing as a man spent the following forty-seven years in the desert, eating only the fish from a nearby pond and some bread to balance her diet.

St. Isolina of Pergamum provided a similar example. Happily married, her kindness made her so attractive that a frivolous young man fell in love and wanted to seduce her, but she rejected his impure desires. With what she had at home, she was satisfied.

Enraged, he resorted to a witch, who by potions and specious words led her to consent. But the trance having past, she felt so sad that she promised herself to regret it for life. So she put on men's clothes and begged to be admitted in a neighboring monastery. She said her name was Isolino and once accepted 'he' attracted the admiration of everybody by the harshness of his (or her) mortifications.

In that place a female inn-keeper lived whom an unscrupulous waiter had left pregnant and, not wanting to take responsibility for the fruit of his manhood, had run away. The landlady accused Isolino of being the father of the child.

Isolino kept silent and did not want to reveal the lie, so was expelled from the community. Then Isolino retired to solitude, took over the little one and fed him with skimmed goat's milk. The roughness of religious life in the open and the hardships tanned his complexion, which had been smooth so far. Some years later he pleaded to be admitted back into the sacred precincts, which was granted him after having been made to swear that he would never leave his cell. He did so, and only after his death when he was being shrouded to give him a Christian burial was

Isolino's true gender discovered. Her son later became abbot of the same place.

Similarly St. Nerea of Bithynia; St. Ann of Constantinople; holy Apolinaria, holy Anastasia of Aegina, St. Hilary, St. Margaret, St. Matrone of Pergia, holy Epiphany of Eleutheropolis, St. Pelagia of Antioch, St. Paola and many others that it would be tedious to name, had put aside female apparel and taken on the appearance of holy men.

And what to say about the famous Edelvithe? A daughter of the Duke of Sotomayor, she had been governess of Prince Uxío, heir to the kingdom in which her father served. At forty, disillusioned with the Court, she wanted to move to the country, where she practiced a penance so rigorous that her bloody shirts were made with fragments of broken glass and the whippings which for hours she imposed on herself with rusty chains impressed some and appalled others. Although she had taken refuge in a cave, where she spent hours as though buried alive, the devils did not rest in tempting her and attempt to make her lose her temper took the nefarious form of voluptuous snakes or aroused hounds. It was said that she ate only on Sundays, Tuesdays and Thursdays, which she kept track of not with a calendar but with secret arts. When the moment arrived and she decided to take the religious habit in the order of Mount Carmel, founded to honor the Prophet Elijah, she chose the convent of men instead of women, as should have befitted her sex, because her head did not suffer on it even the touch of a headdress. Her reputation for holiness made the Princess of Villasobroso invite her to spend some time in the palace, where she shocked everybody who did not know her, parading in a large coach surrounded by illustrious ladies, and blessing all those whom they met on the way.

The bishop of the diocese had summoned her to his presence intending to scold her for conduct so outrageous, However, seeing that she was a woman of high rank, and not the monk whom one would have suspected by her robe, he changed his mind and instead of scolding her sharply as he thought to do at first, with chosen and pious words he tried to encourage her to leave the roughness of the open air and seclude herself in a monastery together with other women. This she outright rejected on the grounds that "she did not want to live amid fulsome and mannered devouts, whose wild fantasy could only increase the already excessive natural weakness of the feminine gender."

On returning to her solitude, she stayed one night in a monastery, and when in the morning she departed, the ascetics who had been so privileged as to approach and entertain her, asserted that the monk's habit of rough serge, very dirty, exhaled an indescribable odor of sanctity. With the extreme heat of that time, you could very well have expected otherwise.

At the hermitage she caused so deep an impression that the abbess was confused and complained of not feeling able to imitate her penance, until God Himself had appeared to her and reassured her that to please Him there was no need to go to such outrageous extremes, as he considered someone's obedience worthier than the blows of leather whips or the fasting and abstinence practiced in the meatless days ordered by the Church.

Animated by the thought of so many exemplary lives, I determined to escape from home disguised as a male to avoid the disadvantages I had met on my first attempt.

Easier said than done. I managed as best I could to get the clothes of my youngest brother, which by chance had been hanged to dry my industrious mother, not without asking God forgive me that theft, to which adverse circumstances pushed me.

The female garment having been discarded, I cut with a sharp stone the treacherous hair and tried too to conceal the roundness of my nascent breasts; then so protected and after looking around and sighing with sadness, I delivered myself to the good fortune that God would give me and without waiting for my father to return, I fled by night, while he was absent.

I run away from home disguised as a man to live in a monastery

To prevent further flights, my father had locked me in a room with a pole barring the door, but he had neglected the window, so I let myself down to the damp ground, and without further delay I went to a nearby monastery, attracted by its reputation for holiness and austerity of the life there practiced.

I knocked on the door and asked to see the abbot. In his presence, I begged him to admit me into the holy residence as one more novice. I told him my name was John. Having been part of the imperial court and become disenchanted with the promises of the world, I had run away from its deceptions and the court intrigues and wanted to devote my life to prayer in the midst of the peace and example of such community. I begged him insistently and stressed that I must be received among his flock, because I just wanted to serve the Lord.

Though my good words seemed to please him, he could not make up his mind to let me in and my fragile appearance did not seem to him to correspond to the strength that as a standard was expected of applicants; therefore, being dubious of my ability to lead the life of denial and rough work prescribed by the rule, which was that of St. Benedict of Aniane, he refused to admit me.

The sweetness of my voice had surprised him. "Brother John," he said, "have you still not changed voice?" And I replied: "Reverend Father, I do not think I would ever change it."

Wondering at my youthful beauty and young age, still he did not trust me and refused my entry, saying that he did not think I could withstand the fasts and vigils that there were practiced; but I insisted, I refused to leave the vicinity of the house, and for seven days and nights I did not move from the door.

I refrained from eating completely, or ate nothing else but the leftovers that, pitying me, another novice sneakily brought me; I slept on the ground when I felt too tired, and carried on zealously the humblest services with which I was only occasionally entrusted to test me.

I remembered the example of St. Arsenius.

Disillusioned by the imperial court, where he had been entrusted with the education of the two children of Theodosius the Great, he wanted to engage in other work more profitable regarding the salvation of his soul.

One day he was in prayer and asked God to illuminate him. What is to be done to achieve quicker sanctity? And he heard a voice saying, "Turn aside from dealing with people and look for solitude."

So he decided to go to the desert to pray and do penance with others who lived in that place.

Once in the monastery, its monks, knowing that he had spent all his life as a senator and high official of the Palace, wanted to make him undergo some tests to see if this life of humiliation and mortification would suit him. The superior received him coldly, and in the dining hall he did not allow him to sit at table, but left him standing in the middle of the room. Then, instead of handing him over a plate of food he threw at his feet a slice of bread and said dryly: "If you want to eat, pick it up and eat it." Arsenius bent humbly, took up that piece of bread, sat down and ate it meekly. Astonished at such behavior, the abbot judged him fit for the monastic life and accepted him as a monk, after making the others to observe: "Behold a good brother, whose example will be of advantage to us all."

I too chose "to be despised in the house of God rather than to dwell in the tents of sinners."

Then I was allowed to enter the cloister, but now it was Lent and the monks observed it by the most complete fasting and extraordinary penances according to everyone's imagination. Some fasted one day a week, others fasted two, others three or four, some stood all day or just sat working for hours.

I stayed all the time at my corner, concentrating on what I was doing and through the forty days maintained the most rigorous abstinence from food, eating only on Sundays the leaves of cabbage that were grown in the garden.

Easter arrived and, astonished at such extreme austerity, the other monks went to the abbot and begged him not to let those rigors go on, worried no doubt that they would hurt everybody because they would feel motivated to follow my example and starvation would consume the weakest.

The abbot went to the chapel and prayed fervently to God to determine what to do in such a surprising case of penance and religious zeal; God enlightened him: everything was fine and there was no reason to worry.

In admiration the abbot hugged me, thanked me for edifying the monks and entrusted them to my prayers.

He no longer had any qualms about counting me as one more among them, but not to leave anything to chance he also decided to watch me to see if I could endure the heavy work, therefore he warned me that, given my inexperience in the discipline of religious life, I would have to submit to the direction of an ancient monk, a novice master.

I replied that not only was I ready to accept the guidance of a master of perfection, but also of as many as would be necessary, because in a holy place like that one, those who by their ordered life would serve me as a guide would not be lacking. He then put me in the hands of the father who acted as director of the novices, though not before saying to him in an aside: "Take care of this useless one, see what can be done with him."

Without wasting time, in the novitiate I addressed the master of novices in the following terms: "Tell me, O Master, what I must do to achieve holiness?" And without a baffled look he replied, "Imagine a canvas on which Jesus Christ is represented perfectly. Copy it in your soul with all its features. Then present it to men."

Comforted with such holy words and grateful to God for the favor that he did me without any merit on my part, I worked without giving a break, tending the garden, keeping the mules and donkeys cleans, attending the many needs of the house, aiding the sexton… Since the monastery was poor and did not have all the copies of the psalter or Book of Psalms that would have been necessary, I learned them by heart, so as not to be left behind in the choir. In October of that year - I had entered the last spring - the abbot who had branded me useless and judged me incapable of heavy work retracted his hasty opinion and found me suitable for the religious life. Talking to another brother about me, he told him that I was "tireless in the task, a man of prayer, exemplary in the observance and heroic in every virtue, especially in charity towards those who shared the life with me."

It was true that often, having finished the work that by duty or office as required of me, I approached a brother who was still toiling and said to him: "Leave it to me, I'll finish, because I'm younger than you." Most of the time I met no opposition and the brothers gladly let me do their work.

One day, up a steep slope nearby climbed an old woman, who had her washing on her head, and I hastened to approach, and though some there made fun of me, I took on her burden and carried it to where it was necessary.

I must say that instead of thanking me, had looked at me with suspicion, as she was not accustomed to such gentleness.

On another occasion I met a poor man who walked barefoot on the rocky road: after handing him my own sandals I went home barefoot. Later I saw a young man who with a gangrenous leg mourned his bad luck: I sucked the rot off the wound and healed it.

Community life does not satisfy me

The trial period ended and when the abbot was firmly committed to admitting me as one more monk of the monastery, I felt that convent life did not call me as much as that of a hermit. My beauty and charm did not fit well in a community of men alone as they became distracted. Once one of the novices who had passed me in the cloister exclaimed, "Either this brother of ours is a woman or is the devil, because I can never see him without feeling impure temptations."

No doubt. To live in disguise among so many males meant danger, so I asked the abbot to be allowed to live separately in the vicinity; I should attend all services, but the rest of the time I would pass alone in my beloved solitude.

The abbot had begun distrusting me, but with my indomitable effort I had convinced him of the strength of my vocation. He resisted at first, but finally gave his consent to my request and agreed to let me live in the neighborhood in one of the numerous caves and hollows abounding nearby.

Without knowing it, I faithfully copied the lives of other servants of God, St. Avitus, St. Romuald, St. Campio - examples of an admirable life all of them.

One day the young Avitus had begged the abbot, Maximino or Mesmino, to be admitted to the monastery; if not as a monk, then at least as a servant. He was ready to refuse to depart from the door of the convent in order to get what he wanted, and would even let himself die of cold and hunger if necessary.

Faced with such holy stubbornness, the abbot, a cautious man, felt no qualms in admitting him. And he was so friendly, helpful and obedient that sometimes some took as supine stupidity his simplicity and desire to please the community.

The abbot thought him a godsend, made him his treasurer and confided to him all that related to the support of the friars. He had to take care that they did not lack what was needed in life, and so he had to arrange the order of the meals, monitor the single store, replenish supplies and keep aside a small part for the many alms.

Unfortunately his way of performing his duty did not please everyone, so that some of the monks criticized him and whispered about him.

The apparent failure led Avitus to want to live an isolated life. He therefore prayed and begged God to enlighten him and make know to him whether it was right to change direction in life. The response must have been affirmative because he entered the cell of the abbot, waited for him to surrender himself to sleep and then deposited under his pillow the treasurer's keys, to let him know that he was resigning from office. He left the monastery and in the nearby forest he delivered himself freely to penance and prayer without having to keep listening to the protests of his brothers in Christ.

He mimicked the hermits by eating grass, roots and fruits of the field.

In the year 520, the abbot Maximino died, and at the request of the Bishop of Orleans and the monks with whom he had shared brotherhood, Avitus left his retirement and agreed to rule the abbey. With humility and example rather than with dry orders he ruled his flock and raised the divine tone of the monastery. Yet he could not forget the peace of solitude.

Again he retreated to it, living in caves or huts made of the branches of trees, in a more distant and less accessible place than the first. He hoped that there it would not be easy for the monks to find him if by chance he was being sought; he had brought with him another priest who encouraged the same desire for retirement. Like the first time, they lived in contemplation and penance, in the distance and silence.

They did not last long, however, because a miracle discovered them. By order of the saint, someone who had been deaf since childhood regained his speech and thereafter it was impossible to silence him. The news spread. Loneliness, goodbye! Those then living had never heard of such a thing, and people came to see and touch the incredible man. Like the disciple Thomas, who only believed in the resurrection of the Lord when he had allowed himself to put his fingers into the wounds, they were people weak in faith. They were unlike the centurion in the holy Gospel, whose servant had fallen ill and so he begged Jesus to heal him, for which he saw no need to visit him in bed, as did ordinary physicians, since it was sufficient that Jesus wanted it and would enforce His will. Like our Savior had done, everybody admired a faith so sublime. In any case, the saint here spoken of catechized, taught, prayed and made others pray. The disciples came and, unwillingly, he had no choice but to establish a new monastery that eventually bore his name.

Through his intercession, in Orleans prisoners were freed from jail. Miraculously he healed a blind man too, and restored life to a monk who was already dead. He also asked King Clodomiro, the son of Clovis and Clotilde, to make peace with Sigismund, King of Burgundy, and his family, whom Clodomiro had captured.

Compared to so many admirable examples, my life seemed ordinary in excess. Because, as is well known to those who understand it, "When a painter desires to be renowned in his art, he seeks to imitate the originals of the rarest painters that he has seen; a rule that also applies to all other trades or exercises that serve to adorn kingdoms and empires. Those who want to be esteemed prudent and patient must do the same in imitating Ulysses, in whose person and work Homer paints a lively picture of prudence and patience; they should also follow the example of the person of Aeneas the Roman poet Virgil has showed us, in whom we see the value of a pious son and the sagacity of a brave and skillful captain; Virgil did not paint and describe them such as they were, but as they ought to be, so as to leave the example of their virtues to posterity."

In the same way St Anthony Abbot had been the North Star, the guiding light, the sun to so many valiant servants of God, who should be copied by all those who militate under the banner of divine love.

This being so, as it is, I thought that the ascetic who best imitates him would be close to reaching the perfection of life in the wilderness.

And Jesus had said: "Blessed are you, the solitary and the elect; you will find the kingdom, because you have just come from it and to it you will return."

Hermit life

St. Pacomio had been the first to show Christians a life of strict asceticism, but within a confined place and under the obedience of a superior and in observance of a rule. It was coenobitic or community life. In the East the two rules of St. Basil were followed; in the West, those of St. Augustine and St. Benedict.

As I said, living in company would not suit me; in many cases my soul would be in danger, so I preferred to leave the monastery and carry on a hermit's life. In such a life monks did not live together in a building, but in separate cabins, although under a common rule. Though isolated from each other, they gathered together for some ascetic exercises, a kind of gym of the soul, and submitted to be led by an outstanding master teacher.

In the vicinity of the monastery in which I had hidden to escape the world and my father, there was an established colony of hermits into which, imitating those of St. Anthony Abbot, disciples were admitted; it was led by the venerable Pafnucio, one of the teachers of greatest prestige at that moment.

Known for its singular asceticism, the name of that community was on everyone's lips. During the week, in his separate cell, each hermit lived in absolute solitude, but on Saturdays and holidays they gathered together to celebrate the divine offices. They were engaged in prayer, observed the strictest silence, made handicrafts, mats, baskets or things like that which besides keeping them busy helped them to dispel idle thoughts and encourage contemplation and union with God. Although they reduced their food to the most frugal and necessary, their happiness, good spirits and even their healthy bodies were to be admired.

In this life what caused me most trouble was keeping strict and rigorous silence.

Healthy in body and soul, well directed by our great teacher, we lived only for God, to whom we had completely dedicated ourselves.

The following fact testifies to the harmony of our coexistence and the spiritual joy that radiated from us.

On one occasion, another ascetic and I were crossing a nearby river and we passed a group of army officers who were strongly impressed by the cheerful demeanor and happiness we exuded; one said to each other: "It's funny how these men are so happy in their poverty."

And I replied: "Rightly you consider us happy people, as it correctly attests our spirit. If we are happy despising the world, is not fair that you consider yourselves miserable by serving it?"

These hard words, coupled with the example that we gave them, produced such an effect on the chief of that group that he returned to his home, distributed among the poor all he owned and became like us a hermit.

In these ways the Lord poured His graces over that hermitage, so much so that, surrounded by a multitude of angels, the Mother of God arrived and let herself be seen by us at the cabin of the director, where she remained while the community -assembled to behold the wonder- intoned and sang a Salve.

Indeed, we monks were like stone rather than flesh. We scourged each other and the common chapel resounded with the pounding of chests; when we got excited or devotion inflamed us, our clamor rose powerfully. We confessed to each other our sins and faults or praised the Lord. God had favored some of us with the gift of tears, so much so that when we shed them, they ran down our gaunt and haggard cheeks in such abundance that they fell to the floor, and the weeping opened deep grooves in them.

We took to extreme mortification and penance. One day, the back of a candidate was flogged before a lot of green wood, because we expected that when he was sufficiently purified or punished, fire would come down from heaven and kindle the logs. The thing was not as incomprehensible as it may seem initially, as it was well known that the Prophet Elijah had had a similar epiphany.

Cold bruised our feet, and rocks and thorns hurt us so much that they would look more like eggplant than human limbs.

Every night a statue of St. Joseph in our director's cell enumerated the faults he had committed during the day. The lips of the statue were parted and the monks called it "the holy talker."

For my life to be more regular and complete, God permitted that - like the patient Job - I was persecuted and even slandered. I was accused of excessive mortification and falling into unacceptable practices. It was true that in addition to wearing the regular sackcloth made with porcupine quills, I wore on my thighs and arms several others of metal wire. But I do not think the deed deserved such scandal.

As the common doctrine of the Church asserts, our Lord has ordered us to deny ourselves, which entails the mortification of the body. You must forget yourself and open your eyes to look at others, as represented by the true Man of Sorrows, a name also given to Jesus Christ.

The malevolent persecution became so great, that for some time I was expelled from my cell and someone even denounced me to the bishop and asked him to banish me to a secluded place.

But God was watching over me. When, required by service, I moved from one place to another, St Nicephorus of Otranto sent me a dog to accompany me, a black and white spotted poodle, which disappeared when the danger passed.

My unusual zeal frightened those who were most mediocre and shy, and some who shared with me such life in the wilderness thought that I, like St. Benedict of Nursia, was demanding too much because, as it was said, I refused "to live by lighting one candle to God and another to the devil," or in other words to live the life of retirement as vigorously as in the world; therefore they wanted to suffer it no longer and sought to get rid of me by killing me.

And when presented with the opportunity, they poured a strong poison in the wine that on the occasion of the feast of Easter and I was ready to drink to celebrate the resurrection of the Lord. But as I used to do with all that I put in my mouth, I blessed the cup, which exploded in pieces.

Realizing that among those people my life was in danger, I determined to get away from there.

I also suffered appalling impure temptations. The most corrupt scenes presented themselves to my imagination and I remembered a young man I had seen some time ago and for whom I had felt a strong and incomparable passion. I prayed and asked for help to heaven, and finally when I was on the verge of fainting and so excited that my shaking legs could hardly hold me up, I threw myself against a bush full of sharp thorns and wallowed in it until all my body was injured and hurt. Well, through those bodily wounds I was healed in the wounds of the soul, and that deceitful temptation went away from me.

Of St. Benedict it was recounted that in his later years he had prayed and fought against the temptations of the flesh for three consecutive years, since apparently lust would not leave him alone. That man was no doubt vigorous. One night he dreamed of a girl he had met at Norcia. Panicked by such a vision, he threw himself naked on nettles, which immediately became fragrant roses.

God decided too that my soul also would be tested with the greatest spiritual darkness. Moved by my eagerness of contemplation, I locked myself in the cell to remain there five days. The first two days I was flooded with celestial sweetness, but on the third there rushed upon me such turmoil and conflict that I was forced to return to normal life. God retires at certain times, for men to experience their own weakness and acknowledge that life is a struggle.

To this life of unconditional seclusion of the world, of prayer and consecration to God, I added the strictest continence and a huge variety of privations and penances.

In all this I showed myself superior. I exceeded all in the austerity of my life, which became proverbial among the monks, but I excelled in a special way through my ascetic practices, always performed in the purest spirit of love for Jesus Christ and in imitation of His passion and with the desire to atone for the sins in which the world wallowed without any moderation. Fervor possessed me and I felt an extraordinary love for God.

So much so that to resemble him further in regard to His divine passion, I made, with the wild gorse that abounded everywhere, a crown of thorns, and constantly wore with special pride its vividly yellow flowers on my head, without taking it off even for sleeping, which was not very difficult because I slept very little.

So much was I driven by the desire to mortify myself and suffer, that I practiced long vigils, and so that sleep did not make me surrender, I stayed outside the hut, burnt by the sun during the day and racked by cold at night.

But such repetitiveness of the days was wearisome so I tried to introduce some variety into life.

Like holy Hyacinth had done before me, in remembrance of the seven deadly sins that offended God, I built seven oratories or chapels, which every day, barefoot and a cross on my back, I visited one at a time, and I always stopped to sing some of the Psalms of David. Thus I had my first glimpses of mystical ecstasy and raptures.

Holy Begga of Landen, older sister of holy Gertrude and St. Arnold's daughter-in-law, had also raised seven chapels, in honor of the seven churches which there had once been in Rome.

Number seven was an arcane number. You must remember the seven-branched candelabra of the Jewish faith, the seven gifts of the Holy Spirit, the seven days of a week God required to create the world and everything it contains, and the seven planets then known. In addition there were the seven days that St. Brendan sailed to the Fortunate Islands also called the Hesperides. Not forgetting popular folklore, according to which every seven years the life of a person begins a new stage.

While living with my parents and siblings, the spirit of religion and piety was the most precious ornament or finial of the family. Thereby they had tried to instill it in me. In that homey ambience I felt for the first time attracted by a lofty ideal and it awoke my penchant for liturgical ceremonies. As a child, in the garden of our home I delighted in raising chapels and mimicking the celebrations and prayers of our Holy Mother the Christian Church, and tried to dress as best as I could to accommodate myself to the rite that at the time I performed.

Recalling those past childish things, I wanted to repeat what I had previously done and attend common prayers in the liturgical vestments prescribed by the ritual of the day in order to follow with devotion and restraint as perfectly as possible the sacred ceremonies. I asked our spiritual father permission to satisfy so devout an enthusiasm, but that master of virtue only allowed me to change, according to the different festivities, the thickness and color of the cingulum of my habit and the material of which the various hair shirts I wore were made. He deemed my proposal a sinful frivolity and excessive fantasy, as it was well known that bright colors excite lust, that is, the appetite and desire for earthly goods, especially those of the flesh.

St. Ildefonso had better luck: to him the Virgin herself had appeared and given him the liturgical vestments. She had not been fussy; she had not made herself difficult nor made a storm in a teacup about it.

I felt called to an even more secluded life

Life in that community did not seem to me a sacrifice.

I began to eat only every other day until I got tired and proceeded to eat only on Mondays. I learned then that St. Macarius of Alexandria had already done this; he had advanced me in the feat, and so if he had come to eating just once a week, I would do better and not even eat that often. I began thus to eat only in alternate weeks, and to imitate him even more, I also spent most of the time in the open air, like him.

No doubt my difficult life pleased the Lord, because I lived healthily and my body did not resent such rigor and penitence. God had given me a body especially suited to coping with the toughest mortification of the flesh and the hardest sacrifices, therefore, always moved by the desire to please Him, I tried to imitate and even surpass any spiritual exercise that I had saw or heard of.

Again discontent ensued among my brothers in faith. They began to murmur and to reproach me for having a wild imagination and asked our superior to force me to follow the rules, in short, to be like everybody else and not distinguish myself, in either good or bad.

Accustomed to the common cilice and wanting something new, I made a rope of wild myrtle and tied my body with such violence that it adhered to the skin and wounded my flesh, making me bleed. Our common teacher intervened, and the other ascetics took it off me by force of water.

On another occasion, in passing with other ascetics by nearby a cave in which had dwelt long years the holy Nerea of Sampayo, I made a halt to pray. I remained prostrate on the ground so long that my companions began to grow impatient. Once finished, I apologized to them.

The saint had appeared to me and had encouraged me to not falter in seeking the way of perfection and continue along the path taken. And she had promised to give me support at any time.

This was the limit for our holy director; having found out about such improbable happenings, he tactfully suggested that I seek another place where I could freely carry out my appalling penance without shocking those who unfortunately were not as heroic as me.

I was not satisfied. That life did not seem harsh enough to me. I pondered what I should do. One day in the chapel, a monk preached the Beatitudes. I asked the Lord: "What shall I do, my Lord, to deserve salvation?" And in a voice barely audible he replied: "The surest path is to leave everything, even the life lived in common with others, and live as an anchorite."

But I had heard of a holy abbess, who, in order to exercise herself in humility, refused to occupy in the monastery the private cell to which she would have been entitled by her office, and instead slept in room with the poorest sisters and mingled with them.

On another occasion, also in the church, praying to God to deign to show me how I could best serve Him, I had a dream. I was digging the ground to lay the foundations of a building. Then I thought: that's it. But a voice urged me: "You have to dig deeper, even more deeply." I kept digging; the warning was repeated twice until I heard, "Enough, now you can safely raise the building."

No doubt. The Lord called me by another way. I left then that community of sainted ascetics and went alone into the wasteland. I walked undecided until I found an abandoned empty water tank. I got down into it and there I spent five days in constant prayer.

Sorry, the other monks looked for me. They took me out of the well and entreated me to come back with them. Lent came and I wanted to pass it without food. I asked advice from my colleagues; they said it was alright, but just in case I'd better take with some water, salt and bread with me.

I wanted to test the anchoritic way of living as a prisoner, so I got into the cabin, and the others boarded up the door with stones and mud and left me.

I spent the first day standing up, then sitting, and finally lying on the ground. Ending their vigil, the others came and broke down the wall, and they found me almost dead. They gave me some water and I was revived. I was twenty-three years old.

But I was determined to live on my own. I thanked them for the amiable interest they had shown me, but I made them understand that God had called me to another life, more lonely and wild.

Even if that life was very ascetic, I did not yet feel satisfied. I hated being constantly surrounded by men and longed to live the same life, but among women. I do not know what impelled me to such a desire. Dressed as a man, maybe I had become identified with the male role and longed for life among women, as a Sultan in his seraglio: me being the only man among many women, without rivalry or threatening jealousy. On the other hand, maybe I was inclined to live in female company because of my true womanhood. Living disguised as a man entailed constant tension, primarily the fear that one fateful day someone would discover my true nature. At that time it would have meant mortal danger. Everybody had in mind the words of the Bible: "Thou shalt not take woman's dress, nor will she masquerade as a boy. They that do so will be put to death."

In the ancient desert there had been women's communities, both anchorite and coenobitic ones. As soon as men ran away from the madding crowd, they were followed by crowds of women, who like bees in a beehive were busy caring for the ascetic dwellings. Some of them kneaded bread or cooked vegetables; others spun wool and the light came down on them like a pleased smile of God. Some meditated in the shade of stunted palms, their white hands hung at their sides because, full of love, they had chosen the part of Mary of Bethany and exercised themselves only in prayer, contemplation and ecstasy. They were called the Mary and dressed in white, while those given to working with their hands were called Martha and dressed in blue. To preserve from the torrid heat the delicate skin and avoid it being prematurely tarnished, all wore the veil, not by virtue, as was erroneously believed, but for hygiene. Nevertheless the youngest ones showed some curls on their forehead, without knowing it, because it was forbidden by the rule.

It was said that when, at the request of the venerable Pafnucio, the courtesan Thais decided to leave Alexandria, sad because of the dissolute and frivolous life she had led as a dancer until then, the abbess of one of those asciteries had placed her in a cabin as a penitent. The cabin had been vacant since the death of the virgin Leta, whose presence had sanctified it. In the narrow room there was only a basic cot, a table and a pitcher, and Thais, when she set foot on the threshold, felt imbued with infinite joy. The abbess had ordered one of the lay maids serving the others: "My daughter, bring to our dear Thais what she needs: bread, water and a three-hole flute."

I live as an anchorite

But to make that dream come was impossible. So I decided to live in solitude.

In the early days of primitive Christianity, it was believed that evil spirits populated the world; everywhere you looked, you ran into one of them: when ploughing a field, digging a well, building a house or a hut, there was always a Djins. They embodied themselves in wild animals, birds of prey, in snakes and lizards; sometimes they were manifested to people as hybrid beings, hirsute and hairy.

One day while he walked deep in thought, St. Anthony Abbot had encountered a centaur, whose terrible and disgusting combination of human torso and equine stomach were intended to intimidate him. Quickly a chorus of other monsters joined the beast, like satyrs, with legs and beards of goats, who terrorized the ascetic and forced him to return to the monastery. The devil incarnate expressed itself in all them. The saint had to get involved in a prolonged and enormous fight against these monsters. Finally they did not do him any harm: the creatures were harmless, as were all those dragons to those who served God faithfully.

I did not fear solitude. The angels watch in the solitude too, ready to chain the devil and help those who defeat him in the fight. Like the hermit St. Paul, I knew that besides the company of wild animals and fierce birds, I could count upon that of angels, who, though invisible, were very close to me, always attentive to protecting me against the powers of darkness and ready to present before the throne of God those merits that through my penance and prayers made me a credit to Him.

Like God had led to the desert His chosen people to speak confidentially to their hearts there, so He had led me. In the wilderness God had indoctrinated directly His chosen people, who never forgot the divine catechism; in those days of pilgrimage in the desert, Israel celebrated his nuptials with Yahweh. I would do the same.

Ruminating about what I ought to do and how from that moment I would manage in my new life, I considered the examples of many holy women who setting aside the vanities and pomp of the fallacious world and fled to the desert to live a hermit's life and died there full of holiness and of the smell of it, so that again finally I will win eternal bliss, although by means not so expeditious as that of the martyrdom I had first imagined.

Having taken the decision, I had only to put it into practice, so I reviewed the lives of many who had preceded me on the narrow path of perfection.

I wished that what had happened to the anchorite Paul when he looked for a place of his to isolate himself and live a life of contemplation would happen to me. It is said that when he returned to his den on one occasion, entering into the very heart of the desert, he found a rocky mountain in whose foothill he saw the entrance of a cave half blocked by a large stone.

Out of curiosity, he entered the cave and found himself in a spacious lobby, in the open, covered by the branches of an old palm tree. He also saw there a spring of purest water that after a brief spurt disappeared into the ground. He took a great liking to the place and decided to settle there permanently. The palm would be responsible for feeding him; the spring water would quench his thirst.

The world was far away and he only had to fear attacks from his flesh and from the devil, which followed him to the hiding place and continually threatened the peace of his soul.

But his solitude was not ruled by the evil spirits, because God also reigned over them there. It was well known that once the demon Asmodeo fled to Upper Egypt and an angel had tied him to a post. Also, sometimes, at dawn there had been seen some people running away in tears and, when asked about the causes of such distress, they had responded: "I weep and moan, because this or that ascetic who lives here has beaten me and I got kicked out ignominiously."

St. Macarius had also sought a wild jungle to live in in complete solitude. He had found an empty tomb and had spent some time there. But since he did not yet feel entirely at home, he had abandoned it to penetrate to the innermost thickness, and to isolate himself even more from the world, he had erected a stone wall around, and bound himself to a rock with chains. He was reasonably assured that it would be difficult to leave the place if his motivation left him, and thus had devoted himself to contemplation.

There the devil had stepped up his attacks to overcome the amazing resistance of so holy a man. Sometimes he horrified him with very strong sounds that made him believe he was in the midst of a horrific battle of titans giants; on others he appeared to him in the guise of terrible beasts or no less frightening goblins and witches, who terrorized him and caused him untold moral suffering.

I craved resembling him. So in order to avoid possible unexpected human visitors, I went into the depths of the thicket, without straying from a stream that flowed there and that for the time being would provide me with what I needed to stay hydrated, and also I looked to see if perhaps there was hidden somewhere a fruit tree, because man does not live by bread alone. In the Garden of Eden, man's first dwelling, there were some, which God had providentially arranged so as to show where the most appropriate place to worship and serve him. On the other hand, such trees often bear fruit without needing any ploughing nor autumn sowing, because as well as the Lord caring for the birds of the air and the flowers of the meadow, he looks after this poor girl too, now in man's clothes, who sought nothing but to please Him in silence and to die in peace after many years and enter His Kingdom.

Unfortunately human improvidence did not have the foresight to plant fruit trees in the forest. Instead it is preferred raise them in orchards, near home, where collecting the ripe fruits needs no effort beyond the stretching out the hand, so that in the thicket there were no fig-trees nor apples or pears, but mostly oaks and the occasional walnut or wild chestnut.

God squeezes but does not drown, I thought, and I agreed to live on chestnuts and walnuts, and if necessary even acorns, that past example had shown to be digestible and even nutritious.

I built with reeds and fireproof refractory clay my oratory –also an elementary chapel- without forgetting the silky moss to cover and fill the cracks, and prepared to spend hours in recitation like those who the divine service devoted themselves.

Such I had learned from books.

I wanted to keep giving myself to the manual labor that in my former state I carried out, namely, weaving mats and baskets, but I found that in those places there were no osiers or rushes or other suitable material, so for the time being I was perplexed at the prospect of having nothing to do in the empty hours. Fortunately the Lord, who was aware of my inclinations and past activities, put himself in my place and had pity on me, providing the remedy which consisted of regularly sending me via an angel abundant and varied reading, which averted the risk that with nothing to do but meditate on the brevity of this life, idleness would corrupt me and lead me astray.

This solution was not as rare as it might seem, as Dionysus of Alexandria had received from heaven an order to read all the books. Printing had not yet been invented; otherwise it would certainly not be easy to obey. It had also happened in other faiths, since the Archangel Gabriel before anything else had advised, if not ordered Mohammad: 'to read.' It was not to be doubted.

Of what I have just said, it should not be suspected that I was tempted to give myself a great life, full of idleness, in which without caring for anything, I would gaze into the sky at the small white clouds passing by. Nothing like that. I saw very clearly my duties to God, who provided thus for my needs – the spiritual ones, at least - and I did not forget to try to achieve by all possible means my eternal salvation, that at that time was given to nobody for free. So I went on keeping to the prescribed fasting, and on regular days whipping my bare back with bundles of the thorny bushes that everywhere grew up abundant. This world was a valley of tears, and we were not in it for a good time, but to love and serve God in this life and then enjoy Him in the eternal one –so the holy fathers or St. Paul said, I do not remember which, but it was not to be doubted.

They would speak out their own experience, I suppose.

Among fasts, whippings and profitable readings I spent my days. I increasingly ate only raw foods, natural and more nutritious than cooked ones. I had taken into account too that to make fire would be extremely laborious, whether striking two boulders together, or rotating with the palms of my hands a stick on the surface of a highly flammable wood, better if resinous; there was also the fact that by doing so I would run the risk that the invention slipped from my hands and set fire to the same forest which gave me maintenance and shelter.

Fully immersed in the contemplative life, I used to meditate on the one of St. Mary Magdalene, which my mother, committed to my education, had read to me and whom in the first years of nascent Christianity some had said was the carnal wife of Jesus Christ, when He was still only Jesus, the son of a carpenter, and not Christ, the founder of a Jewish sect. In one of the apocryphal gospels, i.e., not authorized by the later Church, some had it written in black on white, to the scandal of future generations.

According to this gospel, in the Cana weddings that of Jesus with Magdalene was celebrated. In the weddings Mary, the mother of the groom, was also in charge of monitoring the service to see that no one took undue liberties and everything passed in peace and harmony; she had played the role of a sommelier, the one who ensures the guests do not lack wine and drink it by the rules of the game, which consisted in drinking first the good and aged one and leaving for the end, when everyone was tipsy and did not give a damn for anything, that of lower quality.

No one knows if things really happened that way. In any case, it was said that the couple married in those weddings had retired to French Provence, in the south of the country, where they had cultivated a farm and like any other family they had procreated and cared for their offspring. Obviously they had done it after the passion and death of the divine saviour, which as is evident Jesus Christ would have survived, and from which He would have recovered apparently without any disabling injury, perhaps because of the care that had been lavished on Him by the three holy women who accompanied Him in life and then had seen Him hanging on the Cross.

Already at that time women survived men, their life expectancy was greater than theirs, it seems, so that Magdalene was widowed, and not wanting to remarry, according to what many years later would be recommended by the great Milanese bishop St. Ambrose, she had retreated to a cave nearby and spent her later years there. She was sorry for her youthful wanderings, presumably abundant in promiscuous relationships, and had known (carnally) many men. Satisfying at will the sexual appetite was something condemned by some censorious tongues. She was already returned from the painful ordeal in which she had witnessed the supposed death on the Cross of divine Jesus.

When, once alone and equally contrite for my past errors, I imagined the passion of the Lord, who had meekly died on behalf of all us, the saint had come to my aid, appearing and encouraging me not to falter in my penance.

From then on I progressed a great deal in the spiritual life. I was attracted especially by Christ made Christ, with signs of terrible suffering. Once I stopped in front of an extremely bloody crucifix and asked, Lord, who has put you in such a condition? And it seemed to me that a voice would answer, "Your moments of leisure, which you spend without thinking of me, those are what make me so." And I began to mourn extremely remorsefully.

I renounced then any leisure and other occasions of dissipation and minor faults, for which God began to favor me often with the stillness and prayer of union, and especially on meatless Fridays he began to visit me with visions and internal communications. I felt restless, as I remembered the many saints whom the devil had miserably deceived by fallacious illusions. Though convinced that mine came from a source without blemish, perplexity led me to discuss the matter with the birds of the sky and the beasts of the earth, more in contact with the source of everything than us mere mortals. Unfortunately, they did not keep the obliged secret, and much to my confusion, the news of my visions began to spread.

Alone in the wilderness, by special favor of God animals shared my life and directed me with sermons I never tired of hearing, "no matter how bad they were." I had become so much used to living in the forest and seeing no human being that I sought their company, learnt to speak animal language and talked with them; listening to their complaints, I felt sorry for the ancestors of the abused wolves of Gubbio.

As readers probably know, according to The Flowers of St. Francis, the wolf of Gubbio was a fierce dog that plagued the Italian town of Gubbio, located in Umbria, in the province of Perugia. This European predator had devoured both animals and people. It showed such ferocity that no one dared even to leave the city. Francis of Assisi was moved by compassion for the locals and on his own initiative, without them having requested his intervention, sought the wolf and ordered him on behalf of Christ to do no more harm. Just the as the "saint of Assisi" made the sign of the cross, the wolf closed his mouth, stopped running, walked meekly, and fell at his feet. Led by Francis to the city, the wolf lived there for two years until his death from old age.

I consulted the turtledove, the animal that according to St. Ambrose is the most faithful of all, a model of virtue in a couple, because, "once widowed and having lost her male partner, the female is disappointed and frustrated by the brevity of this love's enjoyment and its bitter results, lavishing more in pain than in love over the loss of the cherished one, she feels a deep aversion to anything that means breeding. So she renounces new links and does not violate charity laws, or break the bonds that joined her to her first partner: she keeps only her love for him, only for him she preserves the name of partner."

The turtledove introduced me to the fox, the smartest in the animal kingdom, who maintained that the devil deceived me, as it was impossible that God would favors a common primate monkey like me.

The proofs that God sent me purified my soul, and His extraordinary favors burned in me with the desire to please Him. They taught me to be humble and strong; they separated me off even more from the things of the world - not just metaphorically, since in some ecstasy I rose three feet off the ground.

On another day I wanted to imitate St. Simeon, called the Stylite. When he was a child, he had been a shepherd's helper and leading a flock of sheep had roamed the nearby mountains.

St. Genevieve also had a similar childhood. On reading her life I found that she had grazed the herds of her father, so I tried to be like her.

Since I had left home, I could not feed the flocks of my father, nor did he have any, apart from those of the metaphoric lambs of his converts to the Christian faith. So I tried to arrange myself the best as I could.

I looked around and saw no herd which could serve my purpose; only the forest creatures surrounded me, as I said, but they belonged to themselves. Reluctant to gather in herds and let themselves to be pushed to a pen, they tolerate neither dog nor shepherd. You might say they were model anarchists.

Holy Genevieve also had a well and a cave to which she retired to pray. When taken by the slumber due to the heat the satiated sheep tended to rest. With her arms crossed, she fixed her eyes on top and was ready to shed the tears needed to receive the inspiration that God Almighty would be kind enough to send her, because that girl was endowed with the gifts of the Holy Spirit.

I wanted to copy her in this too, but unfortunately there was neither cave nor pit at hand, so I decided to look for them as soon as I could. Meanwhile I tried to save time and like her began to pray with my arms crossed, but my circulation was hindered and I felt tingling in them, so I had to bring them down before I would have wished and not yet having reached that degree of mortification I had proposed for myself.

Staring at the cloudless sky (during the day, of course) did not cost me much, as living in high latitudes the sky was rather cool and not as bright as it would have been further south. As to the gifts of the Holy Spirit, I did not know whether I had received them since I had no experience in the matter and that I knew that over my head tongues of fire had never appeared, nor had any dove come down, as allegedly had come down over Jesus in Jordan during His baptism at the hands of the one who preached in the desert, the hermit John.

As we know, Salome, Herod's stepdaughter, was in love with John, called the Baptist, and as he rejected her requests with horror, she asked her father for the head of that impossible man who fed on honey and grasshoppers and prepared the way of the Lord. She wanted it on a silver platter; not in vain had she danced for him, belly dancing, wrapped in only seven transparent veils that left nothing to the imagination.

Herodias, her mother, had pushed her to do so; she felt insulted by John because he admonished the husband who lived in concubinage with her; besides being his niece, she was also his sister-in-law and moreover she was widowed, a conjugal union of which the laws of the Jewish Pharisees, more fundamentalist than the Sadducees, strongly disapproved.

It was clear that in terms of holiness, I was far from being at the level of St. Genevieve, as in no way had my intercessions caused the wonders that by hers occurred. St. German had visited her, and from the sky a medal had fallen, so that the saint had rushed to hang it at her neck like a sacred talisman or 'stop'.

A few centuries later, devout fighters in the Spanish Civil War would hang at their necks a medal on which they had written "Halt", intending to stop in such a way the enemy bullets.

Later a reckless man, insensible to virtue, had insulted Salome and was killed instantly. Also her mother had gone beyond limits. Indeed, carried away by anger, she one day seemed to have got out of bed in a bad temper and she had slapped the saint, and was immediately blinded. But Genevieve was generous and asked God to forgive as she forgave her and return her the sight, to which God agreed and her mother saw again as before.

In her elderly years she lived in Paris, where civil wars raged, and there was famine in the city. But she felt pity for the residents and despite the doors being closely guarded, she had wrapped up in a cloak that made her invisible, and had taken a boat and sailed down the river Seine, the waterfalls having stopped momentarily to let her pass freely. The countryside barns opened on her way and a band of angels had filled her boat with grain her boat and the other eleven boats which had joined her, and filled with wheat, they had all returned to the city.

Parisians had been saved from dying of starvation by eating each other in an act of anachronistic cannibalism. The former heathen savages did not any longer offer human sacrifices to the gods, because since they had converted to Christianity, they had ceased to be nomadic, had settled, and as serfs, that is the rabble, had learned to cultivate the fields on behalf of bishops, clergy, marquises, dukes, and in general all the most powerful ones. They paid the Church tithes for all crops and farm animals, and instead of eating each other, the living ones gave sacred burials to those who died.

It was impossible to follow her in these examples: first, I did not live in the city, but in rural solitude. Although in my country the children of the Emperor Louis made war with each other, there was no famine, and even if there had been, wheat, with which the saint had fed Parisian people, was not cultivated in the fields, because oats were preferred as they were thought healthier for the digestive tract and less harmful to the environment and the sustainable development that Charlemagne's land reform had intended.

As a peculiar detail I'll say that a queen, who had devoutly gone in pilgrimage to the tomb of St. Genevieve, had given as a votive offering to the guardian monks several diamonds, but an informed had discovered that they were false.

Also by then picaresque was de rigueur.

The devil tempts me

Like another holy Paula my song were psalms, my words the gospels, continence my delight, fasting and abstinence my life.

But the devil did not suffer that so easily escape him a soul, and it would have been embarrassing if, letting himself be carried away by weakness and that serene ambiance, he had done nothing instead of struggling to prevent it, as it was his profession and duty. Those who had taken holy orders used to say in Latin, quia in inferno nulla est redemptio, that is, for those who are in hell there is no redemption, so that the devil could not, even if he had wanted, leave me alone and even sympathize with me. Otherwise he would be reproached for letting himself be mixed up and would be accused of suffering from the so-called Stockholm syndrome experienced by those torturers and terrorists who after repenting and becoming friends of the tortured, quit torturing and terrorizing them and even heal their wounds.

That is why the devil tempted me. He knows all. First he wanted to make me feel guilty of the ugly vice of selfishness. He appeared in the form of an elegant, well-dressed gentleman who pretending to pity me and said gently: "What are you doing here, a girl like you, Joan, devoted to this useless life? By living this way you do not give anyone anything. Leave this isolated place, this barren solitariness, and go where you can do something positive and give back to society what you have received from it."

Oh, devious and misleading words!

"You could be a trained nurse," he continued. "You could be one of those who after the battle pick up the injured from the field, bring them to the nearest hospital and wash and bandage their wounds. By doing so, you would return to many the love of life and encourage them to give a farewell to arms. You might also devote yourself to special education of children with problems."

He was careful not to overdo it and pointed to the opportunity to have a husband who, grateful to me for having cured him, would take me with him to his homeland, the land of freedom.

On seeing how much he affected me with his sweet poisonous words, I understood at once that it was evil in disguise, wanting to induce me to leave my life of prayer and penance so pleasing to the Lord to bring me back to the misleading life in the world.

I threw myself to the ground and shouted angrily: "Only by dragging me will you take me out of here! Do it by force, if you can, because I assure you I will not quit this place voluntarily."

To discourage him and make him see that I did not talk for the sake of talking, that this was not bravado, or a boast, or a bluff, I filled with earth a basket that I myself had made, shouldered it and walked endlessly back and forth, over and over until exhausted. I did four hundred paces.

Taking the example of Simon who had helped our divine Redeemer to carry the Cross on the road to Calvary, my guardian angel, who saw me walking overwhelmed, offered to share the burden and help me to carry it, but I did not want to accept his selfless offer, and if anyone there had asked me for an explanation of my seemingly strange behavior, I would have responded in a similar way to St. Anthony Abbot in a comparable predicament: "I torment this body that haunts me so much."

In those ancient times, Christian people were dualistic; they thought themselves split in two, soul and body, and regarded this last one as an object, something you could dispose of at will.

Vanity and pride also tempted me. One day, as in the cases of Pafnucio and Thais, the harlot of Alexandria and the ascetic who left the desert to return her to the Lord, I was reminded of a mime that in my youth I had seen in Ingelheim. He was a famous mime. Everybody pampered him and loved him for his youthful beauty rather than his skill in the art.

Given his pure, angelic voice, some would assume him neutered, in the manner of those who with high-pitched voice sang in the choir at the Episcopal Cathedral. I thought it would be worthwhile in the eyes of God to leave for a while my retirement and go back to the city where that dancer kept on reaping worldly triumphs; I would show him how everything in the world is vanity of vanities and only vanity, and God willing I should persuade him to leave behind those vain pleasures and ephemeral applause to accompany me to the mountain, where we both would live the rest of our life, a life continuously praising the Lord and singing the Psalms of David.

I deemed it obvious that he would accept.

On my knees in my cell, prostrated at the feet of He that on the Cross had erased with His blood the sins of the world, I remembered my own faults and mourned them. For I had been on the brink of consenting to carnal sin. The gossips said that many had surrendered to the charms of the mime. So as a good hermit I mused at length about the horrible ugliness of carnal delights.

In my days of unconscious ignorance, that young man had provoked in me a strong desire of sensual pleasure. After several hours of meditation, I felt as if I had him before me with the utmost distinctness. At first he appeared like the picture of Eros, lying triumphant on a bed of lilies, sparkling with manly beauty, like an dream adored: self-aware, bright and glowing his eyes, pulsing his nostrils, parted his lips, aggressive his muscular chest, exciting, his arms strong like two disturbing chains. At the sight of such an appearance, I pounded my chest and said: "You can see, oh my Lord, how I meditate on the ugliness of temptation!"

I was troubled in the depths of the soul. I bent my knees and prayed this prayer:

"Oh, You, who put in us pity as You deposit in the fields the morning dew! Just and compassionate God, be blessed! Be blessed and praised forever! Put out in Thine servant this misleading tenderness that leads to sin, and grant me the grace to love creatures only in You, because they go by while You stay. Just because this man is Your doing he troubles me. Even angels are at his service.

"Is it not that with the breath of your mouth You have given him life, my Lord? It imposes itself on me to prevent him sinning further with so many women who want him in their arms. In the depths I pity him. His crimes are heinous and just thinking about them makes me shudder in horror so much so that my body hair stands on end. But the guiltier he is, the more I pity him. I cry, seeing him suffer eternally in hell."

As I pondered in this way, I discovered sitting at my feet a lapdog. I was surprised, because I had not seen him before. The animal seemed to read my thoughts and did not stop wagging his tail. I made the sign of the cross and he yawned. Then I wet my fingers in the water from a chipped pitcher that was at hand and again I drew in the air the salvation signal. The strange animal vanished. No doubt, it was the devil. I prayed a short prayer, and again I thought about the mime. I had to go and save him, with God's help.

But some hours later and after thinking it better, I gave up the project, fearing that instead of me persuading him to leave the world, he persuaded me to accompany him back.

On top of it all and in case I remained dubious, Jesus Christ appeared to me and told me this was not any good, that the time I devoted to that fellow was wasted time and that I should remember only Him and nobody else.

Later the devil wanted me to believe that I had not seen Jesus and had only dreamed it.

The temptation of vanity

Suddenly I saw myself fashionably dressed in twenty-first century style, wrapped in silk blouses, flowered skirts, delicate fabrics and lace ornaments. I wore a grey jacket made of Lurex over an embroidered strapless dress and a matching long skirt. The top and the long skirt were grey and glass-beaded. Then, I was wrapped in a shawl of fausse fourrure over a black velvet fourreau dress decoré with butterflies. Or wearing a jacket of matelassé finished with faux fur over a dress in black velvet decorated in polka dots. And even a short jacket matelassé with cuffs of wool boa, matched with an embellished black chiffon skirt.

For those not familiar with it, Lurex is the registered brand name for a type of yarn with a metallic appearance. The yarn is made from synthetic film, onto which a metallic aluminum, silver, or gold layer has been vaporized. "Lurex" may also refer to cloth created with the yarn.

Fourreau or faux fur dresses are sexier than ever. They cling to the body, marking all the curves of a woman. They are clearly favorites among the famous, because all look equally successful. Their length usually extends below the knee, allowing a highly alluring look without falling into vulgarity. Some of them are very bold and nearly transparent.

Matelassé is a weaving or stitching technique yielding a pattern that appears quilted or padded. Matelassé may be achieved by hand, on a jacquard loom, or a quilting machine. It is meant to mimic the style of hand-stitched quilts made in Marseilles, France. It is a heavy, thick textile that appears to be padded, but actually has no padding within the fabric.

The experience did not end there, because then I was enveloped in an ethereal white tulle dress with a corset, combined with a coat of flowers, a tiara of beads and cream laced boots, the whole outfit by top designers. Then, as though behind the scenes of a theatre of dreams, I wore a beige coat, underneath it brown leather shorts stamped with flowers and swans and a headdress with Strass crystals. Next, I found myself in a green dress with a lingerie bodice and a thick knitted cardigan, a scarf of lamé and a necklace of beaded flowers.

I hope you won't judge me anachronistic if - being ahead of my time - I tell readers that Strass is a name for rhinestone, a diamond simulant made from rock crystal, glass or acrylic. Originally, rhinestones were rock crystals gathered from the river Rhine. The availability was to be greatly increased in the course the eighteenth century when the Alsatian jeweler Georg Friedrich Strass had the idea of imitating diamonds by coating the lower side of glass with metal powder. Hence, rhinestones would be called Strass in many European languages. Rhinestones would be used as imitations of diamonds, and some manufacturers even manage to reproduce the glistening effect real diamonds have in the sun.

Already on the verge of fainting because of the harassment of so many impressions, the devil changed his tactics and rounded off his task by making me aware of my skin, too worn and dried out from having lived in the open, so that he led me to think of make-up fluids or creams, eye contour gel, dry rather than wet paper towels that they do not nest micro-organisms, moisturizers, especially a nutritious one made with chocolate, sugar and honey, perfect to end the tension and eliminate cracks due to cold; the whole completed with an in-depth treatment to make me regain the lost charm of youth.

My legs buckled, but by the infinite mercy of God I overcame the ordeal.

I also liked to eat. Here the devil tempted me. Once and by his good offices I received from an unknown source a basket of juicy figs; at once I saw in it the malignant face, so that I was forced to send it to an ailing monk who lived in a nearby cave. But the devil surpassed me in cunningness. The servant of God also wanted to mortify himself, so he sent it to another monk, who, with the same spirit, sent it to a third, and so wandered the gift from rock to rock and from cabin to cabin until the last recluse, no less adept at mortifying himself than everyone else, sent it back to me. The devil knows everything, as a result of being old rather than being the devil.

I ate only vegetables. Among them there are also different sexes and, as with most animals, some fertilize and some others let themselves be fertilized, so that as a rule I avoided eating those whose gender was opposed to mine. At first I felt some scruples, because I hesitated to eat only male plants, in line with my male attire, or only female ones, as would be the most right given my true female nature.

Finally I reached a compromise: I avoided the plants of a definite sex and sought only the hermaphrodites, which in themselves united both genders, male and female.

In monasteries monks never ate animals of the sex opposite to theirs, particularly quadrupeds, as St. Benedict's rule had set down. Neither were plants of the cursed genus farmed and they even hesitated to serve eggs at the refectory table, especially if boiled, because to see them hard on the dish could bring to the mind of the monks not entirely innocent memories. It was well known that in the monasteries of the Greek Mount Athos, no chickens, sheep or goats were allowed, nor dogs nor cows; nor were plants cultivated that in the manner of human females received the seed of the male.

Nevertheless and although given the antecedents or premises it might seem a strange thing, that prevention did not extend to the land, which belonged to that same category as that above pointed out, since it always passively receiving the seed and with time giving fruit, a hundredfold in the best of cases if the winter was mild and rainy at the right time. Moreover, since generally all agreed to call it mother earth and recognize it as such, it would have easily been associated with the sin of incest, when their children threw on it their seeds. But probably such an issue had not come to the mind of the ancient theologians of the Eastern Empire, who were then engaged in discussing the matter of the Trinity and their filioque by which so much blood was shed.

As regards to the filioque, it meant the contention of those who argued that the Sacred Spirit, the third person of the holy Trinity, came simultaneously from Father and Son, that is, from the two, against those who in turn claimed that it only came from the Father. It seemed nonsense to equate to the father any one of his children.

The word filio-que meaning "and the child."

It was entered into the Creed and since then, Catholics, who call the Pope the Bishop of Rome, take as proven that the Holy Spirit proceeds at one time from Father and Son.

For seven years, I fed only on edible plants and some cereal grains and for the following three just a few crusts of bread a day and a little water. I must say that it was desert bread, baked in primitive ovens, almost without any kneading and badly sifted flour. It retained thus all its vitamins and nourishing properties, to which was no doubt due the fact that I never get sick and my health did not suffer. From the time of the Greek Aesculapius it was stated that, "Diet is the best lancet."

If due to neglect or prolonged drought one day the stuff was lacking and I ran the risk of dying of starvation, a raven watched over me constantly, hovering over my head with a loaf of bread in its beak. For all the years of my separation from the world, it did not miss its duty a single day, and never failed to place the bread at my feet, if I was not paying due attention to my natural needs. If the day was one of fast, God sent me by the same messenger only half a loaf.

Such are Lord's wonders.

The temptation of gluttony

But the devil tempted me also from another side. One evening at my hut I was sad, hungry and thirsty. I felt depressed. Then, the fallen angel, who saw my temporary weakness and wanted to take advantage of it and see whether I would succumb to the ruse that with the Divine Savior all of us had failed. As he had done with Jesus, he encouraged me to turn into golden and crisp bread the numerous stones that were abundant in my environment, but as I discredited his lack of imagination and laziness in inventing new tricks, his self-esteem was crushed and led me into a trance. (He might have suggested I transform into wine the running water so abundant in those parts, as Jesus had done at the Cana weddings. But it seems the idea did not come to his mind.)

Hallucinating, I found myself in the midst of a feast of kings. White linen and purple hung covering the walls, fastened in place by strings of red and purple silk, silver rings and marble columns; on a pavement of emerald, marble, alabaster and other precious stones rested couches of gold and silver. Drinks were served in gold cups and glasses of various artistic forms, and good wine flowed generously with regal munificence. And I saw before me a table full of delicacies, on which spider crabs were not lacking, eel, different caviar, lobster with garlic, and for dessert, the savory meat fondue. It made my mouth water and I felt like I would faint; I could not help it, I reached out and wanted to give myself a feast, but it all vanished into thin air, while with humiliating laughter the evil tempter was mocking me.

On another occasion I had a dream. Jesus appeared to me, His mortal wife, and not wanting my flesh spoiled by so much austerity, made some cheese and gave me to eat the curd.

God did not allow the fasting to endanger my life. On one occasion I felt listless and without appetite. At lunch I sat motionless in front of the bread and water that used to be my daily food. Suddenly I saw at my side, standing, the Lord Jesus, who was dressed in His tunic of Arimathea linen. He unfolded the napkin he had with Him, knotted it at my neck, as if I was a baby, and broke bread and fed me a small snack, while saying: "Eat, my child. No wonder you're upset. But you must not lose heart, because nothing lasts forever and even this shall pass." Without adding anything more, He finished the task and left. From whence He had come, I suppose.

Whenever the temptation haunted me of putting some variety in the menu and nostalgically I dreamed of the northern Spanish dish of cap i pota that on festivals my mother cooked, having inherited it from her Basque ancestors I sourly remonstrated with myself by saying: "Glutton, you're a glutton; you have had some wine and oil and bread with tomato. What else you want? Will you never be satisfied?"

With little miracles God eased my pain. One day I was consumed with fever, had a dry and sore mouth and could not swallow anything. But I felt the whim to eat a watermelon. If my loneliness did not prevent me from satisfying the desire, it was impossible anyway, as it was not an area in which such fruits usually ripen. But suddenly there appeared one of my monk neighbors who brought me a gift, precisely a portion of a juicy watermelon.

More than bodily food I missed the spiritual type. For a whole month and due to what I have above said, I could not receive the Holy Communion. When anyone asked me if I did not think this was the worst of my hardships, I replied that if God had so decided, I was not one to raise any objections.

Those clashes left me exhausted. And tired of this constant spiritual warfare, I directed bitter invectives to the devil saying unto him: "Do I owe you something? What do you want? Go away and let me alone!"

But he laughed at me and did not let up.

The temptation of political power

Then, after I had resisted the temptation of gluttony, just as in the wilderness Jesus had been tempted with political power - "And he said to him, All these things will I give you, if you will go down on your knees and give me worship" - the devil tried to lead me to identify myself with empresses such as St. Helen, the mother of Emperor Constantine, who travelled widely, made a cruise of the Rhine, had known the world, had been in the holy places of the Holy Land and had finally been rewarded by God who allowed her to discover the remains of the true Cross.

He also wanted me to identify myself with the Empress Irene of Constantinople, a basilisa – as those queens were called - who had been commanded to blind her son and had become infatuated by a precursor of the Templars; with Theodore of Byzantium, the empress who loved Justinian and bravely saved him from the mass uprising on the famous race track. Also, though less well known and popular than the others, because she was born in northern Europe and in a country then considered savage and uncivilized, Ireland or Scotland, with Boadicea, the battling queen and famous warrior who had led her people to countless victories against primitive neighboring peoples. Finally, since I ate greens, like those ascetics called pascolants – those who graze or pasture - he tempted me by showing me another king, Nebuchadnezzar, who had preceded me in eating on all fours the grass of fields.

To sweeten the deal, the devil then offered me prodigious treasures of pearls, precious gems and gold, and made me imagine myself dressed in satin, embellished with the rarest jewels and arousing the admiration of friends and strangers who, fascinated, fell prostrate at my feet and with the incense of their fallacious flattery tempted me to become conceited. But I defended myself by reminding him of that Paul, the holy hermit, who covered his nakedness with a tunic made of palm leaves and did not suffer for it. I also recited: A thousand graces spreading, He passed through the groves in haste, and merely by looking at them He clothed them with His beauty.

The wiseacre called me the devil and a bluestocking.

Without mentioning the blessed St. Anthony, who had never taken a bath nor changed his clothes, knowing neither lotions nor perfumes despite his living in the desert, where, as experts said, because of the heat you should bathe several times a day to endure in life.

To get rid of temptation, I began to flog myself with bunches of nettles, but then Satan attacked me from the angle of sexual desire. Here, he also went through a period of uncertainty; the devil did not know at first whether to tempt me with images of strong young men, or with those of voluptuous women, because, like me, he was unsure of my sexual identity. But at last, after drawing lots, he made up his mind and showed me an effigy of the Queen of Sheba, for whom King Solomon had lost the north and every other point of orientation. To her he had dedicated one of the first poems in the world, the Song of Songs, which according to St. Ambrose had been composed to celebrate the love of Jesus for His Church, the mother of all.

To others it was an epithalamium or metaphoric nuptial song of the connubial relations of the Jewish people — their marriage with Yahweh.

It was thought that the people of Israel were possessed by this God, and lay (that is, had sexual intercourse) with Him (metaphorically, of course). They were the female part of the couple, and Yahweh, the male part.

The devil moved onto Zenobia, Queen of Palmyra, who had defied Roman legions when the emperor commanding them had summoned her to surrender. She had responded to him on the same level and did not want to submit. Next he brought forth Phryne, the Athenian courtesan with whom Aristotle used to chat when on the bed or couch; his love of wisdom did not prevent him of being in love with such famous a hetaera.

Then he introduced me to Omphalia who by her charms seduced Hercules to such a point that at her feet he devoted himself to the spinning of wool and some other tasks no less inappropriate to his sex, while in the meantime he regained the strength to use the cudgel again in the loving endeavor. This task was not at all among the twelve that the Goddess Hera had ordered him to accomplish.

And so on. But since his magic did not seemed to work, he thought he had missed the target and so changed pace. He tempted me with love, through which women are commonly tempted. First he made it to appear in the figure of Antinoo, who committed suicide for love of the emperor Hadrian. Unable to overcome the loss, and after dedicating to him a city, this Roman emperor was never again his former self.

As he had no success here, he put me before Priapus (the son of Aphrodite who personifies sexual power), armed with all his carnal and monstrous attributes. Resistance was more painful to me here, but pouring on my head a bucket of ice-water, I passed the test without damage. As a main course he made me dream that in the amphitheater of Rome I was struggling with a muscular black Egyptian man, a real stallion, whom I overcame and had him yield to my will, after which the prefect of the city, who presided over the games gave me some golden apples following the pleas of the feverish crowd, and named me supreme champion. Remember the golden apple that Paris had given to Venus, one of the three Graces in the famous contest.

The temptation of lust

However, the attack from the angle of legendary characters failed, so to bring me down he tried the grossest part of reality. Behold, my handsome boy costume, without I knowing it, had won me the affection of a beautiful young girl named Katherine, who had followed me into the woods. As soon as I noticed her presence, I threw myself on gorse and brambles and wallowed until the burning aroused me, then I grabbed a handful of them, and scourged the young girl with the burning bouquet. The outer fire managed to extinguish the inner one, and she, repentant, wanted to share my way of life and loneliness. But I drove her out and flung her headlong into a pond. I never heard anything more about her so I figured out that once again the devil had tempted me.

Though the enemy kept assailing me, especially by impure temptations, with beautiful young men who invited me to fornicate, sometimes the Lord appeared to me in all His glory and majesty, surrounded by angels and saints, impalpable pure spirits all, who left me frustrated in the flesh, though then I felt renewed in my strength to persevere on the path chosen and consoled myself. To my mind came the case of the blessed abbot Equitius, whom sensual provocation troubled in youthful years. He continuously prayed for a remedy for this evil, until an angel came down and comforted him, and since then, just as before he had been famous for loving women, was now famous because he loved men.

Like two drops of water resemble each other, that angel resembled the angel Moroni who would later appear to Joseph Smith in prayer. After telling him that the religions of that time were worthless because they all had corrupted the gospel, he revealed where the Book of Mormon was buried, and appointed him prophet and founder of the Mormon order, or the Latter Day Saints.

When she was little, St. Frances of Rome saw her guardian angel that never forsook her. He followed her, and as a special favor he sometimes allowed her to admire the splendor of his figure.

"His beauty was incredible," the saint had said, "He was whiter than snow and the blush that animated him exceeded the flush of roses. He turned his constantly open eyes to the sky and his long hair, the color of burnished gold, encircled his face with countless and delicate curls. He was wearing a blue-white tunic, reaching to the ground, and sometimes red lights flashed from him. Such light radiation emanated from him, that on his clarity night matins could be read, if the occasion would arise".

Frances' father was an early Voltairian and rather skeptical so he did not quite believe her. Sick of her insistence, on one occasion he required her to do him the honor of introducing him to such a supposedly imaginary creature. Without difficulty, she took the angel's hand, and attaching it to his father's, she introduced them; so he saw him and no longer doubted his daughter's good sense.

When I heard about this miracle, I too, like that learned man, harbored many doubts. It was not likely that the angel never closed his eyes, because, at least we mortals here below, have to blink at a given rate to keep them duly moist, if we are to believe those who deal with the matter. On the other hand, if you do not take your eyes away from the sky and walk without looking where you put your feet, you risk falling into a hole, as had happened to the Greek philosopher Thales of Miletus, who without ceasing, like this angel that now occupies me, turned his sight to heavens trying to extort from them the solution to the many mysteries that populate the universe. But again it comes to my mind that angels are not ordinary beings, but can fly, like birds, and never walk; although often they are represented in paintings and altar-pieces wearing golden and stylish ankle boots and sandals such as used to be worn in the time of Constantinople the Porphyrogenitus. As I have said, the descendants of the emperors (the basileus) were wrapped in purple clothing and not in vulgar linen rags when they were born by the duennas that took care of them.

Aside from the sublime happenings adorning the life of that holy Frances, I must say that in the same way as St. Anthony Abbott had fought the temptations of the flesh, I fought my own by always keeping myself busy and avoiding leisure; I wove two-handled reed baskets and wicker bags or sacks and incessantly intoned devotional songs.

CHAPTER 6 - My fame spreads; people come, acclaim me and confer on me the holy orders

The temptation of heresy

To no avail were the devil's evil wiles. All his efforts were thwarted. He could have spared them. As scarce food and solitude had put me off the heat of the flesh better than any devotion, the attack should focus on other targets than carnal lust.

The vision of carnal pleasures and voluptuousness was followed by religious doubts. I went through painful moments of spiritual dryness, in which I thought with futile pride of my efforts in pursuit of the glory of heaven, and felt tempted to take in exactly what the Lord God had said: "Do not worry about your life, what you will eat or what ye shall drink, nor about your body, what you will wear. Consider the lilies of the field - how they grow: they toil not, neither do they spin. Set your eyes on the birds of heaven, they neither sow nor reap nor gather into barns, and yet your heavenly father feeds them, if the Lord cares for them, much more will care for you, oh, those of little faith!"

Do no treasure for morrow and let God any care.

I see the devil, he appears to me

Besides causing me some temptations and secret internal troubles, the devil also caused me some almost public ones. It was impossible not to know it was him. I was once in prayer and he appeared to my left, an abominable figure, especially as I saw his awful mouth, because he spoke. It seemed that from his body came out a great flame, clear, without any shadow. I was frightened. Grinding his teeth, he said that so far I had escaped him, but there was no reason to declare victory, because in the end he would get me.

I felt very scared and made the sign of the cross as best I could; for the time being he was gone, but soon returned. Twice it happened. I did not know what to do. I had some holy water, I sprinkled him with it and he did not return.

Again he was tormenting me five hours uninterruptedly with such terrible pain and distress, inside as well as out, that it seemed to me I would not be able to endure. I did not know how to fend. When aches and bodily malaise became intolerable to me, I used to pray and plead with the Lord to give me patience to endure until His Majesty is served. I did so this time. God wanted me to know that I was tempted by the devil, because I saw near me a little abominable black creature who with grins and grimaces expressed his despair at seeing that he could offer nothing against me and I always overcame him. I saw it and laughed and no longer feared, despite the great torment: I could not resist any longer the blows to the body, head and arms. The internal unrest was the worst, because in no way could I reassure myself.

My long experience of these incidents has taught me that in order to escape the hellish agents there was nothing better than holy water. Though they also flee from the cross, they return quickly. But the virtue of holy water is great. When I take it from the shell that contains it, I feel comforted beyond any measure. An interior delight and recreation floods my soul and comforts me.

It is an admirable thing that the Church has disposed. The strength of the words with which it blesses the water encourages me a great deal; it is this that communes with it and makes without comparison the difference between it and common, unblessed water. First I sprayed myself, without success, and then I sprinkled the devil with it, which left immediately and took away from me all evil. I just felt tired, like I'd been beaten to death.

Even if the devil does not own my body and my soul, he can do much harm when the Lord allows it. What would not, if the body and soul were his?

Recently, it happened again, but had not lasted as long as before. I poured holy water on every corner and then smelled a smell like sulfur and rotten eggs, a terrible stink.

The true servant of God is not afraid of these scarecrows that are just looking to scare him. A night of souls, I was praying; and after saying an evening prayer and reciting a very devotional series of them, I saw the devil seated on the prayer book to interrupt me and stop me from finishing; I crossed myself and he went away. I resumed where I had left off and again he was there; until I poured on him holy water, I could not finish the prayer. Then I saw that a few souls were leaving Purgatory, and I thought the devil had appeared to me to delay their departure.

Again, while I was still living together with the other monks in the hermitage mentioned earlier, and when I was in the rapture such as I had started experimenting with, I saw a great fight of devils against angels. For the time being I did not know what that vision meant, but fifteen days later there broke out in the monastery a scandalous quarrel of a group of monks distinguished by their extreme zeal in enforcing the rule against another who was more lax. That fight was very detrimental to the community.

On another occasion I saw myself surrounded by a gang of demons. I felt as if in the midst of a great light that encircled me and did not let them approach me. Thus God prevented them from endangering me.

Despite all the defeats, the enemy of souls would not give up. He persevered in the attacks and made pass in front of me the heretics who until then had threatened to divide Christianity and tarnish the clear mirror of its faith: Gnostic, Manichaean, Novatians, Donatists,

Macedonians, Arians, Luciferians, Pelagians, Nestorians, Apollinarists, Monophysites and many others. I saw Priscillian, according to whom the soul is born of God and confronts evil; angels teach it, and then it descends through the circles where the evil principle catches it and links it to the various bodies. The soul attaches to bodies as though it were a chirograph - a written document in the handwriting of the author, by which it acknowledges a debt - that Christ pays up and fixes to the cross with His passion.

He also taught that the names of the patriarchs are parts of the soul - Ruben, the head, Judah, the chest - while body parts correspond to the signs of the zodiac - Aries the head, Taurus the neck, and so forth. In such a way and according to him the origin of darkness is as much as the prince of the world. He also held that Christ had not been engendered, because he was eternal.

To punish his blunders he was beheaded at Trier.

The devil then pointed out Donatus, for whom the sacraments which an evil cleric administers are worthless. Then he pointed out Arius, for whom Christ was a creature and not the creator, though created first. By no means were the Father and the Son of the Blessed Trinity the same. Then Pelagius, who denied any original sin and therefore that any baptism deleted it or redeemed it the redeemer. Man can do good by himself; he does not need the grace of God.

As it happens, Pelagius was wrong, as were the very ill-fated doctrines of all others.

Then to confound me and prevent me knowing where I was, the devil showed me all the idols, tender images of Eros, Venus Aphrodite, Astarte, Apollo, Persephone, the satyr Marsyas... and finally the most diverse gods and false prophets from Moloch to Cibele, Buddha and Confucius.

But such pitfalls were of no help to him. With the Lord's aid, who can do everything, I overcame them and left the crucible refined, which amounts to saying, pure and without gangue. Blessed and praised be the Lord, amen.

To the Holy Church the devil is not a symbol, but an actual reality, material and concrete like a stone, though impalpable. Sometimes it enters into a man or woman and takes possession of them. He also takes possession of an irrational animal. To expel him from the possessed one, first you must make sure that it is a real possession, not a common psychosomatic disease. A few tests will confirm or reject the evil presence. They should not be disclosed because the madman could change his behavior. Common vomiting, like that of insults and nails or glass chunks, and levitation, are suspicious. An irrefutable proof is that the alleged madman speaks dead or unusual languages that he has not learned. If a child a few years old suddenly speaks Phoenician but he is not one, he is not a Phoenician (to be a Phoenician is the same as having ability to trade or negotiate and get the most benefit), then there is no doubt that the devil possesses him. Exorcism begins by reciting selected passages from the Holy Bible and reading the litany of saints. Eventually God is implored to carry out the removal. There are some cases more complex than others. An exorcism can last from hours to weeks or months. When done by the Apostles, the devil ran off immediately, but if done by a common priest, no one knows for certain how long it will need, weeks, months may be.

The devil does not choose his victims: people open the door to him. Witchcraft, spiritualism, santeria, that is, healing by means of witchcraft, the Ouija... all of them are invitations to the devil.

I also wanted hoped that as the Lord had given His disciples the power to cast out evil spirits and to cure every disease and illness, he would grant it to me these powers too. After telling them: "Heal the sick, raise the dead, cleanse lepers, cast out demons," he had sent them to preach.

I perform some miracles

With regard to miracles, at first I went through a period of aridity and drought: my skills were poor, I did nothing right. I mean here the adult ones, since in my childhood I had accomplished a few quite successfully. Then I remembered that the hermit Macarius had done them only at the end of his life, when his vocation and his holiness offered no doubt.

I had to wait; to get in the queue.

It was recounted that once a priest who suffered a sore head wound had sought Macarius for help, and the holy man had refused to do anything and even rejected him, because God had revealed to him that through that sore he punished an ugly sin of the flesh. Finally, the man seemed genuinely sorry for his mistakes, so the saint had laid his hands on and healed him.

In the Gospels you can find a similar episode. Perhaps the Macarius story was a copy. According to Luke, a widow had insisted that Jesus healed a relative of hers and he had rejected her because she do not belong to the chosen people of Israel and therefore was not eligible to be an object of the miracles of a Nazarene Rabbi. But she had replied with such grace and spirit to his reasons that the Lord, pleased with so much wit and discretion, had granted her wish.

Intelligence, love of life, obtains everything. It is irresistible.

Also it was said about a holy servant of God that she was so advanced in sanctity, that even in life had performed a miracle: the candles lit on the altar of the Virgin had burned longer and were not consumed as fast as usual.

The few that I did seemed to occur despite my will, as if they gained independence from me and did not take me into account; those I would have preferred did not happen nor when I would have liked them to occur. In the end the thing was frustrating.

I could rightly be accused of excessive self-love, because in the end I was nothing but a docile tool in the hands of the Lord, who deigned to manifest through me.

In any case, I wished to do great miracles that left people speechless, such as the miracle of the shoeing of the horse, attributed to St. Eligius.

This saint had to shoe a horse and the brute animal did not take it easily kicked, neighed and didn't keep quiet; in short, he resisted. But the saint did not let himself be deterred; for him this unholy rebellion meant very little, so he cut off that horse's leg and set it on the anvil to shoe him comfortably, after which he replaced the limb on the animal. So he was appointed patron of blacksmiths and at the side of Lake Constance in Switzerland the Eulogiusritt is held, and in his honor the horses are blessed.

On reading the miracles of so many holy men I remained fervently amazed! About St. Severino it was told that one day he had been asked to expose the members of a recent destructive cult whose nefarious practices had won in the village many adherents. He condescended to do so, and as usual, had preached to the people and asked the priests to fast for three days. Then Severino ordered every home to be given a candle that everybody would later carry to attend the divine services in the temple. So it was done. Then all of them prayed to the Holy Spirit to send His light to expose the evil, and suddenly as if by magic many candles ignited, while others remained put out. As expected, these belonged to the wicked.

How many wonders occurred in those happy ages!

In the same city it came to pass that the many locusts of a plague of them invaded it, and as was de rigueur, the villagers requested by means of a prayer the help of God. Those of all sexes and ages went to the temple, even those who no longer prayed with the voice, "And when everybody begged with faith, one of them rose and, leaving the others devoted to what he believed their vain prayers, went to the fields to do on the spot something more positive. Apparently he was counted among those who believed that God helps those who help themselves." And oh, amazing wonder! His harvest was consumed that year, while those of everybody else went unconsumed.

I lived in the greatest seclusion, so having no dealings with anyone, the chance to heal wounds or restore anyone's health were not offered to me; therefore I attributed the lack of miraculous events to my condition as a novice in ascetic and holy matters. I hoped that with time and if the Lord was served, the tide would change and I would be granted thaumaturgic powers.

The thing was not impossible; to others they had been granted. In Alexandria, the courtesan Thais to whom I referred believed that the saints of the desert had inherited from the apostles the power to punish offences against the true God. She had heard it said. Nothing would save those whom they condemned; it sufficed to them to touch with their crook the wicked ones for the earth to open and swallow them. Why should I not be like those holy men?

People of the bad life, mimes, dancers, married priests and harlots, feared them to death.

My exemplary life attracts imitators

I lived happily in my solitude. I struggled with all my might to advance on the path chosen; eager to learn from the martyrs the secrets of the Kingdom of Heaven, and to imitate their virtues, I assiduously read their lives and those of so many other ascetics who had preceded me in tormented living.

In the middle of a life of such austerity, and receiving from God preferential treatment, I attracted other hermits to the dense forest in such a way, that many had already gathered around me and asked me to allow them to follow my spiritual direction.

About St. John Climaticus we are told that when he was first isolated, his erudition and sanctity had been transcendent and people flocked to him for advice and guidance.

The same happened to me.

Many women asked me to guide them. As the humble person I was, for me to instruct others was hard and at first I did not do it very willingly, but I was then assailed by the scruple that if I wanted to be charitable I had to yield. In a similar position to mine, the holy Syncletica used to say: "A treasure is safe only when hidden; to uncover it means to expose it to the greed of the first to arrive and to lose it too; virtue is only safe if secret; if ostentatious it will dissipate like smoke."

I reconciled myself to the idea, and not to offend anyone tried to endow my words with modesty and good faith, which greatly impressed the audience. By means of varied and diverse examples and parables I urged others to charity, to awareness, accountability and all other virtues.

Little by little I let myself be conquered. The drops of patient compliments finally pierced the rock of my humility.

Finally I accepted some devotees.

I was loved and appreciated. Not long ago I lived alone, but my wisdom and virtue went by word of mouth.

Though it was said that there had never been in those mountains an ascetic as good looking as me, no one suspected my womanhood. They began to call me John the "angelic." Traits of an angel were attributed to me, such sparkling eyes and soft skin and hairlessness, and no one was considered fitter than me to lead others on the path of holiness.

On one occasion one of those who had put himself at my disposal felt sad because in spirituality his efforts did not give the fruit he would have wished, so he tried to let off steam by coming to tell me his troubles.

I let him speak freely and when he had finished, I consoled him by saying, "Do not stop at this temptation and be sure to repeat to yourself:

my love for Jesus compels me to persevere here until the end; I have decided to stay in this exile, if only to please him and do His will."

That fellow quitted me comforted.

My fame did nothing but grow. They granted me the favor of attributing to me a spirit bordering on the sublime and word spread that I led my disciples along the path of perfection with tight and secure reins.

Fortunately for those who were willing to surrender to me their will and put themselves into my hands without conditions, mine were never as hard as had been those of the hermit Marino to whom I have referred elsewhere. This man had taken under his direction the future St. Romuald. And walking under the oaks, the teacher made the pupil recite twenty psalms here; a few steps further, forty, and so on. The young one, who had had little education, often stumbled and said a few words by others, so his mentor, it is unclear why the preference, hit him with the stick in his left ear, until one day, with the greatest humility, the patient informed the executioner: "Master, hit me on the right side, because on the left I am completely deaf." For that pedant, no doubt, virtue was taught by blows. Spare the rod and spoil the child. Who loves you, will make you mourn.

Old masters had learned their primer.

Old masters had learned their primer.

But that unsought popularity bothered me. I began to miss my primitive isolation. I felt I was not called to lead any movement. To lead anyone. A trait that -according to some - shows intelligence. That courtship of young people who left me neither sun nor shade threatened to end my stamina. They were my fans, OK, my supporters, but it was a burden. Enough was enough. So to keep my distance and rise a little above the vulgar crowd, I called my closest friends and asked them for the love of God to raise in a clearing of the forest a column or pillar ten cubits in height, which I then increased to fifteen and finally to twenty. I stopped there. I was beginning to feel the giddiness of heights. And since regarding the proud the prophet had said, "The harder will be their fall", I feared to go farther.

(Remember, the cubit was the measure of length that God had said to Noah when he had built the Ark. Noah's Ark, the first Diluvium. The universal one.)

While those devotees were busy building for me the column, I occasionally made them be served mead as a drink, that is, honey diluted with spring water, which as usual I asked from the angels who provided me the essentials. But fearing that my generosity was to overwhelm the patience of such kind servers as they, when on one occasion the drink was scarce, I poured it into cups with holy parsimony, but oh, wonder! I had feared in vain, because if I thought I had poured the last drop, the pitcher was still full to overflowing.

Erected at last was that profane pedestal and I retired there and stayed some time in the open, exposed to rain, sun and wind, the morning dew and the frost of winter. I did not sleep, ate only once a week and during Lent I abstained from eating anything at all. My mind was preoccupied with the comparison of Jesus, who spent forty days and forty nights in the desert where Satan had tempted Him, had not eaten a bite or drunk a sip of water, which we would now give, thanks to those who warn of the risk of dehydration. But those were times of faith and science was yet to come. No one reasoned, nor needed to, because somebody else thought for others and they just obeyed. It was more comfortable and more practical, especially for those who ruled.

In any case I spent in prayer most of the day and night, standing or prostrated, and when standing, I bowed continually to hit the ground with the crown of my head, which was thought a unique act of incomparable holiness; another saint had preceded me in doing it. At the great festivities and without tiring or weakening, I prayed all night with my arms raised to heaven. I must admit here that, despite such praying, wars did not stop. Maybe they please the Lord and you should not ask him to stop them.

I would have liked to resemble St. Benedict and a nun who had imitated him, for whom the hard floor on which everybody else slept seemed excessive luxury, so they rolled on nettles, fasted the whole year and only spoke with God.

But the devotees did not leave me alone. They again insisted and begged me to please not leave them to themselves, as they felt weak and in need of a strong hand to lead them. They urged me to preach doctrine to them, from my height, real as much as metaphorical.

In the end I consented. I resigned myself to the bath of crowd. Since for no merit of mine it seemed I had to be a wise and knowledgeable one, I agreed to share with others what I had learned.

I was reminded of the parable of the Divine Savior about those who having received a gift from God, hide it under a bushel rather than put it on a stand. It was not right that I concealed my gifts, because everything comes from God and we are not anything other than His instruments or channels through which He passes onto others what they should know to attain eternal happiness. By special incomprehensible provision of God, some are His spokesmen. And just as in the vicinity of Constantinople the blessed St. Daniel had done, I asked to put a railing on the platform, to use the whole as a pulpit and avoid falling into the void in case, carried by excitement and falling prey to the wicked demon, I felt tempted to try to fly to illustrate better the flight of souls to paradise.

At first, confused by the attention paid to me and eager to regain solitude and with it my prayers, I contented myself by answering with eyes downcast the questions put to me. But gradually I began to take in Christian charity the desire to please. I believed I could not let go my kind visitors without having welcomed them warmly and taking interest in their troubles. I had a heart so grateful that to bribe me a single date from a palm tree was enough. Soon everyone commented on how lovely my conversation was.

Visitors were amazed that at my age, somewhat mature, I still retained the charm of a young person, added to a kind of grit certainly coming from my years of isolation and due to my many readings, my meditations and my suffering. My sound discernment, my open mind captivated everyone who heard me.

A devotee arrived to say that because of me he spent unaware the daylight hours, and with the desire to see me again in the morning, the nights too.

They said my speech was funny and sparkling, sweet and serious at the same time, and my conversation was simple and sensible. My words radiated so soft a heat that it melted the hearts of those who approached me, without burning them. Among other gifts, I had the so-called gratia sermonis - the grace of frank talk- and pulled along my listeners.

But I just did not feel quite at ease with myself. The words of the Apostle Paul had come to my mind: "In the church of God let women be silent; they should not preach in the pulpit, nor read in the chair, nor print books." But then I realized that to those who saw me I was not Joan, but John, so what that saint had said did not apply to me. He rejected women, and me, Joan, a woman dressed in a man, was in the eyes of others a young male, so everything was in order. I did not get lost in Byzantine hesitation. Some other holy fathers had insisted on the same. To St. Augustine women had not been made in the image and likeness of God. And to St. Ambrose, man was perfect, as perfect is the square compared to other polygons, while I was imperfect, a woman, nature's trick on the human species to continue living, a triangle of only three miserable sides.

And to put the Holy Scriptures at the reach of common people meant risk; much more anything that seemed to contradict it even in the least. Only authorized clergy was allowed to read them, and even then, preferably in ancient Aramaic. As very few in the West knew something of that lost language, laws tolerated it to be read in Latin to chosen audiences, that is, the noble and learned, while to simple people they used to preach in rustic language and then only the basics.

To do otherwise would amount to casting pearls before swine.

So instead of risking going too far meddling with the Bible, I determined to speak of the ancient myths that from the lips of my mother I had heard. Since church authorities were wary of those who spoke of the sacred without the authority that would have been given to them by the appropriate academic degree, I decided to have recourse at the profane, especially it did not cast a shadow on the sacred. To St. Romuald only the philosophy contained in the Holy Scriptures was worthy of its name.

In knighthood books, to be a knight you had to receive a blow on the back, and to participate in the ancient Greek mysteries, you had to go through the rite of initiation. But I had gone through none of them.

Due to all that I have pointed, added to the already mentioned danger of being a false male, I was in danger of being taken by an Alumbrado, one of those illuminati, a mystic Spanish sect seeking illumination by God and union with Him; they used to gather in corners, outside the temple, to discuss the word of God, so they were said to be adepts of secret places and doctrines.

God help me not to oppose the Church! I would rather not see myself forced to say like the famous Don Quixote: "With the church we have bumped, folks!"

St. Romuald did not wash his frock

Perhaps because I was a female, I hated what some ascetic holy men used to do concerning a particular issue. One of them, Pietro Damiani, headed a monastery and encouraged its monks to leave the body, beard and hair without any grooming; above all it was important to tame nature by dint of mortification, and to persist in it. Not in vain had his master, St. Romuald, boasted of not having washed his frock even once in his life.

Unfortunately, even pure and reformed monasteries were dominated by the rivalry and competition for a better position in the

Kingdom of Heaven. It is clear that in this case it was a pious rivalry, not a vulgar one seeking benefits only in this earthly underworld.

There is no wonder about this if that passage of the Gospels in which the disciples asked Jesus who would sit next to Him in His Kingdom is taken into account. With that they had earned a good slap on the wrist.

Also in other respects were such male specimens distinguished from their peers. According to Damiani, all his monks should discipline themselves daily for as long as forty psalms, sixty in Lent and seventy in Advent. Without the abbot preventing it, some went further and whipped themselves during the recitation of an entire psalter and more. In this a saint called Dominic Lorigado won the palm; having fitted tightly to his body a lorica or iron cuirass he used to take off only to flog himself. The lorica was a small armor garment of steel plates overlapping each other like the scales of a fish or winter shingles and roof slabs. When a monk died, all the others had to fast for seven days and give themselves a thousand blows. To avoid routine and loss of purpose by force of habit, by trying various forms of flogging they discovered that mutual flagellation appealed to them more. Someone ventured that such a thing was perhaps indecent, but that abbot defended it and calm his scruples. To him, flogging in a spirit of humility and patience was the most sublime spectacle and delicious: "O quam iucundum, o quam insigne spectaculum!" He exclaimed in a famous treatise he had composed: "De laude flagellorum."

According to that exemplary man, cardinal, saint and Church father, if a punishment of fifty lashes was lawful and healthy, even more so would one of sixty, a hundred, two hundred or even a thousand or two thousand be.

He might well be called a joyful man, so much did he enjoy giving others the rod, as he had given his father.

Once in a fit, that unhappy father had killed a subject, and feeling sorry at his deed, he had sought relief in one of the convents of his son, but after a while, perhaps because he believed in having more than would atone for the crime, he had thought of leaving. When his son heard this, he would not consent, and after chaining him by the feet he had him beaten with a hazel with such a fury that the poor old man resigned the project and stayed put until he finally died.

Nevertheless his biographers, apparently romantic people, said that in the depths of Pietro Damiani flowed a source of tenderness and there grew the flower of mystical poetry. When he spoke of Jesus Christ and the rapture shone through him and he showed the intimate fervor of a lover should anyone mention Sodom and Gomorrah,; he delighted in the cross, felt the infinite and indescribable fragrance of the wounds of Christ and savored the nectar and honey of the blood dripping from Him.

So it has been told.

A great devotee of the Blessed Virgin, he encouraged all to follow suit. Maybe because of this he was distinguished for attacking nicolaitism, the name given to many clerics' custom of living with concubines, that is, women to whom the Church had not married them.

That holy abbot had launched furious invectives against the concubines, tigers, lions, snakes, courtesans, prostitutes, harpies, a race of sin, servants of Satan, who had made fall into the abominable sin of the flesh so many servants of God. As he claimed, the virgin Christ, son of the Holy Virgin, could trust his body in the Mass only to virgin priests. Those who had the misfortune of having a wife could not have apostolic zeal.

When inspired, he wrote verses of beauty as high as those dedicated to the glory of paradise, in which he expressed the thirst for God of his soul: "Ad perennis vitae fontem - mens arida sitivit."

He crowned matters by loathing all terrestrial philosophy, animal and devilish, compared to the sublime scientists who taught the holy gospel.

A Pope Leo inducted him a doctor of the Church.

However he was not the only doctor who hated the other sex. St. Jerome called marriage the eighth deadly sin and in a poetic rapture proposed, "To break with the axe of virginity the nefarious yoke." To a young Eustochy, a woman devotee of him, God knows why, "He wrote a letter in which he extolled the pleasures of chastity." To which a malicious person noted that perhaps the man had never tried those of lust. He also said that even by thinking you could lose your virginity and that the best defenses known to date were the cilice or sackcloth and avoiding treats at the table.

He would know, since he said it.

My devotees want relics of me

You should not believe that the life of an ascetic was all was peaches and cream; it also had its drawbacks. My fervent devotees vied to seize chunks of my habit or anything that I had blessed or touched. Fortunately they did not reach such extremes as had the suitors of St. Romuald. His reputation among the peasants was such that, having learnt that he planned to leave, they hired a murderer to kill him and have free access to his relics and remains.

None of my fans stepped up their zealotry to the point of considering relics the trees and shrubs of the forest in which I lived, perhaps because they did not know about the alms received by a famous monastery which boasted of owning as a precious relic a tree of the earthly paradise of our first parents.

At least the vegetation was winning.

I talked to animals

I commonly spoke to animals, and they transmitted to me their knowledge, especially about healing the sick. From them I learned the healing powers of many wild plants, a knowledge that I added to those learnt from the healer and midwife who had attended my mother at my birth. I had almost forgotten them, but during my new life in the solitude of those rough places, little by little I recovered them. I needed to heal the animals seeking help when due to hunters, pollution or natural causes they were injured or suffered some kind of harm.

My dealings with forest beasts should not surprise anyone. Shortly before he died St. Payo of Navia saw a lion that with claws and nails dug him the grave. Then he knew that God was calling him to his bosom, So he went to visit all his brothers in penanl commonly spoke to animals, and they transmitted to me their knowledge, especially about healing the sick. From them I learned the healing powers of many wild plants, a knowledge that I added to those learnt from the healer and midwife who had attended my mother at my birth. I had almost forgotten them, but during my new life in the solitude of those rough places, little by little I recovered them. I needed to heal the animals seeking help when, due to hunters, pollution or natural causes they were injured or suffered some kind of harm.

My dealings with forest beasts should not surprise anyone. Shortly before he died, St. Payo of Navia saw a lion that with claws and nails dug him a grave. Then he knew that God was calling him to His bosom. So he went to visit all his brothers in penance and one by one kissed them the cheek, wished them peace and lay down happily on the ground where placidly he slept in the Lord.

People came to me looking for help. Word spread that in both people and beasts I was able to cure ailments that doctors and veterinarians of the time could not heal, so I was considered the best of all of them.

My recipes for poultices and plasters were specially appreciated.ce, one by one kissed them the cheek, wished them peace and lay down happily on the ground where placidly he slept in the Lord.

People came to me looking for help. Word spread that in both people and beast, I was able to cure ailments that doctors and veterinarians of the time could not heal, so I was considered the best of all them.

My recipes for poultices and plasters were specially appreciated.

They set me a trap

Leo IV, then the reigning Pope, was sick in bed, and my therapeutic and thaumaturgic abilities being known they sent a delegation to consult me on his illness.

That delegation was formed by the personal physician of His Holiness, who as is easily understood saw me as an unwelcome competitor and gladly would have preferred to know nothing about me; he was accompanied by a cardinal legate, to whom the pope's death would have meant a good chance of rising to the papal see, because at that time the bishop of Rome was chosen by popular acclaim and in the curia as much as in the city that Cardinal had friends who supported his candidacy.

To test me and put me in evidence, they asked me that by examining the urine sample they had brought with them in a jar, I diagnosed the ailment of the Holy Father.

I suspected their trap and prepared myself for whatever might happen. After carefully sniffing and even tasting with the tip of the tongue the liquid in the container they handed to me, I discovered it to be the urine of a pregnant woman.

How would I avoid falling into the trap they so cunningly had laid me? I reflected an instant and then answered: "Let us admire the omnipotence of God by the miracle He is about to perform; within a few months, his holiness the Pope is going to give birth at the Vatican."

The envoys were confused, I had proved my skill and exposed their deceit without uttering a single word of accusation. Those present shook with laughter and for the time being everything remained as it was. The Holy Father was suffering an acute attack of gout. He liked overeating and drinking too much. He only needed to moderate at the table.

Also in two hours of bright dialectic St. Augustine had defeated and ashamed the Manichean bishop Fortunate, who to preserve his honour found no alternative but to resign his seat and go live elsewhere.

Louis the Pious having died in 840, his son Lothario, who had succeeded him, came to visit me. And in a token of reverence and respect he removed from his head the imperial crown and put it in my hands.

He had already visited me at other times, disguised and incognito to see me freely.

At last the bishop, astonished at my penance, ordained me priest.

Though he was a layman and a heathen, in only a week St. Ambrose was baptized, received the sacraments, the holy orders and the episcopal consecration: he was neither the first nor the only one in the history of the Church to know so fast a promotion.

CHAPTER 7. Joan is Pope; she loves God, becomes pregnant and gives birth to a child.

No woman will be a priest because for Eve mankind is fallen.

S. Irenaeus

Women won't be allowed to speak in churches, nor teach, baptise, offer the sacrifice or claim the priesthood fitting the male.

Tertullian

If women had been called to priesthood, in the New Testament Mary also would have been a priest... but she was no granted such a grace.

St. Epiphane

If man is the head of women, it is unfair that the rest of the body crowned the head.

Didascalia and Apostolic Constitutions

The model of women is Mary, and the holy Virgin has nothing of a bishop.

Evdokimov, Greek prelate orthodox.

They urge me out of retirement to be bishop and Pope

Pope Leo IV had died, so it was necessary to find a successor. There were in Rome two political factions, one that was pro-Lothario, Emperor of Germany, son of Louis the Pious, and the other that was pro-Roma, and wanted to keep the papacy independent of the other side of the mountains. There were ups and downs, disputes and various proposals. Finally someone thought of a third way and he remembered me. After so many warring popes entangled in the intrigues and plots of power, they wanted a calm Pope, independent, not in debt to anyone. So they thought on me.

People cheered me, and because of my virtues they wanted me as their shepherd.

The fate of all those who became famous and popular was very sad and to think about it changed me profoundly. I desired even more than before to meditate in loneliness on the gospel and to serve the Lord, whose empire is endless. As the very God had given me to understand, harm comes to the world because we do not know the truths of scripture. However the grace of God was preparing me for another spiritual dignity about which my distracted soul had not thought before. Once Leo, bishop of Rome, died, a popular vote chose me to succeed him in the episcopate. I declared humbly my layman and lonely hermit condition, unaware of the ways of the world, but it was to no avail, because from the column where I preached, Church dignitaries raised me to the chair of St. Peter. I stated then to those who listened to me: "A heavy burden has been imposed on my unworthiness, I feel oppressed, I teach before I have learned, I am constrained to preach the good before having practiced it; like a barren tree, I cannot offer fruits of good deeds, I can only submit leaves, my words."

I came to say what St. Paul before me had wisely said: proboque video meliora, deteriora sequor. Although I know the good, I cannot avoid doing evil.

All were charmed by my modesty and they were even more convinced they had chosen correctly.

But there was a prelate who out of prudence or perhaps fearing the wrath of the party which had proposed another candidate, hesitated to vote in my favor. "My brothers," he said solemnly to those present there, "Be careful not to take from the Lord His legitimate child, in whose penance he is pleased."

He was too afraid to go against the sacred canons, which prohibit conferring suddenly holy orders, without following the established procedure, to those who had never had them. But certainly inspired by God, who had already decided to elevate me to the papacy, I went ahead and told the holy man: "If you hesitate in agreeing to consecrate me, if you fear men more than God, who so calls me to serve, he will call you to account for the souls of your sheep."

These words decided the good prelate, who agreed wholeheartedly to my ascension to the throne of St. Peter.

Marching slowly in procession, the papal delegates arrived at my column and stopped.

"John, called the English", Pascal, the primicerius, addressed me. "By the will of the supreme Maker and the people of Rome, you have been elected Pope and Bishop of the Roman See".

The primicerius, was the highest rank in an institution.

Then they all fell at my feet to be blessed.

Finally by the Emperor's order I had to leave my retirement and accept the honor of being Bishop and Pope.

En route to Rome, where the will of the Supreme (Maker) called me, my devotees assaulted the convoy. A rich farmer standing at the roadside begged me to stop at his home, where he had arranged a snack or refreshment to honor me; from thirty miles around he had brought his children, grandchildren, sons- and daughters-in-law, servants and other relatives, for me to bless them. His cattle were there too and the tinkling of its bells mingled with the murmur of the prayers of all - who were dressed as for a feast - remained on their knees.

That picture touched everybody; by its noble rusticity as well as by the abundance of tasty dishes on the numerous tables it recalled biblical patriarchal times; but I did not stop and after blessing all of them, I went on my way.

At Bologna the monks of the neighborhood came forward, and seeing them barefoot and wrapped in their worn cloaks, I was touched and thought I relived those old days of the holy fathers, when Christians were still few and the religion of our Lord was taken more seriously.

They had brought two small images and begged me to accept them: one of Jesus as a child and another of His smiling mother, the Holy Virgin, and all along the parade were lanterns, small altars, drapes, and curtains, bouquets of flowers, votive offerings and streamers. Suddenly the child's image came to life and for all the duration of the route he did not stop jumping from the hands of the disciple who took him in my place to a little altar and from there back again.

Thus preceded by the favor of the Son of the living God, I entered the holy city amid an enthusiastic crowd that cheered me and sang while bells sounded and everyone praised me in the name of the Lord.

God knows well that I would rather not have been Pope if I could escape. I wished I could live like those old Sibyls, who only gave good advice and dressed in burlap cloistered themselves in stone cells.

I was elected to the papacy, but it was not expected that I would change anything. Everybody hoped that I would be a mere transitional pope. Given my past life, they counted on a move from one papacy, active and warlike, to another of privacy, more interested in the realm of spirit than in this earthly world; more likely to get people to recognize themselves as sinful than to ignite minds in favor of a political enterprise. A papacy of small steps and gestures, as it was understood that John VIII, that is, me, was not going against the model that had preceded him. Regarding substantial changes, there would be no surprise, as a change of climate would suffice.

I was also considered a Pope of great learning, with a higher doctrinal level than my predecessor, and able to dispute with great intellectuals.

I'd devoted myself to study; my preparation was really exceptional, and I was versed in mythology, medicine and moral theology. Hidden in the bushes, I had given myself even more to the reflective task, and as I said, I was often credited with a wisdom and knowledge above average and from me many sought advice. I was supposed more than able and virtuous enough to be Pope.

As I said, in the cathedral school I had studied with the wise Raban Maur.

Disguised as a man, I argued with the most famous doctors: St. Ansgar or Oscar whom the Scandinavians made their patron; the monk Beltran and the abbot Lupus de Ferriere, who had come to see me on my column. I spent a few years there, and with my universal knowledge I showed such eloquence that everybody admired me; my speeches and improvisations caused such enthusiasm that they won me the title of Prince of the Wise.

Nobles, cardinals, priests, deacons and monks felt honored by my friendship, and admiring my talent and purity formed a great party that at the death of Pope Leo raised me to the papal chair. In St. Peter's Basilica, in presence of the envoys of the Emperor, three bishops consecrated me.

The scene of my coronation

To welcome me in the palace of Rome and after preparing me as best they could for what was awaiting, the curia had organized a party. The opportunity demanded it. Carpets, draperies, crosses that the rarest gems garnished, lamps between the columns, mosaics of golden reflections, the melodies of clergy and choristers, the cheers of the faithful.

I was touched, like in transport. I did not quite arrive to convince myself that I had been raised so high up to that supreme dignity.

And I said to the cardinal that led me: indeed, father, this seems the heaven the Lord has promised us.

No, son -he retorted; it is only the anteroom.

Dressed in scarlet silk interwoven with gold thread and riding a white palfrey also adorned with a caparison that gold and silver enhanced, I rode to my apotheosis. All along the Via Sacra, doors and windows had been decked with streamers and pennants of various colours. The road had been paved with fragrant myrtle. The public crowded together at the side and never stopped cheering. Under command of their master, papal guards gave me mounted escort. Thus the long procession made slowly its way toward the Lateran Palace that the Emperor Constantine had given as a present to the Church. When at noon the procession stopped at the cathedral of the Pope, up there the sun shone in all its splendour. I got off the horse and followed by cardinals, bishops and deacons formed up in accordance with the respective range, I climbed the steps and went inside the illuminated basilica.

Replete with ancient and elaborate ritual, the coronation ceremony took several hours. Led by the hand to the sacristy, two bishops vested solemnly me in alb, dalmatic and pénula or cloak before approaching the high altar for the singing of the Litany of the saints and perform the lengthy ritual of consecration or anointing. During the recitation of the vere dignum, a hymn that opens the consecration of a new Pope, Desiderio, the archdeacon and two minor deacons held over my head an open book of the Gospels. Then followed the mass itself, sung, which lasted longer than usual, because numerous special prayers were added befitting the importance of the occasion.

While the ceremony lasted, I kept hieratic and dignified under the weight of the liturgical vestments, which like those of any Byzantine prince gold and silver ornamented. Despite the magnificence of those clothes, I felt inadequate and dwarfed by the enormous responsibility being laid upon me. I thought the so many who had preceded me in the dignity felt surely as I felt now and yet they had managed to carry on.

Meanwhile the heavens seemed to accredit many miracles and the much joy to the anointing of the first woman Pope. Due to the huge crowd that filled the square, the carrier of the sacred chrism could not enter the Basilica, so that the Bishop of Ostia, who officiated at the coronation, begged the Lord to deign to remedy the lack, and in the clear air of that cold morning a blue pigeon was immediately spotted carrying in its beak a vial filled with a miraculous balm, and this bird fluttering gently placed it in the hands of the priest. He took it with humble thanks, and anointed and consecrated me with that heavenly oil. Named the "Holy Ampulla", this little bottle came down from heaven and is kept in St. Peter ad Vincula and it has used to consecrate with this miraculous oil all the Popes of Rome since.

Archpriest Eustatio, primicerius because he occupied the highest rank, recited the final blessing: God Almighty, extend your right hand, bless with it your servant Joannes Anglicus and pour over his head the gift of your grace, amen.

A page came forward bearing on a cushion of white silk the triple crown of my dignity, and after raising it into the air the Bishop of Ostia put it on my head.

Long live to our illustrious Lord Joannes Anglicus, bishop of Rome and Pope of Christianity by decree of God -recited Eustatio.

And while the choir intoned the Laudes, I turned my face to the assembled.

I was already Pope.

I went to the staircase and the crowd cheered me. Thousands had been standing for hours to greet me. Now excited they shouted: Pope John! Pope John! Pope John! Long live our Pope John!

I raised my arms and felt transported. God had willed it. Any doubt and fear I could have felt that morning had vanished.

Here I must tell of something I had dreamed before all this had happened. In a vision of the type I used to have in my loneliness, the Lord had come and after showing me a rosebush had said: "When this plant flowers, your life will change; you'll be called to another state. Pray and watch, because you know neither the day nor the hour." Then with His own incorporeal hands he had given me, with both types of bread and wine, the Holy Communion. And on exactly the day I had been anointed, it in the spring of 855, next to the road where the procession passed I had seen bloom a profusion of rosebushes. Then I remembered what long ago I had been told.

I am Pope and become pregnant, they find out and intern me

From my very arrival at Rome, I was dazzled by the glare of the sun on the white walls, on the marbles of ancient monuments and sculptures; everything was humid, a breath of air brought strong odors of thirsty plants, the heady scent of jasmine which burned in the heat. I grieved for the abominable sins that by force would be committed in a land where even the climate unnerved souls. I had always heard that in such latitudes, when tempting humans the devil had it easier than in the northern areas. There was something violent in things, and - I do not know what - something fugitive in people. Oh, the lies that were told everywhere! And the exaggerations! Everyone was talking loudly, shouting. Enough to make you go crazy! People of that land were not for me, born in the north.

Rome's heat scorched and parched my soul. It was like hell. Never in my life had I been so timid and cowardly as I felt in that city. I did not recognize myself any longer. Though I kept trusting in the Lord as I had always trusted, I felt that now He wanted me to understand it was His spirit that sometimes encouraged me, and that without His mediation, I alone could do nothing.

I was Pope. I never would have aspired to such heights. But God had been set on raising me to that post. It is true that I had wanted to be holy; I had aspired to be better than anyone else and my parents had wished it too, they had been eager for me to reach it.

I had satisfied their wishes. God's ways are inscrutable. The Lord writes straight with crooked lines.

Who better than the vicar of God on earth?

During the early days in this new position in which the will of the divine Lord had put me, I prayed hesitantly and begged Him to show me how I would serve Him better in fulfilling my new duties.

One day while in prayer I felt my spirit lift with impetus and with my senses in abeyance I was admitted to the secret counsel of God in which it was said that four things should matter to fathers before all, namely, to live at peace among themselves, to not be extravagant in building churches because you carry God in the heart, to live if possible lived separate from the world, and finally to teach by example rather than words.

When I came down again to the ground, I remembered all that, and after convening my vision I hastened to inform them about what in the dream-world had been strongly recommended to me, but with the precaution of hiding the source, because I feared to shock them if suddenly I let them know that I had dealings with God, the Holy Virgin and the other inhabitants of the celestial court. Not all spirits are ready for the ineffable.

They listened to me attentively and did not comment on anything. Surely they attributed my words to the piety that because of my past life I was supposed to embody. I must say that unfortunately things continued as before, as it costs a lot to change habits and even more the old thinking. Over the years people's mind becomes ankylosed and they are unable to test new ways.

My mystical loves. Ecstasies, swoon, rapture, levitation

As I implied, I lean to the contemplative life more than the active. I have also told that I was considered a transitional Pope, one who had been chosen more by compromise than by true affection.

Therefore, combining the force of circumstances with my most intimate inclinations, I decided to live apart from any worldly endeavor and develop in me as much as possible the feeling of love. I would be a mystical Pope rather than one immersed in worldly business.

I've also told that once back from my attempt to convert Muslims to the true faith, my father had wished me married and that after thinking it over quietly I decided not to satisfy his desires, to love God exclusively and serve Him in this life and then enjoy Him in the eternal.

I was Pope; I spent most of the days in my room delivered in contemplation and slowly let myself become inflamed by the love of the Divine Savior. As the First Letter of St. John rightly reminds us, God is love, and he who abides in love abides in God and God in him.

Now I want to speak of love. In a world where at times vengeance is justified by God's name and even the obligation to hate and violence, love is more important than ever. There is no better remedy than love. What you need is love.

God fills us with it and we must communicate it. I did not want anything but love. Carried away by love I wanted to write what this feeling inspired in me; I wrote then a pamphlet which I called Concepts of the Love of God. But I had some scruples and consulted with the Curia whether I should publish it. They discouraged me, so I kept it in the drawer of a cabinet and forgot about it. However later a saint wrote something like it and she won the laurels that would have belonged to me.

After the love of God, sexual love supersedes the other loves: love of country, profession, work, family or friends. In it are inextricably involved body and soul, and to man is promised a seemingly irresistible happiness.

We should oppose the misuse of the name of God and the ambiguity of the notion of love.

Like Angela of Foligno I thought that the passion and death of Christ is the greatest show of love the Son of God could have given to humankind. Like her, I felt such a devotion to the cross that if by chance I saw a picture or image depicting some scene of the passion of Jesus, fever seized my limbs and I fell ill.

One day, while passing through the papal chapel, I saw the bust of an Ecce Homo that someone had just left there. This was an image of Christ wounded and natural-looking. As I watched it, I felt much disturbed at the sight of it, because it represented well what for our sake He had endured.

At such a moment I felt how poorly I had thanked Him for those wounds, so that my heart seemed to break, and shedding more tears than those that the Magdalene would have shed in a similar situation, I threw myself on Him and begged Him to strengthen me once and for all to not offend Him anymore.

That grey effigy that the wounds hurt and blood grooves stained, that bloody face under the crown of thorns, that cloudy and sore look of the anguished eyes, showed me my smallness.

I realized Jesus's love surpasses all the joys of the earth, all delights and all pleasures.

Meditating on the passion, I was more vividly aware of the seriousness of my past sins and mourned them with more pain. "In this contemplation of the cross, I burned in such a fire of love and compassion, that standing by it, I resolved to strip myself of all things, and once free of them to devote myself entirely to Christ," I could have said, imitating a saint who in these feelings had preceded me. By the Cross, I learned to be the great confidante of the Lord.

One day looking at a crucifix, I felt suddenly imbued with such an ardent love of the Sacred Heart that I felt it in all my extremities. That delicious feeling came from seeing our Savior unpinning His arms from the Cross and hugging my soul. Also it seemed to me that in the ineffable sweetness of that divine embrace my soul entered His."

Other times the Sacred Heart invited me to put my lips on His side wound and drink the blood that flowed from it. Burned by this fire of love, I melted into an ardent desire to suffer martyrdom for Christ.

The example of St. John of Carinthia kindled my zeal too. One day, seeing an image of Christ carrying the Cross, he ran, transported and stumbling, to embrace a black wooden cross on the white wall of the cloister of the monastery and right there an ecstasy seized him.

In the consecration or during the worship of the Sacred Host, the Lord rewarded me with numerous visions. Approaching this sacrament will never be excessively praised; if you meditate on the great love that it contains, you'll feel your soul transmuted into that same divine love.

My soul knew the ineffable mystical experiences, the admirable raptures and the contemplation of the mystery of the Holy Trinity. My ecstasy was to give chills even to people stronger than me. In them I dealt intimately with the divine, who entrusted to me heavenly secrets. I tasted the ineffable sweetness born of intimate contact with God.

I shall now speak of the transport or elevation; by others also called flight of the spirit, rapture and ecstasy.

Union with God in contemplative prayer brings about only internal effects, but those of the elevation are both internal and external.

Rapture happened to me as if the cloud of divine glory had come down to earth, and sucking the soul, as clouds inhale the vapors of land, would lift it; and the cloud ascends to heaven carrying the soul, and begins to show it things of the promised kingdom.

It seems the soul is no longer in the body, which lacks natural heat, so it cools, but amidst the greatest sweetness and delight.

The rapture is like a great sorrow without pain, without knowing why; like a wound that the love of God produces in the soul, you do not know where or how, nor if it is an injury, or what it is: pain is felt so pleasurably that it make us complain.

With no hurt, you cause pain but without pain you undo the love of creatures.

When God's love touches the soul, the love one felt for creatures goes away without any sorrow.

Here is no place to resist. In contemplative prayer, if one resists, to be strong and suffer the pain it causes is enough. But here there is almost never a remedy, but the momentum is so strong and sudden that you see and feel this cloud or eagle get up and take you with its wings. You realize you are being carried you don't know where, because though it is pleasurable, at first you feel fear; and it takes courage to risk everything, come what may, and abandon yourself in the hands of God, and go willingly to where we are taken, even against our will.

One day, when at Matins, I felt the rapture in the presence of a large number of people, and I would have liked it more hidden. It is useless to resist and you cannot hide yourself. It is stronger than you. You feel such confusion that you do not know where to go to not be seen. I wish I had none of these external manifestations and would be content with common prayer. Anyway it is nothing you can do but praise the Lord for one another.

I felt timid and cried for those gifts as much as for my sins, but I could do nothing. I did not seek the ecstasies and visions, did not ask for voices or consolations, but God loved me, and long years ago when still I hesitated, before devoting to Him my virginity, He had chosen me and drawn me sharply to Him, and I was as unable to prevent such spiritual raptures as is water to prevent the sun evaporating it and becoming a cloud.

Last Palm Sunday I was enraptured in such a way that could not swallow the Sacred Host. When I regained consciousness I found my mouth filled with blood. It was a redeeming blood and I was flooded with joy, for the Lord in the rapture had said to me, "Daughter, I want you to profit of my blood. With many pains I shed it, now enjoy it with so great a delight as you feel; I want to pay for the banquet that you have offered me on such day as this."

He referred to some years ago when I used to always receive communion on Palm Sunday, for my soul to serve as a dwelling of the Lord. I used to think Jews had been very cruel to Jesus, because after their great reception and singing hosanna they had let Him go to have lunch far away, so I asked Him to stay with me.

On that day I did not take any food until three in the afternoon, and gave to a pauper what I used to take at the fall of night. Jesus had compared me to Mary Magdalene saying: "While on Earth, I had her for a friend; I have you now I'm in heaven."

One morning, in communion, the priest broke the Sacred Host to give communion to a brother too. I had told him that I liked to receive it whole, not because I did not believe that our Lord was also complete in any piece, however small, as he had given me to understand another time.

But this morning Jesus appeared to me as usual, very inside, stretched His right hand for me to see, and said, "Look at the wound that the nail made in me; it means that from this day on you are my wife; until now you had not deserved it, but from now on you'll have in mind my honor, not only as Creator, King and God but also as my true wife. My honor is in your hands, like yours is in mine."

These nuptial vows differ from the usual ones between man and woman. At weddings with God, there is never anything but spiritual love, because all is love with love and its operations are extremely delicate and very clean so they are hard to describe with accuracy, but the Lord knows very well how to make us feel them. Nothing is further from them than corporeal pleasure; and between the spiritual transport and tastes that are given by the Lord, and those enjoyed by those who marry commonly, there is such an abyss as cannot be measured.

The spiritual weddings were a great heavenly feast at which attended a multitude of angels and archangels.

From that moment on, He appeared at my side in all circumstances, while eating or sleeping, praying, or walking, it became commonplace, an everyday event in the life of husband and wife.

We had loved each other for so long! We both had suffered so much; we had fought so hard for one another, side by side! And even in the fight, we shared so many joys! Our marriage had borne fruit in wondrous works. I never stopped talking to my husband with pure trustful adoration. I thought well of what He saw fit; what He wanted, I wanted too, and I knew not what would eventually end that spell.

My soul lived in close intimacy with God, but at the same time I kept longing for it. God spoke to me and snatched me into ecstasy. I rose and He drew me to him, and like when the wind raises up a straw, I felt a very sharp wound that I would never wish healed.

The King gives his most precious jewels to his wife, consciousness of the greatness of God, with complete self-knowledge and perfect humility and a contempt for earthly things unless they are employed in serving Him. Without fear of ridicule, I wished I could to scream to the world the wonders of this great God of Heaven.

Oh, what a holy crazy! I was no longer afraid of hell, I did not think of eternal salvation or eternal damnation, because the only important thing was love. The soul and spirit are one, as are the sun and its rays.

Continuing in the same way, the soul and God were like two candles came together so closely that all the light was one, or the wick and light and wax were all one. Finally the soul is in God and God in the soul, as when from the sky drops water into the ocean or river and then there is only one body of water and the water fallen cannot be split from that already there, as if in a room were two windows through where light entered, that although split comes, it becomes all one light.

Such is the intimate union of spiritual marriage in the secret chamber where His Majesty reigns. In this temple of God, in this home of Him, only He and the soul rejoice in deep silence.

The wife's powers are doubled, not to enjoy, but to serve.

I was so impressed by this surrender of God that I was not myself any longer and felt stupefied, so I prayed to the Lord that He would make me worthy of the wedding or get rid of it, because I was not able to cope if it kept on being as it was. All day my excitement lasted. I was then flooded with grace and at the same time confused and distraught, knowing that I was not up to such gifts.

Like the holy martyr Teodota, I wished that in future my heart was only in that of Jesus and His mother Mary, or that the hearts of Jesus and Mary were in mine, and would communicate in it their movements. I wished mine was not shaken or moved, except under the impression received from them.

Like St. Paula, I was in love with the Word made flesh and His divine words; I had memorized the Scriptures.

From my early childhood I carried in the deepest recesses of my being, nursed with milk from my mother, the name of my Savior, the only son of God, I kept it in the depths of my heart, and everything that I was presented with before without that divine name, though elegant, well written and even full of truths, was not enough to snatch me from Him.

I offered the Lord my heart and introduced it into His. With His heart He bartered mine and gave me eternal glory.

Once, amazed at my angelic features, one of my assistants said, "I have never seen such a smile, revealing a state of total ecstasy."

One day a more than miraculous experience changed my life. I was sitting on a terrace overlooking the river Tiber, where there was a still boat. Suddenly the air was full of music the like of which I have never heard. It was at once sad and mysterious, and yet had a hidden melody of joy, as the movement of deep water.

I stood up, went to the boat and paddled toward the sound. And so I reached some rocks where the music was more forthcoming, but not louder than if heard at a distance. As if in a trance, I climbed the rock to meet a young man reclining there, who created that sound, but he did not have any instruments and his lips did not move. I had the impression that he himself was the music. He took me in his arms and the music still sounded around us and I knew a delight that surpasses the limits of imagination. I joined him and achieved an ethereal perfection of unity, against which any ordinary sexual union is no more than an obscene, poor representation of reality. I have said a young man, but of course it was not anything human, but a spirit, an elf, and the fullness of everything you could wish. We made love while the sun was setting in the west; darkness lasted until it rose again in a mottled pink sky behind the mountains. And that music did not stop sounding.

Then he closed my eyes with a kiss and whispered that he would be part of my life forever and we would meet again. And I woke up when the sun fell flat on the rock and there was no sound but the sea, and I was alone. Sea urchins know him because he belongs to the sea, and to the sea returned. One day he'll call me from there. Then it'll come as no surprise to anyone that I despise common sexual unions like I feel contempt for roosters that assault chickens in the corral.

Imbued with love for the Almighty, like in the famous Song of Songs, enraptured I told him: "Let him kiss me with the kisses of his mouth: for thy love is better than wine. Because of the savour of thy good ointments thy name is as ointment poured forth, therefore do the virgins love thee. Draw me, we will run after thee: the king hath brought me into his chambers: we will be glad and rejoice in thee, we will remember thy love more than wine: the upright love thee. I am black, but comely, O ye daughters of Jerusalem, as the tents of Kedar, as the curtains of Solomon. Look not upon me, because I am black, because the sun hath looked upon me: my mother's children were angry with me; they made me the keeper of the vineyards; but mine own vineyard have I not kept. Tell me, O thou whom my soul loveth, where thou feedest, where thou makest thy flock to rest at noon".

How delicious such words spoken by the Beloved.

"While the king sitteth at his table, my spikenard sendeth forth the smell thereof. A bundle of myrrh is my well-beloved unto me; he shall lie all night betwixt my breasts. My beloved is unto me as a cluster of camphire in the vineyards of Engedi. Behold, thou art fair, my beloved, yea, pleasant: also our bed is green".

"I am the rose of Sharon, and the lily of the valleys. As the apple tree among the trees of the wood, so is my beloved among the sons. I sat down under his shadow with great delight, and his fruit was sweet to my taste. He brought me to the banqueting house, and his banner over me was love. Stay me with flagons, comfort me with apples: for I am sick of love. His left hand is under my head, and his right hand doth embrace me".

"The voice of my beloved! Behold, he cometh leaping upon the mountains, skipping upon the hills. My beloved is like a roe or a young hart: behold, he standeth behind our wall, he looketh forth at the windows, shewing himself through the lattice. My beloved spake, and said unto me, Rise up, my love, my fair one, and come away. For, lo, the winter is past, the rain is over and gone; The flowers appear on the earth; the time of the singing of birds is come, and the voice of the turtle is heard in our land; The fig tree putteth forth her green figs, and the vines with the tender grape give a good smell. Arise, my love, my fair one, and come away. O my dove, that art in the clefts of the rock, in the secret places of the stairs, let me see thy countenance, let me hear thy voice; for sweet is thy voice, and thy countenance is comely".

"I sleep, but my heart waketh: it is the voice of my beloved that knocketh, saying, open to me, my sister, my love, my dove, my undefiled: for my head is filled with dew, and my locks with the drops of the night. I have put off my coat"

I might go on without pause. Love is a virtue; love can rise naturally to heavenly thoughts.

How worthy of love is the one that crosses the paths of life! How beautiful are his feet and how his face glows!

I made myself obedient to the most extreme annihilation. I surrendered myself meekly with soft and absolute submissiveness.

I not only resigned myself, but happily allowed myself to squeeze the distilling oil of peace, humility balm.

It is God's revenge. It is the success of His grace. Step by step, resignation after resignation, because holiness is slow and sluggish embroidering, I've gone deeper into the love of one who deserves the sacrifice of our "I" and then, after killing it in its vicious bud, it becomes a new creature, new-born from water, spirit and blood.

From the seventeen years old I sought a place to love, but Jesus found in me a soul suitable to redeem.

One day I saw at my left side an angel in bodily form. He was small rather than large, very beautiful, so bright on the face that looked like a cherub, from those who look closest at God. He carried in his hand a dart of gold, long, which flames licked. I felt that with it he penetrated my heart not once but several times, down to the very entrails. When he removed it, it seemed to take them out and left me burning in unspeakable love of God. So great was the pain I could not help but complain, and so ineffable its softness that far from wishing it gone, I would rather it last, because the soul is not content with less than God. Although the body was involved to some extent, it was not a physical pain, but spiritual. It was so pleasant a wooing between the soul and God that I wished it on everyone.

When I felt so pierced and burnt by divine love, I walked as though fascinated; I would not see nor speak, but burn with fire, which for me was a greater glory than all in all creation.

I had three kinds of visions of myself, but those that took place "by means of communication" exceeded them all.

My beloved gave me repeated "kisses of love", until he consummated the transforming union. The ecstasy of strength seized me and carried me up from the ground. Underfoot a force raised me with an impetus so fast and so strong, it was as if a cloud or an eagle caught me and took me with them.

One day, the twenty-fifth of June 854, I was as usual doing nothing in my palace chambers when suddenly the ecstasy overwhelmed me. I started to feel weird, to feel strange and I found myself briefly transported to paradise. I lost consciousness of where I was. I saw a crowd dressed in beautiful robes, that gave off light never seen before; all seemed transparent yet corporeal, sounded sweet music, music that exalted the soul to the seventh heaven, which was not produced by vulgar instruments, grossly sensible, but ethereal, all radiating a heavenly glow. Everything was immersed in an atmosphere made of impalpable light and sound. And simultaneously the presence of God was felt. God was invisible, but it was clear He was there. God in three persons was one and three at the same time. It felt like the presence of only one true God and at the same time was of three divine persons. This was the rapture. It was not the first to fill me with joy. But that day seemed to be unique.

Imperceptibly I went rising off the ground. In a few moments I was three feet off it. All was quiet.

Surrendered, given, trusting, and not expecting anything bad.

Others had preceded me in loving divine beings

In preferring the love of God to anyone else, I was not original. Many others had preceded me. Holy men fell in love with Mary, while holy women fell in love with Jesus. Before all, this love was spiritual and mystical, but it would be hard to rule out physical love, although I'm not the most suited to it.

An aspiring Church father had said wittily that, "Just as no one removes from a relationship its sexual component, nor is it removed from the relationship with the divinity." What a free spirit was expressed in those profane words; adding that though without God you enjoy sex, without sex you do not enjoy God.

Returning to the subject, holy men usually expressed their love with a kiss on the bosom of Our Lady, while that of holy women was expressed in intercourse, more or less disguised, with the spiritual husband.

In countless legends, Mary appeared exciting and tempting and gave her lovers sensual satisfactions in addition to spiritual ones, covering them with milk, letting herself be wooed and caressed, forcing her devotees to leave their earthly girlfriends and enter a convent.

For instance it was said that Abbot Odilon threw himself down to the ground every time the name of Mary was pronounced in his presence was pronounced; he had a kind of sublime epileptic seizure, apparently pleasurable; and in the Steinfeld Monastery, the monk Hermann had lived in total loving intimacy with the Blessed Virgin.

This Hermann was a son of wealthy parents who had come down to almost into poverty, and since he was seven years old he had been very devoted to the Virgin. In his leisure moments he used to go to church to contemplate rapturously an image of Our Lady. On one occasion he deprived himself of eating dessert, a simple apple, and offered it to the child Jesus, who gladly accepted it. Again, as he arrived barefoot to worship her, the Virgin provided him with proper footwear according to the weather. It also was told that he stayed for hours lying in the greatest ecstasy before the altar of Mary.

The holy Mary gave her breast to many devotees. Of blessed Alan de la Roche, a famous preacher of French Brittany, it was said with admiration: "In such a way Mary responded to his love, so that before the very Son of God accompanied by many angels and chosen souls, she married Alan and with her virginal mouth gave him a kiss of eternal peace, gave him to drink of her chaste breasts and as a sign of marriage she put a ring on his finger and at his neck a necklace made of her own hair" (that of the Virgin was apparently curly).

The Holy Virgin felt for him a special predilection, so she often visited him, apparently to instruct him on how to reach salvation and become a good priest and a perfect religious man in addition to a perfect imitator of Jesus Christ.

On one occasion she had said to him: "In your youth you sinned without limit, but I have obtained from my son your conversion; I have interceded for you before him and if necessary I would wish to endure all sorts of penalties just to save you, because I take pride in making sinners grieve for their past mistakes."

Our Lady the Virgin gave us here an example of what love truly is. On another occasion some horrible demons tormented that holy man and tempted him until he was reduced to the greatest of sorrows and little less than despair, but she, the Holy Virgin, consoled him and her presence dispelled all that darkness and cloud.

St. Bernard of Clairvaux had enjoyed the intimate favors of Our Lady too. As he himself said, "This holy kiss (which he gave to Mary) has an impact so violent that the bride gets immediately what comes from her, and her breasts swell and overflow with milk." When he did not kiss her, the angels sprinkled him with the milk from her breast. And he prayed to the Mother of God: "Monstra te esse Matrem." With that she immediately uncovered her chest and nursed him: "Monstro me esse Matrem." Already in his childhood he had seen in a vision how the child Jesus came "ex utero matris virginis." Mary's womb fascinated him.

As to female saints, the Blessed Margaret Ebner slept next to a cradle in which there was a wooden image of the child Jesus. One day she heard the Lord say: "Do you love me above all things?" And as she shut up apparently puzzled, he added, "Because if you don't breastfeed me I'll leave thee." Then obedient, Margaret had brought to her bare chest the image, feeling an indescribable pleasure. But Jesus had not calmed down, importuned her, appearing even in dreams, so that she admonished Him: "Why do You not be more considerate and let me sleep?" But He responded, "I do not want to let you sleep, you have to take me in your arms." So that eager and happy - she says – "I took Him out of the crib and put Him in my lap. It was a child of flesh and bone." Then I said, "Kiss me, to forget that You've robbed my quiet." He hugged me, grabbed my neck and kissed me. Then I asked Him to let me see the holy circumcision. He showed it to me."

Also Elisabeth Beckün enjoyed the love of Jesus, who "very secretly" approached her and sat on a bench in front of her. Then she jumped up full of joy, as though beside herself, and took Him in her lap and sat in the place He had occupied and paid him flattering compliments, but did not dare to kiss Him, until, torn by desire, with sincere love she spoke thus: "Oh, my heart, perhaps I'll venture to kiss You?" And He replied: "Yes, by the desire of your heart as much as you wish." So has been written.

Another wife of Jesus used to sing to her beloved: "Ointment poured forth, tireless and willing bustler that turns on me and devours me with the kindest of fires. The pleasures of my soul want to pour to the outside or toward the bottom, but the spirit sends all upwards."

In the monastery of Helfta (near Eisleben), Mechthild of Magdeburg ignited and consumed herself in the bed of love. She had to love with all her atoms: "We must love and love/ and you can start anything afresh." She could not deny love anymore, she had to pour love forth. "I, an unworthy sinner, when I was twelve years, being alone, kissed the Holy Spirit, in an exceedingly blissful flux," she confessed. And she flowed ever more frequently, whether singing, "Love springing/ sweet watering", or "Oh God, your love flows!" Or when she felt like a "dry field" and pleaded: "Eh, dear Jesus Christ, send me the gentle rain of your humanity." Meanwhile, she consistently asserted that she wanted to live and flow immaculate and pure.

Not only did she run after the Lord; he too wanted her and was love-sick. "My Lord, You are all the time ill of love for me", revealed to the saint. And he sang softly, "You have to feel pain without end/ in your body"; "You are my pillow", "My bed of love"; "Feel the stream of my ardor"; and in turn he flowed and again made her flow.

"If I shine, you burn, if I flow, you flow."

The "rock sublime", as she called Him, "wanted to live with her as a husband." He promised her a sweet kiss on the mouth and urged her to "allow Him to cool inside her the ardor of His divinity, the longing of His humanity and the joy of the Holy Spirit." Repeatedly, the three persons of the Holy Trinity contended for her and made her delight very varied; when she received Our Lord, from on high the three, Father, Son and Holy Spirit intervened passionately. It was the energy of the Holy Trinity and the holy fire from heaven, so warm.

Mechthild sighed: "Oh, Lord, You pamper too much my muddy dungeon." And the divine husband replied: "My dear heart, my queen, what haunts your impatient senses? If you get hurt to the depths, then with all my love I anoint you."

Often, God consoled her in the bed of love.

Some maids loved until they lost consciousness. Gerburga of Herkenheim, whose body the sweetness of heaven penetrated as a vibrant source of life, was seized with such ardor that she collapsed unconscious.

Of Elisabeth Von Weiler a colleague wrote: "Her sight was so high and so screened with grace that she often remained lying one, two, three days, so her external senses did not perceived anything. Once when she lay in that state, there came to the convent a noblewoman. Not wanting to believe that our sister had lost consciousness thanks to the grace, she approached her and plunged a needle into her heels. But due to her ardent love, Elisabeth felt nothing."

St. Catherine of Siena also was lying for hours in "a state of apparent death" and although she was also subjected to the test of needles, "The feeling of love held all her limbs"

At twenty-six, St. Catherine of Genoa could not stand the heat. "The entire world's water," she cried, "would not cool me in the least." And she threw herself to the ground: "Love, love, I cannot endure anymore." A supernatural fire consumed her. She put her hands in water and made it boil, until even the glass was heated. Some sharp darts of "heavenly love" also reached her. In one case they wounded her so deeply that she lost her speech and sight for three hours. By sign language she implied that red pliers grabbed her heart and other internal organs. And kneeling before her confessor she felt in her heart the wound of the immeasurable love of God.

Like her, Madame Guyon at nineteen noticed when she met her confessor "a deep wound that filled me of love and enchantment, a wound so sweet that I wished it never healed."

Saint Mary Madeleine dei Pazzi, who used to flog herself and lacerate herself with thorns, often remained standing still, "Until the outpouring of love came and with it a new love penetrated her limbs." She often jumped out of bed, frantically clutching a sister and crying, "Come and run with me to call the lover." Then she ran around the convent like a maenad roaring and shouting: "Love, love, love, ah, no more love, it is enough." In the garden, according to her confessor, she tore "everything she could lay her hands on" and, whether summer or winter, because of "the great flame of heavenly love that consumed her" and that she sometimes put out by pouring well water "on her breast", she tore her dress. "She moved with incredible speed" and on May the third, in the choir of the chapel on the Feast of the Invention of the Cross, she rose nine meters high to hold a crucifix. Then she dropped the holy body, uncovered her breasts and offered them to the Lord for the nuns to kiss them.

Amor vincit omnia: love conquers everything.

Beatified Angela of Foligno, the same one who drank the water where lepers had taken a bath, did not give herself to Jesus, but he pursued her in love. "My sweet, my dear daughter, my beloved, my temple!" He languished for her. "All your life, your food, your drink, your dream, yea, I love your whole life. I'll do great things through you in the eyes of everyone. Beloved daughter, my sweet wife, I love you so much! Almighty God has given you lots of love, more than any other woman in this city. He has delighted in you."

In Silesia, the clerical singer Angelus Silesius had written a booklet, Holy Pleasure of Souls or Spiritual Eclogues of the Psyche in Love of God in which he said: "Soul in love! Here I give you the spiritual eclogues and romantic yearnings of Christ's wife to her husband, with which you will please yourself at will, and in the deserts of the world you'll long for your beloved Jesus, your treasure, intimate and loving, as a caste turtle-dove."

Church hymn-books were full of poems such as, "Oh, Rosemont, come and kiss me!"; "Lodestar of souls in love"; "That I be in love, your mind in love causes it"; "Prince of heights, You promised me marriage", and the like.

A poem in church (which was sung to the tune of "Jesus in my heart, my delight") began: "Come, my dove, pure pleasure, come to our flourishing bed. Fiery pleasure, oh, chaste bed, in it my love finds me, of the sweet marriage between us you dispose the yoke, so you offer yourself, so you penetrate, my spirit wants you to pierce it, and only your game finally suffers…"

In another book of songs shone these stanzas: "I look for You in bed until morning, hidden in the bedroom of my heart, I quiet You or call You, I follow the crowd and they see me follow You, Jesus, for love. I have Him, I retain Him, and do not want to lose Him, I wish Him to accept and embrace me, and I should like Him to enter the room of the mother to enjoy her favors."

Other spiritual writings radiate the same spiritual wooing: "My love, my darling, my husband, I lie in Your lap, come into your heart, You'll never get rid of me; I want to be pregnant of You…"

And so many others.

Pietistic circles used to identify the wound in the side of the Crucified with the female sexual organ. Some metaphors gave some to think: "Deeper, deeper, to the side comes a little bird just arrived to sing exultant pleurae glory and in the fresh wound to accommodate itself. The primitive magnet attracts it; in a tender rapture it stands erect and there is nothing more estimable than that beloved body which it is holding.

The pierced side of Jesus was the "wounded ahejilla"; "the wound of little cloth"; "wound of the little fish"; and was written that "It slides into the little side hole", "delves into it", "gnaws", "licks it".

"Ay, to the opening of the spear, bring your mouth and kiss it; it must be kissed."

And the phallus was extolled as "most secret member" of the "marital ointments."

The foreskin of Jesus attracted the curiosity of many male and female servants of God.

The Church Fathers had wondered whether it had rotten; if it had become too small or had grown miraculously; if the Lord produced a new one; if He had it at the Last Supper, when he turned the bread into His body; if in heaven He had it and whether it was suitable to His greatness; what was the relationship of His divinity and the foreskin, if His divinity extended also to the foreskin; and as a relic, if it could be truly identified, if it was to be worshipped, like other relics, or simply venerated.

At least thirteen places boasted of owning the real foreskin of Jesus: the church of Lateran, Charroux (near Poitiers), in Antwerp, Paris, Bruges, Bologna, Besançon, Nancy, Metz. Le Puy, Conques and Hildesheim. An angel had given it to Charlemagne who had brought it to Rome.

A monk exalted Jesus's foreskin as a ring of commitment to His wives. "As has been written by a maiden who was made a saint," said the holy man, "in the mystery of circumcision, Jesus sends His wives the precious flesh ring of His foreskin. Not hard, reddened with sardonyx, it bears the legend 'By the Poured Blood', and another inscription recalls the love, that is, the name of Jesus. In the workshop of the pure womb of Mary, the Holy Spirit produced this ring. The ring is soft and if you put it on the appropriate finger, it turns a stony heart into one of compassionate flesh. It is glowing red because it makes us able to shed our blood and to resist sin and because it makes us pure and pious beings."

St. Catherine of Siena, who rolled on the ground screaming and begging for the "hugs" of this "sweet and dear young Jesus", carried on her finger the (invisible) foreskin of Christ, which he had given her. And often with much shyness she declared to her confessor that she saw the ring constantly; not for a single moment would she cease to notice it; and once dead, several pious people praying at her remains also saw the ring, but it was invisible to the rest. The same grace was granted to two young people in French Aquitaine who had the stigmata, Célestine Fenouil and

Marie Julie Jahenny; in the latter, fourteen men saw the ring that had swelled and reddened under her skin.

A nun at Vienna, Agnes Blannbekin, had also known about the divine prepuce.

Almost since adolescence, she had missed that part that Jesus had lost: the untraceable skin of His penis. Every time the circumcision celebration approached, she used to mourn with deep and very sincere compassion that Christ had shed His blood from the very beginning of His life. And on one of these holidays, just after communion, she felt it on her tongue. "While I cried and felt sorry for Christ", she recounted, "I started thinking about where the foreskin would be, and suddenly I felt on my tongue something like a little piece of skin, like the film of an eggshell, of a superlative sweetness, and I ate it. I had scarcely swallowed it before I again felt on my tongue the sweet skin, and once more I ate it. I did it a hundred times, and I found that the foreskin had risen with the Lord on the day of resurrection. It was so great, the sweetness, that when I ate it I felt in all my body a sweet transformation."

I conceive by virtue of the north wind

Since by renouncing profane love I had deliberately deprived myself of ordinary intercourse, if I did not want to die sterile and without descent I had no recourse but to leave to a spirit the conception of my offspring.

So it was. I suddenly felt as if a gust of subtle wind had come silently into my room. At the same time I imagined myself naked. It was as if suddenly I no longer felt on my body the touch of clothing. I was still dressed, but I wore an incorporeal garment, impalpable, like a spider web, infinitely thin, infinitely slight and immaterial. I was at once clothed and naked, yet certain of being dressed; I was not aware of finding myself exposed to everybody's sight such as I was when my mother had brought me to this world. My modesty did not suffer. Immersed in the trance of joy and suspense, levitating in the air, I became a spirit without losing matter. I felt a sweet voice saying, "Rejoice, Joan, you have found favor in the eyes of God. By the Holy Spirit you'll conceive a child, whom you will give the name you see fit. He shall stir scandal, but you will never be forgotten, you, his mother. Past centuries, you will be talked about, for being the first of your gender to preside over the Church that represents God on earth."

Thus spoke the voice. The angel of God possessed me. And he added: "To pay for your sins and convert sinners, you must choose which you prefer: the nine months of your pregnancy and the suffering of shame and humiliation when your child is born, or having thirty-eight hours in the pains of purgatory?" To which I replied: "I prefer thirty-eight hours in purgatory." Then I felt as if I was dying and began to suffer.

After having spent thirty-eight hours and three hundred and eighty and three thousand eight hundred without my martyrdom coming to an end, I finally asked: "Why would the Lord not be true to our deal? He told me to endure thirty-eight hours to purgatory and I've been in it three thousand eight hundred."

"How many hours do you think have you been in purgatory?"

"Over three thousand eight hundred!" I said.

"Do you know how much time has passed since you chose what you proposed? You have not spent even five minutes and imagine that three thousand eight hundred hours are gone!" On hearing these words, I felt scared and yelled: my God, I prefer then to continue the pregnancy and give birth in front of everybody. And that voice announced: "Well, you wanted it; you will suffer here on earth living the passion as Jesus has lived it before. You will feel the shame with which the crowd of fools will deluge you; they will spit on you and hit you, their cries of hatred will panic you; but you need not fear. God has decreed it and He will always be with you."

Here stopped the voice of the Lord. I felt that again everything was the way it used to be. The wind was not blowing any longer. All was quiet and again the room was ordinary. I no longer levitated suspended in the air. I was kneeling at the prie-dieu or kneeling stool at the foot of the bed as if nothing had happened. But I had not dreamed it. Feeling that he existed in mortal flesh and blood, the child I housed inside me showed signs of delight. And I knew that the announcement had been fulfilled.

Finally, in His infinite sweetness and providence God had hearkened to my pleading; He granted me the gift of doing miracles, the gift that I had so much desired. I would give birth to a son, and there is no miracle comparable to that. In front of it, everything I had hitherto carried out was less than nothing. What worth was the turning water into wine, with five loaves to feed a crowd or even to heal a leper by touching him, compared to the wonder of giving life to a living being? God would never make me a greater gift.

But for the time being and after a few hours reality imposed itself. Not everyone would necessarily share my enthusiasm for this gift. For nine months I would have to disguise my new condition, act as if nothing had happened. It was not necessary for anyone to know anything about it. Since I had been assured that He would always be with me, once the date of the birthing arrived, God would provide.

Nevertheless the thought of what had inevitably befallen me filled me with anguish. The same as Jesus Christ had suffered in the Garden of Olives, I also suffered. When night arrived, I sweated blood and water like Him. I sweated with fear and grief, and after kneeling on the cold marble slabs paving my room I prayed, saying: "God almighty, if You wish, drive this burden off me; but Your will, not mine be done". Then directly from heaven an angel appeared who comforted me. And entering into agony, I prayed harder. My sweat turned like drops of blood falling to the ground. And wanting to call my assistants, I found them asleep in the contiguous chamber, careless of what should befall me. To myself I congratulated them because over them did not hang the responsibility that I confronted. But they continued sleeping.

Those dark hours of sad anxiety finally elapsed and with its invigorating glow came the new day; and alone with myself I meditated on the wheel of life. History repeated itself. There was nothing new under the sun. Just as my mother had been fertilized by the Boreas or north wind in which the Holy Spirit had materialized, now He had fertilized me. As Jesus was born to a virgin mother, not possessed by male flesh, my child will be born of an untouched mother, by the will and the effect of God.

I spoke before about the miracle and wonder of conceiving a living being. It was no lesser one to conceive without resorting to annoying sexual relationships, and even more so when my age was already advanced, because without me realizing, amidst all the exhausting works and anxious concerns the days of my fertility were gone. Even if I was not yet an old woman, because all that I recount here had happened by the time I was scarcely thirty-two, the age of the promises of early youth had long since gone away.

I was not the first and certainly would not be the last one to whom such miracles happened. Apart the Blessed Virgin, to whom Jesus was born, St Elizabeth, her cousin, St. Anna, her mother, and Sarah, Abraham's wife, all conceived in an uncommon way, some when they had no more hope of it, others without intervention of a man. It also happened to holy Ilduara, a woman of already advanced age; to her an impalpable angel had announced that by the intervention of the Holy Spirit she had been made pregnant with a son who would later be called St. Rosendo in blessed memory.

I was absorbed in these thoughts when suddenly there came to my mind the idea that it was always a male angel that announced the miracle, and never a female one, and always a male demon that tempted people, and never a female one. It was assumed that to serve Him and sing His praises God had created spiritual beings of an unique genre, in no way similar to men, which very well might be interpreted as a hateful and incomprehensible discrimination of the most High. Despite the fact that - as is well- known – "angels have no sex", the issue was odd.

Also odd was a story of Gnostic origin, if I am right, according to which on one occasion three angels had become infatuated with three mortal women. How could they have fallen in love if they had no sex? It was something to ponder.

I do not know the extent to which such thoughts would have been considered heretical. In any case, I consoled myself with the idea that given the infallibility generally attributed to me, faith was not something given beforehand: I made faith.

Back to reality: the ordinary days meant for me a hideous martyrdom. Increasingly the most uncomfortable inconveniences plagued me. Nausea was continuous, I hated many dishes that delighted me before, I suffered endless headaches, no position in bed allowed me to sleep comfortably, I had a fever and my thirst was insatiable.

Fortunately no one even imagined what was happening in front of their eyes.

Days passed and I did not quite accept the fate God had designated me. One morning, still in my bed I heard the rush of so many who in the palace devoted themselves diligently to their duties, unconcerned about anything else, and I started crying and asked the Lord why He had chosen me for such bitter passion. One day, by His mercy, He made holy Lidwina appear to me, who like me had lived long years of suffering and martyrdom, and she said: "To produce a better fruit, God prunes more the tree He wants most, and children love most who makes them suffer more." Then she advised me to put in front of my bed a crucifix, and from time to time look at Jesus crucified and compare myself with Him, and think that if Christ had endured such suffering, surely it was because holiness is achieved through pain.

At first I refused to follow the advice of the saint; how easy to talk when you are not concerned, I thought, a little annoyed. But soon I repented of my ingratitude and begged her to be patient with me, because as it was said Zamora was not conquered in one hour. Notwithstanding that, I avoided looking at the crucifix and cried and felt very unhappy. But then suddenly I began to stare at Him and meditate on the wounds of Christ in His anguish and torment and His most holy passion; recalling the sufferings of Jesus totally changed my way of thinking and suffering. From then on I did not ask God any longer to take from me the cup of bitterness that He had handed over to me, but I begged Him to give me courage and love enough to suffer as Jesus had suffered for the conversion of sinners and salvation of souls.

I came to love so much my sufferings that I repeated: "If to prevent pain a short prayer were enough, I would not pray."

I found my true calling, that is, to convert sinners by means of my pains. And I devoted myself to meditating with all my force on the passion and death of Jesus. From then on my suffering became to me a source of spiritual joy and as many "weapons" and "nets" with which to make sinners depart from the path to hell and direct them to heaven.

The Holy Communion and meditation on the passion of our Lord gave me courage, joy and peace.

Then again I received from God the gifts to announce the future to many and to heal sick people praying for them. Two months after conceiving the being I carried in my womb, the ecstasies and visions to which I was accustomed redoubled. Only now they became more intense. While the body was abandoned and lifeless, I was speaking in rapture with God, the Blessed Virgin and my guardian angel. God showed me sometimes the suffering of Jesus Christ in His most holy passion. Others allowed me to contemplate the torments of souls in purgatory, and even the joys that await us in heaven.

After each ecstasy I devoted myself more and more to saving souls through my suffering offered to God, but when those visions ended, my anguish grew at seeing how my pregnancy came to term, but also increased the love with which I offered everything for our Lord.

Little by little the fruit in my womb was imposing itself on me, without feeling that he invaded me. Fortunately, given the loose papal robes nobody noticed my precarious state, which otherwise would have caused a scandal. Despite my plight, no one saw me sad or discouraged, but rather the opposite: happy for suffering for the love of Christ and to convert poor sinners. And oddly enough, even if my misfortune was so overwhelming, I gave off a heady scent with which everybody around me felt the soul filled with a burning desire to pray and meditate. The fourth of April 857, Easter day shortly before three in the afternoon, I had a vision; I saw how in eternity it was woven for me a beautiful crown of awards, but it lacked a little bit to complete it. These were the last days before delivery. Patiently I offered everything to God and then I heard a voice say: "With a little pain still yet to come, your crown will complete. And you'll be ready to give birth in peace."

I thought I heard the sound of a crowd invading my room, the steps of an army of people, the touch of their on with the flagstones, the flight of their spacious robes that agitated the air around me, and when I was about to call my servants and hold them accountable of the unexpected invasion, I realized that such this joyous crowd of gentlemen and ladies dressed in the utmost splendor were ten thousand martyrs who had been chosen to prepare me for the passion and then invite me to share their eternal joy in heaven.

The streets of Rome are my Golgotha and my Way of the Cross

And as I was taken in a procession of praying, going on horseback, clad in pontifical vestments, followed by a large crowd of men and women, who spread their cloaks on the ground, for my horse to trample on, and the whole multitude of merry attendants began loudly to praise God for the greatness with which He had covered His representative on earth, saying: "Blessed be the pontiff who comes in the name of the Lord!" "Peace in heaven and glory in the supreme heights!"

Some members of the Curia, whom disorder scared more than injustice, wanted to curb such enthusiasm and asked me to silence those who so exulted, to which I reassured them saying, "if these were silent, stones would shout." So that quietly they let me go.

The women wept with emotion. And turning to them, I told them: "Roman women, do not weep for me, but for you and your children. Because not far off are the days when it will be said: 'Blessed are the barren and the wombs that never bear, and the breasts that never nurse.'"

And when the procession came close to the Basilica of St. Clement, the delivery pains attacked me, so acute that I could not help letting go and fell off the horse, while crying, Lord, Lord! Why have You forsaken me? In the midst of horrific screams, confusion and excitement, under my disorderly clothes I gave birth to a child.

They shut me in a convent

I write this confession by my superior's mandate. At first, before the sheet of paper, I did not know what to say or how to begin. Words failed me and I thought my life was in sight of all and it was expected that I would relate what everyone already knew. I felt like those birds that someone has taught to speak, but then are shown to know nothing more than what they have learned and repeated. But then I thought that the Lord would put at the point of my pen what He would dictate to me; if I have succeeded in something, it was not on my own, because my little understanding and ability in these things would be worth nothing if the Lord, in His mercy, had not have filled the gap. He finally calmed me down and encouraged me to write. He appeared and showed me the plan of the work as a beautiful crystal maze, in the manner of a temple with seven entrances and rooms - as many as the chapters of this story I write – and in the final one was the king of glory, with the greatest splendor.

On another occasion, when I was writing alone in my cell, the jailer came in and distracted me. I suddenly felt transported in an ecstatic trance, and after recovering my senses, the blank pages before me were full of fine writing.

To the venerable priests, deacons, abbots, monks and novices, dear brothers in Christ, religious and gospel preachers, who had appointed as our holy bishop, good leader and tender father, to all those living under religious observance, I, a miserable female of Basque origin, the last and least in life as much as in deeds, I dare to write, for the sake of posterity and those present, the story of my life that sin has stamped.

Though lacking the necessary experience and knowledge because I am just a weak woman, I would like, according to my lights, to summarize here the events of my life and offer you something to help remember them. And to undertake a task for which I am so inept, I pray God to take away from me any presumption whatsoever. Your authority and kindness together with divine grace have enabled me to describe the wonders of the Word made flesh, which lived in this world, suffered and rose for us.

It did not seem appropriate to let those things fall into oblivion, nor remain silent about what God today has shown to His servant.

It took much audacity for me to write this story when so many holy priests would do it with much more art than I do, but I'll obey humbly my betters. Hoping that you will excuse me and grant me benevolence, trusting also in the grace of God, I offer this narrative written in ink and dedicated to the glory of God, from whom everything comes.

I'll say how this sinner came to earth and lived her early years, how she submitted to monastic life and imitated the life of saints. I'll say about her youth, the time of her maturity and of her old age, even her last years on earth, combining and organizing the corresponding facts in a continuous thread. Amen.

Finished the 17th February 2006

About the author

I was born and then it all started. I was a child, I was young and now I am elderly. I planted a tree, I wrote a book and I have begotten a lot of children. Something of a hippie in England, I saw a bit the world, I hitch-hiked to Sweden, north, and to Naples, south, I travelled through South America, went on a cruise up the Amazon river and I was an extra in some movies. I played saxophone, studied violin and taught quantum Physics, I read tarot cards, I practised yoga and jogging and now I do walking. Ah, I abhor Stieg Larsson and have not finished reading James Joyce's Ulysses.

Printed in Dunstable, United Kingdom